CBA
CIRC

THIS BOOK SHOULD BE RETURNED ON OR BEFORE THE LATEST
DATE SHOWN TO THE LIBRARY FROM WHICH IT WAS BORROWED

| AUTHOR | CLASS |
|---|---|
| CREASEY, J. | A F C |

**TITLE**  The House of the Bears

# THE HOUSE OF THE BEARS

In the middle of the moors lies The House of the Bears, which is the home of Sir Rufus Morne. Decorative bears can be found everywhere in and around the house.

Dr Palfrey has been asked to examine a patient but when he and his wife arrive, the invalid is no longer there.

Morne's daughter has just been dreadfully injured in a fall from the minstrel gallery, and bearing in mind two recent accidents, this must surely be attempted murder.

# THE HOUSE OF
# THE BEARS

John Creasey

First published 1946
by
John Long Ltd

This edition 2000 by Chivers Press
published by arrangement with
John Creasey Ltd

ISBN 0 7540 8567 8

Copyright © by John Creasey 1962

**British Library Cataloguing in Publication Data available**

081321816

Printed and bound in Great Britain by
Redwood Books, Trowbridge, Wiltshire

# CONTENTS

## Book I

## THE HOUSE OF THE BEARS

1  The House of Morne          7
2  The Baying of Dogs          20
3  *Post Mortem*               31
4  'I want Dr. Palfrey'        38
5  The Third Post              48
6  The Papers                  55
7  The Cottage with the Parrot 64
8  Trunk Call                  78
9  Dead Rose—and Garth         86

## Book II

## THE SHADOW

10  Everything on the Table    102
11  The Town Which Shook       111
12  Gathering of Friends       120
13  Gathering of Clans         133
14  Theatre Royal              137
15  The Bridge                 147
16  The Mines of Morne         159
17  The Mine                   171
18  The Submarine              180

## ACKNOWLEDGMENTS

I would like to express my warm thanks to Thomas B. Gill, Esq., Manager of Gough's Caves, Cheddar, and to the management of the Theatre Royal, Bristol, for their freely given permission for me to set some of the imaginary incidents of this story in Gough's Caves and the Theatre Royal respectively.

No person or persons depicted in this book are based on any persons connected with these two concerns, because *all* the characters are wholly fictitious.

# Book One

## THE HOUSE OF THE BEARS

### ONE

## THE HOUSE OF MORNE

'HAVE we much further to go?'

'I don't think so. Only a mile or two,' said the driver.

'I'm not looking forward to the return journey,' declared his wife. 'How long will you be at the house?'

'It depends on the patient,' her husband told her, 'and what Halsted has to talk about. But he'll know the road and can lead us back.'

'I hope so,' said his wife, feelingly.

Now the road sloped upwards and the hillocks became hills, some of which were wooded. The same melancholy bleakness reigned, the mist was thick in the deeper hollows, and some of the hill-tops were high enough to hide the sun. In their shadows the land and sky seemed the same dark purple.

The driver switched on the headlamps. Great beams shot out and caught the mist, filling the air with garish light. 'It's better without them,' said the driver, and switched them off. 'Look out for an inn on the left, darling.'

'An inn, out *here*?'

'Halsted said so. It stands on its own at some cross-roads, where we turn right. It's only half a mile from there, mostly through the grounds.'

'What kind of place is it?'

'I don't know. Its owner impressed Halsted. England is still old England here. Feudal lords and ancient retainers—and the doctor little more than a courtier, or so I gather. The Mornes have lived in the same house for centuries.'

Now the road was straight, but the driver went slowly.

'There should be iron gates,' he informed his wife.

'*Can* the place be a moated castle?'

'It would be in keeping.' The driver slowed down to crawling pace, for a patch of thick mist covered the road and he could see nothing but its sluggish greyness. Even when it thinned, he did not quicken the pace, but leaned forward, hoping to catch a glimpse of the gates.

Suddenly, frighteningly, something moved in front of them. It was a man, rising as if out of the hard road, arms outstretched, mouth wide open, an eerie figure and frightening. Glaring eyes shone in a pale face. The driver jammed on the brakes. His wife, exclaiming, was thrown forward. The figure stayed there, unmoving. The car went slowly on, brakes squealing like a wild banshee might ; and then, when it seemed that they would run it down, the figure was swallowed up by the darkness.

'Sorry,' said the driver, breathlessly.

'What—was it?' His wife's voice was hoarse.

'A fool with a twisted sense of humour,' said her husband.

As he spoke, the lights shone upon a gateway, where great iron gates stood open. On either side of them was a wall, standing much higher than the car. As they passed through, men came running, some carrying weapons which looked like guns and might have been broomsticks. Silently the men split into two groups and ran silently past on either side. They ran in single file, all glancing towards the car but vanishing as they passed the headlamps. Shadows seemed to brush against the windows. Then they were gone, and only the faint mist and the straight road lay ahead.

'Were they chasing the first man?' the woman exclaimed.

'The same thought struck me,' said the driver. 'Or perhaps they like running about the moor in this weather!' His flippancy struck a false note, and he drove in silence for a few hundred yards until the beams of the headlamps shone upon a fountain in the centre of a great courtyard. The arcs of falling water glinted silver in the headlights. Here the road divided, and the driver took the left-hand fork. Soon they saw the front of the house. It was dark, built of great stone slabs, with long, narrow windows—all of them unlighted.

The road swung right. The headlights showed the great porch, with colonnades and steps leading to a massive door. The driver pulled up outside it, and he and his wife sat back in silence. The only light came from the car. Now that the engine was silent, there was no sound.

'I don't think I could stay out here alone,' said the woman, slowly. 'I don't think I've got the nerve.'

8

'You're not going to stay out here,' said her husband. He got out, opened the door for her and helped her out. They walked up the steps, the man counting: '. . . five, six, seven, eight.' Their footsteps sounded very loud. The man took out a torch and shone it on the door. They saw the great iron studs, the tiny slit for a letter-box, the old iron handle and chain of the bell, and the great knocker, which was the shape of a bear. The iron studs were shaped like the heads of bears, their ugly snouts thrust forward and eye sockets empty, giving a ghoulish effect.

'Here goes,' said the driver.

He pulled the hanging bell, and as he released it a clanging din broke upon them, startling them both, echoing and re-echoing inside the house. It continued for a long time, gradually growing fainter. The woman clutched her husband's arm, then drew her hand away and called herself a fool. The man continued to shine his torch, even when he heard sharp, ringing footsteps. The door opened, but no more than a foot. A dim light shone inside, and against it was the outline of a woman, her hair drawn tight over her head.

The man shone the torch straight into her face. Long, narrow, pale as death, it was in keeping with this eerie place. She blinked large, gleaming eyes, moved her head to one side, then turned and looked into the hall.

'No!' she called. Her voice echoed.

A man's voice sounded deep and clear, but as if from a long way off.

'Then send them away. Send them away! I want no one else here tonight.'

The woman turned and looked at the driver, who had lowered his torch so that it shone upon her black-clad bosom.

'I am sorry. Sir Rufus is not at home.'

'*Send them away!*' called the man. '*Send them away!*'

The door began to close. The driver of the car put forward a foot to stop it. The woman repeated: 'I am sorry, Sir Rufus it *out.*'

'I think there is some mistake,' said the driver. 'I have an appointment here with Dr. Halsted.'

'Who are you?'

'Dr. Palfrey, from London.'

'*Doctor* Palfrey?'

'Yes.'

The woman turned her head again and called: 'It is a

doctor.' She opened the door without waiting for a response, and Dr. Palfrey and his wife stepped into the hall. There was no light on; the glow came from a doorway in one corner and seemed a long way off. The hall seemed to have no ceiling and no sides; all those were lost in darkness, except the wall near the lighted door. A tall, heavily-built man with a great mane of hair, appeared in the doorway.

'Do you say it is Halsted?'

'No, another doctor,' said the woman. 'Come this way, please.' She walked across the hall, her footsteps echoing on stone flags or muffled as she trod on carpets and rugs. The callers followed, Mrs. Palfrey still touching her husband's arm. As they drew nearer the doorway, they saw that the man's hair was red; it caught the light, and was like a halo of fire.

He backed away and waited for them in a smaller room, but one which was large by ordinary standards. A blazing chandelier hung from the high ceiling. Heavy furniture stood against the walls and about the room; in a great stone fireplace a mass of wood embers glowed red, and the rich, warm scent of wood smoke lay heavy on the air. The man was standing near the door with his back to the fire; the light from the chandelier fell upon his heavy, handsome face and strange amber eyes.

'I don't understand,' he said. 'Who are you?'

'Dr. Halsted asked me to meet him here for a consultation at half past five,' said Palfrey. 'I am Dr. Palfrey.' He gave the man his card. 'Are you Sir Rufus Morne?'

'Yes. I am glad to see you, Doctor. There has been—there has been——' His voice broke, and he turned away.

'A serious accident,' interjected the woman. She was tall and very thin, and her black dress was unrelieved by any touch of colour. Her hands and face seemed parchment white.

'You must do something!' cried Morne. 'She's dying—oh, God, she's dying!'

Palfrey glanced at his wife with quick reassurance, and nodded towards an arm-chair which was drawn up close to the fire. On a table near it was a decanter, glasses, a syphon and a box of cigarettes. Morne turned towards another door and led the way, Palfrey and the woman followed. They went along a wide stone passage and then entered a room as large as the hall. It had dark panelled walls, a polished wood floor strewn with rugs, and another fireplace with leaping flames. At one side a grand piano was open, with music on the rest and more music on the floor, as if scattered by a gust of wind.

10

A group of three people stood a few yards from the piano, and a man knelt by the side of a girl who lay on the floor with a cushion under her head. Her face was deathly white, and her lack-lustre eyes stared upwards. Slowly, agonizingly, she turned her head from side to side, moaning with each movement. The sound floated through the big room and seemed to gather volume, and the echoes clashed with each other, making a regular sough of torment. The girl was brightly clad in green, and her auburn hair spread over the cushion like a canopy.

The man kneeling by her was trying to put his right arm beneath her shoulders.

'Don't move her, please,' said Palfrey, crisply. He opened his bag as the kneeling man looked round in surprise. He took out a hypodermic syringe and a small phial, broke the top of the phial and filled the syringe. 'Take your arm away from her,' he ordered.

The man obeyed, and stood up. He was short, thick-set and dark.

Morne moved as Palfrey stepped forward.

'What is in that? What are you going to do?'

'Send her to sleep,' said Palfrey. 'This is morphia.' He shook off Morne's detaining hand and bent down.

The girl had fallen from a great height. Her right arm was bent at an odd angle; so was her left leg. There was a dark bruise on her forehead, but none of these things worried Palfrey so much as the wooden stool near her; it looked as if she had fallen upon the stool, striking it with her back.

He stood up, still looking down at her.

'How long has she been like this?'

'About a quarter of an hour,' said a youth. He was good-looking in an effeminate, sallow way, and his yellow hair was overlong and swept back from his forehead. 'I was playing. Loretta was leaning over the gallery, and——'

He broke off with a catch in his voice. Palfrey glanced up. Immediately above him was the rail of a minstrel gallery. A piece about a yard long was hanging over the edge. He noticed that the woodwork was heavy and magnificently carved.

'She just fell,' continued the youth, whose name was Gerry. 'It was dreadful!'

'I wonder if one of you will fetch my wife, who is in the next room?' asked Palfrey, and then added, abruptly: 'No. I will. I think it would be better if everyone else left the room. Get a drink,' he said, and reached the doorway. ''Silla, will you lend me a hand? There's been a nasty accident.'

The girl had a strong likeness to Rufus Morne. Her face, now in repose, was very beautiful.

Palfrey made a rapid examination.

There were compound fractures of the arm and leg, and he did not spend much time over them. He examined her head; there was no serious injury. He felt her back, prodding the ribs gently. His lips tightened, and he shot a quick, bleak look at the stool. She had undoubtedly fallen across it, smashing her ribs. Only an X-ray could tell the full extent of her injuries, but she could not be moved except by ambulance, and it would take three-quarters of an hour for an ambulance to come from Corbin, the nearest town he knew in that bleak Corshire county. It would take three-quarters of an hour or more to come, over an hour to get back; it would be too long; he must find a way of getting her to hospital more quickly than that. There might be one nearer.

He asked the manservant.

'There's the sanatorium, sir. On the other side of Wenlock Hill, about five miles off.'

'Do you know if they have an operating theatre?'

'I don't know that, sir.'

'See if one of the others can tell you,' said Palfrey.

The man hurried off. Palfrey finished his examination and stood up. Voices came from the next room, and the short man came in with firm and heavy tread.

'There is an operating theatre at the sanatorium, Doctor.'

'Good! Will you telephone for an ambulance at once? Tell them to expect the case immediately and prepare first for an X-ray and then for setting compound fractures.' He did not want to cause too much alarm.

While he waited for the message to be sent, Palfrey stood looking up at the minstrel gallery and the hanging wood. He could picture the girl leaning over and calling down—laughing, perhaps; he pictured her as laughing freely, a gay, vivacious spirit. Leaning over the rail and laughing, unaware of coming disaster.

Had age so worn the wooden post and rail that, at the pressure of her body, they had broken? The posts were thick, the rail was thicker; he could see that the carving was of bears, rampant and couchant, the bears of the House of Morne. Or, perhaps, soon more aptly, the house of mourning.

12

The great front door opened as Palfrey went inside for the second time that night. A footman stood aside, and Sir Rufus Morne came hurrying from the inner room.

'How is she?'

'You mustn't expect too much yet,' Palfrey told him. 'She is comfortable, the operation gave little trouble, and there is a good chance that things will go well.'

'Tell me the worst,' Morne demanded, abruptly.

Palfrey said: 'The spinal column is damaged, but the surgeon at the sanatorium does not think irretrievably. I have telephoned to Anstruthers, who is quite the best man, and he has promised to come from London early in the morning.'

'I see,' said Morne. 'You have been very good.'

'I'm glad I arrived when I did,' said Palfrey.

'I have remembered that Halsted told me that he was consulting someone else,' said Morne. He ran his hand over his mane of red hair and turned towards the inner room. 'I cannot understand why he allowed you to make the journey, but, as it happened, it was timely.' Morne was speaking slowly, without looking at Palfrey. 'A friend of my daughter's was taken ill while staying here. The illness puzzled Halsted. Unnecessarily, I think. At least, the patient left this morning. Halsted was telephoned; I'm sure that he was telephoned.' He looked at Palfrey, and glanced away. 'He would have been here himself had he not been warned.'

'I suppose so,' said Palfrey.

'I am afraid I cannot think clearly about anything except my daughter's accident,' Morne went on.

'I didn't know she was your daughter,' said Palfrey.

'Oh, yes.' Morne stepped into the smaller room, where Drusilla and one of the well-dressed women and the thick-set man were sitting in front of the fire, which was now blazing. Huge logs were crackling, and brandy glasses were warming in front of the flames. 'So much has happened so quickly, I had no time to introduce you.' Morne was very formal as he spoke to the woman, who looked remarkably like him but was of smaller build. 'Dinah, this is Dr. Palfrey—Dr. Palfrey, my sister, Lady Markham. My brother-in-law, Sir Claude Markham.' He paused. 'You must be famished, Dr. Palfrey.'

Palfrey gave a quick, diffident smile.

'I am, rather.'

'My sister tells me that I must try to eat,' said Morne.

'She is quite right.'

Morne stood for a moment with his back to the fire and studied Palfrey, who did not look an imposing figure. He was rather thin, his shoulders sloped and he had a slight stoop. His fair, silky hair was curly, and shone in the light from the chandelier. His nose was a trifle prominent and, with his full lips, created the impression of a weak chin. His large eyes looked dull.

Palfrey glanced at Drusilla.

Obviously she was puzzled by this household, probably by something which happened while he had been away with Loretta Morne. Palfrey could tell that from her manner, from the slight lift of her eyebrows. She looked warm and comfortable, however, and smiled assent when Markham suggested talking with Morne and Palfrey in the dining-room.

Little was said. Morne toyed with his food, occasionally roused himself to look after his guest, but for the most part sat brooding.

Palfrey studied him closely. The man had a magnificent forehead; his good looks were remarkable, although he was a little too fat and had a heavy jowl. His red hair waved, unruly, full of vitality. His amber eyes were shot with red. Everything about him suggested strength and perhaps an ungovernable temper.

In a different way, Markham, too, was impressive; he looked fit, and his hair was raven black; his heavy chin was shaded blue by incipient stubble. A broad nose and full lips, fine grey eyes and a broad forehead, all contrasted with Morne. He was nearly as silent as his brother-in-law. Now and again, Palfrey caught Markham looking at him intently; almost, he thought, suspiciously.

'Shall we go into the other room?' asked Morne at last.

'Yes,' said Markham, getting up at once. 'You and your wife will stay the night, Dr. Palfrey, won't you? You know what it's like out. You probably won't reach Corbin in the fog.'

'Yes, it is bad,' said Palfrey. 'Thank you.'

Morne said: 'I can't think clearly. Thanks, Claude.' He looked at Palfrey with a faint smile. 'You will accept my apologies for my absent-mindedness, I'm sure.'

'Of course,' said Palfrey.

Was there something else the matter besides the girl's fall? Was the brooding silence of the red-haired man wholly caused by that? Were those quick, penetrating glances from Markham just an expression of curiosity, or was the subject of Dr. Halsted, who had sent for him and, apparently, had forgotten to cancel the appointment, deliberately neglected? Or could they think only of the girl as she had lain moaning, with her head turning from side to side?

Lady Markham was talking to Drusilla in a soft voice.

'Yes, since she was a child she has always gone up there and looked down; she preferred to hear the piano in the gallery. She always stood in the same spot, resting——'

'Dinah!' exclaimed Morne.

'Oh, Rufus, I'm so sorry.' She looked at him rather blankly. 'I was just telling Mrs. Palfrey.'

'Choose a time when I'm not here, please.'

'Of course, Rufus!' The woman looked a little frightened, and drew her skirts closer about her legs. Morne offered cigars, pierced one, lit it and then, without speaking, turned on his heel and went out.

'I'm so sorry,' murmured Lady Markham, in distress.

'We quite understand,' Drusilla said.

'Such a *terrible* shock.' Lady Markham looked at Palfrey. 'My sister has collapsed, Dr. Palfrey. She has gone to her room. And poor Gerry, he is distracted, *quite* distracted. Ever since he was a child he had played to her and she has laughed down at him. How often I have gone into the music gallery and heard her laughing; so lovely, so happy. I'm sure she would have been perfectly happy with Gerry. I feel so sorry for him. For it to happen in *such* a way.'

'It's been a greater shock than you realize, Dinah,' said Markham. Palfrey saw the look he gave his wife; eyebrows drawn together, a cold glint in his eyes—an angry, exasperated glance. 'I think you'll be wise to follow Rachel's example and go to bed. Don't you think so, Dr. Palfrey?'

'It might be wise,' said Palfrey.

'But, Claude, our guests——'

'Please don't worry about us,' said Drusilla, quickly.

'I will come upstairs with you,' said Markham.

He took her arm. She said good night effusively, then meekly went away with him, leaving the Palfreys alone in the room.

The firelight danced on Drusilla's dark hair; she looked superb in her severely-tailored suit of wine red. Palfrey watched her as she stared at the fire, following the line of her profile and the gentle fall of her throat, the line of her shoulders.

'It's an odd business,' he said.

'I hated this place before we got here,' said Drusilla, 'and I hate it ten times more now!' She was quite serious. 'I don't know why, Sap, but there's something——'

'Uncanny.'

'Have you noticed it?'

'Yes. It isn't imagination. Halsted not turning up gives it a really odd touch. They expected him, you know. The woman who opened the door thought I was Halsted, and told Morne that I was not. Now they pretend that he wasn't due. It's odd. And there are other things. There were no menservants about when we first arrived. The woman, presumably the house-keeper——'

'She is. Mrs. Bardle.'

'——opened the door, but would not have done had a foot-man been available. Before we got here, those men ran out. It looks as if the menservants were set on some other task. That man we saw, in front of the car, might have been a fugitive, perhaps. He was certainly a badly frightened man. In the head-lights, I thought our imagination was playing us tricks and giving him the pale face, the desperate look in his eyes. I'm not so sure now. If he were running away——'

Drusilla interrupted. 'Aren't you going rather fast?'

Palfrey said restlessly: 'I don't know. Where's this patient Halsted wanted me to see? A man ill enough to be kept to his room, ill enough for Halsted to want another opinion, didn't just get up and walk out. Morne says that he left this morning, and also says that he was a friend of the girl's.'

Drusilla did not speak. Palfrey lit a cigarette and threw the match into the fire.

'And this atmosphere—it's fantastic! Neither Morne nor Markham spoke more than a dozen words during dinner. The only one who's shown any inclination to talk is Lady Mark-ham. Morne shut her up and Markham took her away.' He thrust his hands into his pockets. 'She said one thing which I can't get out of my mind. "For it to happen in *such* a way." Morne barked at her; Markham looked at her as if he could have murdered her. I'm not exaggerating. "For it to happen in *such* a way"—as if she had expected it to happen some way or other.'

'The accident would naturally upset them,' Drusilla said.

'Markham isn't upset. Markham is calm and calculating, and looks at me as if he's trying to read my mind.' Palfrey laughed mirthlessly. 'Coming for a walk?'

16

He took her hands and pulled her up. 'I want to look at the minstrel gallery,' he said.

They went into the music room and found a doorway which led to a flight of steps. The doorway was covered with thick curtains. Only a faint light shone on the stairway, and Palfrey, taking one look, said quietly:

'That's the way up. Will you wait here and warn me if anyone comes?'

'Ought you to go?'

'Yes,' said Palfrey. He smiled, and pushed aside the curtain. The steps beyond were of stone, well worn in the centre. The walls, too, were of stone and hung with tapestries, although the staircase was narrow. There were two bends, both awkward to ascend in the poor light, but at last he reached the top and stepped into the gallery itself. There were four levels, where the musician could play, each platform two yards wide, making the gallery larger than it had seemed from below.

He went to the front cautiously. He stood a few feet from the gap, looking down at Drusilla, who was near the door.

He studied the wooden balustrade. The bear carvings were beautifully done and the wood dark from oiling; it had been oiled recently. He gave it closer attention, and could see signs of wear but nothing to suggest that the wood was rotten. He went closer to the gap and there saw that the wood had powdered away, as if worm-eaten. He wished the light were better, and switched on his torch. He studied the wood closely. It was not worm-eaten, it had just rotted. He prodded, and found that it had gone soft. He walked the whole width of the gallery, running his fingers along the balustrade, but at no other point was it soft, only at the one vital spot where Loretta Morne had always leaned and laughed down at Gerry.

Drusilla turned and beckoned him.

He hurried to the staircase and down the stairs, and Palfrey pushed aside the curtain in time to see Markham striding into the room. The man stood quite still, his lips set tightly, and Palfrey did not move.

Markham said: 'Have you been upstairs?'

'Yes,' murmured Palfrey. He looked abashed, but met Markham's gaze steadily. 'Left alone, one gets restless.' He smiled. 'It's remarkably odd, isn't it?'

'Dr. Palfrey——' Markham began, and then stopped himself and turned away abruptly. 'I am sorry. We are all on edge tonight, Dr. Palfrey. Please come and sit down.'

**17**

The smaller room was warm; soon they were sitting down and smoking, and Markham was exerting himself to be friendly. He told them that Loretta, as Lady Markham had said, had made a habit of going up to the minstrel gallery whenever the piano was played. He emphasized the fact that there was nothing unusual about it.

Palfrey murmured something unintelligible.

'I just cannot understand why Halsted failed to tell you that his patient had gone away,' said Markham, abruptly. 'He's usually a most reliable fellow.'

'Yes,' said Palfrey. 'I've known him all my life.'

Markham looked at him intently. 'Have you?'

'School, Balliol, Guys,' said Palfrey, nursing his knee. 'For no one else would I have come out here. After getting his letter, my wife and I decided to take a week's holiday and fit the visit in. Corshire isn't our favourite holiday haunt.'

'It's all right on the other side of Wenlock,' said Markham, 'where there's an entirely different climate. The temperature is often ten degrees higher. Remarkable, isn't it?' He talked freely, almost volubly, drawing a picture of the bleak, fog-ridden moor and the bogs which lay about further to the north, contrasting the scene with the sunny valleys on the south side of Wenlock Hills, which ran down to the sea and faced the broad Atlantic.

A clock struck eleven.

'It's getting late,' said Drusilla.

'I'll show you to your room,' said Markham. 'Mrs. Bardle will have prepared it by now. You're in no great hurry in the morning, I understand.'

'None,' said Palfrey.

'Then take it easy,' said Markham.

The main staircase lay to the right of the front hall. It swept round, giving an impression of the vastness of the place. The floor here was of wood, with bearskin rugs; the heads of bears appeared on the walls and on the furniture, even in the lofty room with a four-poster bed into which Markham led them. A fire was burning; comfortable easy-chairs were drawn up to it, whisky and brandy were on a fireside table, and books lay ready to hand.

Markham said good night and left them.

'It's a cheerful room,' Palfrey said.

'It's all right now that we can shut off the rest of the house,' said Drusilla. 'Did you see how Markham looked at you when you came down from the gallery?'

18

'He was very angry indeed.'

'What did you see up there?'

'Enough to make me curious,' said Palfrey. 'I wish I were an expert on wood. How could one tiny patch be soft enough to break while the rest was hard and firm?'

'It could have been worm-eaten,' said Drusilla.

'No worm-holes.'

She sat on the side of the bed, staring at him.

She said: 'Are you seriously suggesting that—that the balustrade was tampered with?'

'Yes.'

'You must be wrong!'

Palfrey said savagely: 'I believe it was an attempt at murder.'

'You can't——'

'I can't prove it. I shall have a damned good try.' He stood staring at her, frowning. 'I don't yet know how.'

'I don't see what you can do about it,' protested Drusilla.

'That's simple. I shall tell the police.'

Drusilla could find nothing to say.

'I'm not sure that I ought to wait until morning,' said Palfrey. 'But I don't think anything can be altered. The soft wood certainly can't be hardened. I'd better wait. And we'd better get to bed,' he added, with a lighter note in his voice. 'As you say, my sweet, I may be entirely wrong, and I hope I am.'

'I've been thinking,' said Drusilla.

She stopped at the sound of a tap on the door. Palfrey looked round and the tap came again. 'Come in,' he called, and stood waiting expectantly.

Morne appeared, still fully dressed. His forehead was furrowed, the hand by his side was clenched, as if he were exerting himself to retain his composure. He looked at Palfrey without speaking, and closed the door behind him. He walked to the fireplace slowly, steadily, then turned and stood with his back to it. He was trying to speak, but the words would not come. Something in his manner was frightening. Drusilla looked sharply at Palfrey, who stood grave-faced by the door.

At last Morne said: 'I am sorry to behave like this, Dr. Palfrey; my sister has reminded me that a Dr. Palfrey won some renown in Europe during the war.' He paused. 'He was engaged on Secret Service work. Are you that Palfrey?'

Palfrey waved his hand. 'As a matter of fact, yes.'

'Why did you come here?'

Palfrey said: 'Halsted asked me to come for a consultation.'

19

'Will you give me your word that there is no other reason for your visit?' demanded Morne. 'I am serious, Dr. Palfrey. It is a matter of great importance. Have you told me the truth?'

## TWO

## THE BAYING OF DOGS

PALFREY eyed the man levelly as he replied: 'Risking considerable dislocation of my work, I agreed to come here to see Dr. Halsted's patient. The patient has disappeared. I had no other purpose in coming, and I am sorry that the weather prevents me from leaving tonight.'

Morne said: '*No* other purpose?'

'None at all. The possibility wouldn't occur to you if you weren't overwrought,' said Palfrey. 'You ought to get to bed.'

After a pause, Morne said: 'Why do you say that the patient has disappeared?'

'Hasn't he? And hasn't Halsted?'

Drusilla raised a hand, as if to remonstrate with him. Palfrey deliberately avoided catching her eye. Morne raised both clenched hands in front of him.

'I did not know the patient was going to leave. I was out this morning when he left. My daughter told me that he had gone. I know nothing more about it than that, Dr. Palfrey.'

'I am concerned about a great deal that has happened here.'

'I don't understand you.'

Palfrey said deliberately: 'If your daughter dies, in my opinion it will be a matter for police investigation.'

'What do you mean?'

'I mean I think the wood of the gallery was tampered with,' said Palfrey.

'What grounds have you for saying that?'

'An inspection of the wood of the balustrade,' said Palfrey. 'Have you inspected it?'

'No.'

'Will you do so with me?'

'I will,' said Morne. He moved at once towards the door.

In the gallery, Palfrey indicated the soft wood. Morne examined it closely, giving it his whole attention.

20

Palfrey said: 'No other part of the rail is soft like that. The rest has been properly oiled. The first thought that sprang to my mind was that the wood was worm-eaten. That would be un-usual—if this part were touched, other parts would be also—but it was possible. But there are no worm-holes; nothing suggests that the wood just rotted.'

'How could it be softened?' demanded Morne.

'I don't know. I only know that it was. The police will con-sult experts.'

'I see.' Abruptly, Morne went down. At the foot of the steps he turned, stretched up just inside the staircase, and took some-thing from a ledge in the wall. Then, to Palfrey's surprise, he pulled a door to; the door had been flush with the wall behind the curtains, and Palfrey had not seen it before.

The 'something' was a key. Morne locked the door and put the key into his pocket.

'I shall telephone the police at once,' he said.

Morne went into the next room and telephoned to Corbin Police Headquarters.

'I'm glad you've done it,' said Palfrey, as he rang off.

'I am glad you prompted me,' said Morne. He hesitated, and then went on in a voice filled with pain: 'This was the third accident to befall my daughter in as many months. I did not wish to believe the obvious—that someone was attempting to murder her. I am glad you forced the issue.'

After saying good night to their host, Palfrey and Drusilla went to their room.

'Not a pleasant evening,' said Palfrey. 'There's a key in our door, so we can sleep in peace.'

Drusilla turned abruptly and he saw alarm writ large in her eyes.

'Hallo, what's the matter?'

'You said there was a key,' said Drusilla.

'There was.' Palfrey looked at the keyhole. He remembered the key, a large one in the old-fashioned lock. He was quite sure that he had seen one, but it was not there now.

'Which piece of furniture would you like me to drag across the door?' he asked, smiling.

'It isn't funny,' said Drusilla.

'It certainly isn't,' agreed Palfrey. He went to one of the easy-chairs, which rolled easily on its castors, and pushed it beneath the handle of the door. It fitted tightly, and when he tried to open the door without moving the chair he found it impossible. He tucked his arm round Drusilla's waist and said: 'Don't look for hidden doors and passages, that's going too far.' He went across to the dying fire and picked up the whisky. 'What you want is a night-cap,' he declared, 'and you'll sleep like a top.'

Drusilla did not appear to agree with him.

A sound echoed in his ears, not near, not far away. He lay between sleeping and waking, just conscious of tension, listening for a repetition. There were vague, muffled noises, which seemed a long way off and were not loud enough to have disturbed him. Then, almost outside the window, the deep baying of a hound startled him and made him open his eyes wide.

Red light was reflected on the ceiling. Red, then yellow, darting swiftly here and there. There were shadows, too, one central one, the shadow of a huge bear. The flickering light made the thing look alive, the tongue seemed to poke out and lick at the grinning chops.

Fire!

Palfrey put his hand on Drusilla's shoulder, squeezing gently. She stirred. 'Wake up, 'Silla,' he called. 'There's a fire.'

Palfrey pulled a chair to the window, so that he could see beyond the recess, and saw the tongues of flame licking out and then receding. Dark smoke billowed up from the same direction.

He stood on tip-toe, staring down. Between him and the flames he could see the silhouette of a bear; below that was the fire, coming from a bowl which jutted out from the wall. Further away there was another, and he felt a deep sense of relief. He turned, to see Drusilla pulling the chair away from the door.

'False alarm,' he said, 'it's coming from flares—oil flares on the walls.'

'What on earth for?' asked Drusilla.

'That's what we have to find out,' said Palfrey. He looked blue with cold. 'What's the time?'

'A quarter past six.'

In the hall one chandelier was burning.

Palfrey hurried to the door. It was ajar, and, when he pulled it, swung heavily. The light from the flares came into the room; the whole porch was burnished red. A cold wind struck at him as he stepped forward and went down the steps.

The scene was fantastic: half a dozen horsemen, several riderless horses, turning and stamping, lit by that lurid light—a scene that might have come from the Middle Ages, for the red glow shone on the clothes of the riders as if on metal. Markham was having trouble with a big black horse. The youngster, Gerry, was sitting erect and still, looking towards the gates. They were open, lit by flares like those on the walls of the house. A single horseman sat his horse in the gateway.

The courtyard was momentarily silent. Then suddenly there came a long-drawn-out sound—the baying of a hound some distance off. Coming out of the surrounding darkness into that scene of infernal wildness, it made Palfrey jump. A woman sitting on a grey horse exclaimed: 'They've found something!'

Palfrey looked at her. It was not Lady Markham but the other woman, who, he had been told, had gone early to bed the previous night—Morne's other sister, Rachel. She made a splendid figure, vital and eager.

Markham said: 'All ready?'

'All except me,' murmured Palfrey.

Markham glanced round at him, and for a moment his expression reminded Palfrey of their encounter at the foot of the minstrel staircase.

'What are you doing here, Palfrey?'

'Something disturbed me,' said Palfrey, mildly. 'I'm curious.'

'Mind your own damned business!' snapped Markham.

He jerked the reins. His horse moved off, and the others followed, a glittering cavalcade of prancing horses and silent riders. There were six riders altogether ; he guessed that three were grooms. Two horses, bridled and saddled, were left in the courtyard, but there was only one other man, the old servant who had helped with Loretta the previous night.

The cavalcade passed through the gateway. They turned left, off the road. Only Palfrey and the old servant were left. As Palfrey lit a cigarette, he saw the flash of torch-light not far beyond the wall. It shone on a horse and rider. He felt suddenly angry and determined not to be put off so cavalierly, and hurried down the steps. Before the servant knew what he was about to do, he had climbed into the saddle with a quick, effortless movement and gathered up the reins.

'You mustn't ride out, sir!'

'Why not?' asked Palfrey.

'The moor isn't safe for those who don't know it!'

'Do you know it?'

'Oh, yes, sir, but——'

'Then come and look after me,' said Palfrey. He gave a

23

gentle pull at the reins, and his horse moved off.

It was very dark.

They were beyond the glow of the flares, although sometimes Palfrey could see them leaping and dancing in the distance, too far away now to show the outline of Morne House. They were like meteors in the darkness of the night. The wind was bitter, but he was warm from the ride, and his first doubts had gone ; he was right to do this, and the old servant approved, or he would not have followed.

Palfrey could see the pale blur of his face. 'If I tell you what has happened, sir, you won't let Sir Claude know, will you?'

'No,' Palfrey promised.

'Thank you, sir. Sir Rufus is out on the moors, afoot. He left at five o'clock,' said the man. 'He was followed, of course, but the fool lost him.'

'Followed, *of course,*' thought Palfrey. How far could he try this friendly fellow. Aloud, he asked: 'Why was he followed, do you know?'

'He is always followed,' said the guide.

'Does he often go out?'

'More often than he should,' said the guide. 'The moor is in his blood, sir ; he can't help himself ; it calls him and he goes out. Once he was lost all night. And the moor is dangerous in March, more dangerous than any other time of the year.'

'I see,' said Palfrey.

They rode on in silence for some minutes, and then the man said:

'I am greatly worried about the master.'

'Surely he knows the moor well?'

'I wasn't thinking of that, sir. Last night——' The man paused, but his deep, clear voice seemed to echo about them. 'Last night he tried to kill himself, sir. Sir Claude stopped him, sir. I was there. He picked up a sword and thrust it towards his chest, sir ; it caused a wound. Hardly a scratch, but it caused a wound. Sir Claude is afraid that he has gone out to—to try again, sir.'

It was easier now to understand why Markham had been angry. This affair, in his opinion, was none of Palfrey's business. This was a proud family, and it was in grievous trouble.

The groom began to talk again. It had been three o'clock before he and Sir Claude had taken Sir Rufus to his room and left him, convinced that he was then safe. He, the servant, had stayed outside the door ; the master had not gone out that way.

24

He had left by the window, which they had found open. The groom on night duty had been by the gates, and had known nothing of the earlier trouble. Immediately the man had returned, the flares had been lighted.

'Why?' asked Palfrey.

'To guide the search party and the master, if he has lost his way,' said the groom. 'On such a night it is impossible to keep your bearings, sir, but you can see the flares for many miles.' He turned, and Palfrey, looking round, saw the faint glow of the flares ; they seemed to be still now, but he could imagine them roaring and dancing.

The flares were lighted whenever any member of the household was out after dark. The groom took that as a matter of course.

Palfrey said : 'You've been very helpful. What is your name?'

'Ruegg,' said the man. 'Ruegg, sir. We will need to ride single file again now.'

During the conversation, Palfrey had almost forgotten their quest. Now he looked about him, but could see nothing. He was puzzled by the continued silence of the hounds. He was puzzled, also, by Ruegg's frankness. Why had the man chosen to talk so freely? It was on his mind so much that he called out and asked.

'You are a doctor, sir. A doctor might be needed today.'

'Ah, yes.'

'And'—a pause—'it's my opinion you saved Miss Loretta's life last night, sir. But for you, they would have lifted her. I was against lifting her.'

'And rightly,' said Palfrey.

Towards the right, he saw a faint trace of light, not from the sky but at ground level. He watched it grow brighter. It was a long way off, but soon he identified it. There were two cars on the road with headlights full on. Ruegg said nothing. Palfrey wondered if the police had started out from Corbin.

'*Look, sir!*'

There was a note of excitement in Ruegg's voice. Palfrey thought he had seen the cars, but the man was pointing to the left. Palfrey followed his gaze. Several torch-lights were flashing. Now, faint across the dark land, they could hear the baying of the hounds, a deep, excited sound which kept on and on.

'They've found something,' said Ruegg. 'It's by Mylem Pond. We're near a road now, sir. We can gallop.' In a few moments they left the marsh and Palfrey felt the hard surface of a road

beneath him. His horse was eager, with smooth, easy movements, a lengthening stride and then a full gallop; the hoof-
beats were loud and drowned the sound of the hounds at first.
Gradually they drew nearer to the lights and to the baying;
nearer still, and Ruegg called over his shoulder:

'Slow down, sir. Slow down!'

Palfrey drew level with him. 'If questions are asked,' he said,
'you can say that I started off and you were forced to follow
me, in case I got lost.'

'Thank you, sir.'

Now they could see trees which shone in the light of a dozen
torches. The horses were standing free; men on foot were
clustered by the edge of a pond, some holding the straining
hounds. Palfrey could not identify any of the people until he
dismounted and drew nearer. Then he saw that Markham,
Gerry and the woman were watching the men with the hounds,
men whom Palfrey had not seen before.

Markham called out: 'Get into the water, men!'

'Aye, sir.' Four men joined hands, left the hounds together
at the side of the pool, and stepped into the water. As the faint
grey light stole over the eastern sky and the rain came down
more heavily, it was an eerie scene. The men walked slowly.
The water was shallow near the edge, but soon reached their
knees, then half-way up their thighs.

Palfrey said: 'Do you think he's there?'

Markham turned and looked at him; obviously he had been
warned by the galloping horses of the new arrivals. He did not
speak, but turned away. The tension grew. Palfrey, sensing the
hostility of the man by his side, thought more of that than of
the possibility of Morne being in the pool.

A man in the water stumbled. Gerry gasped. Markham went
forward, ankle-deep in water. The men there drew closer together, and then one of them called:

'I think this is it, sir.'

'Get him out!' shouted Markham.

The men bent down, going shoulder-deep in water, until two
of them straightened up and the others heaved. A dark shape
came out of the water, limp, lifeless. Torches were shone
towards it, but the man was face downwards and covered with
mud. The body was put on the dry ground and gently straightened out. Torches shone down into the pale face——

*It was not Morne.*

It was a smaller man than Morne, nearly bald, his mouth

26

gaping open. Palfrey needed no telling that he was dead. He shouldered his way forward, filled with increasing alarm, to see that face more clearly. He stood at the drowned man's feet and looked down and recognized Dr. Halsted.

'When the others realized that it was Halsted, two noticeable things happened,' Palfrey told his wife later. 'Markham was relieved ; so was Morne's sister Rachel. I looked round and saw her sitting in the saddle, smiling, as if she had not a care in the world. That was odd in the circumstances, for Morne was still missing. On the other hand, Gerry, who is Markham's son, looked frightened out of his life. Imagine a man who sees a ghost, and you can see Gerry as he stared down.'

'How long had Halsted been dead?'

'I think he had been in the water at least twelve hours,' said Palfrey. 'It looks as if he were drowned about the time he should have arrived here last night.'

'I suppose he *was* drowned?'

'We can't be sure until after the autopsy,' said Palfrey. 'I hope the Corbin police will let me be present for that. No reason why they shouldn't, as far as I can see. The outward signs are of drowning.'

'No—no marks of violence?'

'None,' said Palfrey.

'And Markham isn't back yet,' said Drusilla, nursing her knees. 'If they find Morne drowned too——' She broke off, and stood up and went to the window. 'And that child in hospital with her back broken. It's devilish.'

'Yes. Dark, evil forces at work,' said Palfrey. 'A most curious business in every way. I feel that I have a personal interest now that Halsted's dead.'

'I suppose that *was* murder?'

'There's no evidence yet,' said Palfrey. 'He might have got lost in the mists last night. If so, where is his car? The police Johnny downstairs told me that he left Corbin by car at a quarter to five. That gave him good time for the journey. He was seen on the outskirts of Corbin, on this road. He wasn't seen again, alive, as far as we yet know.'

'What are the policemen like?'

'Dour, as you'd expect. They lost no time in coming out, you notice ; Morne made them jump to it. I gather that it was still misty round Corbin when they started. So far, they haven't had a lead. No one has told them why Morne telephoned them, and they seem to have jumped to the conclusion that he was talking of Halsted's disappearance.'

'Why didn't you put them right?'

'I'd rather wait until Markham's here,' said Palfrey, 'and, better still, until Morne returns. I've arranged with Ruegg to tell me if they propose to leave. There's one snag,' Palfrey added. 'Morne put the key of the staircase door in his pocket, and presumably he still has it.'

'I see,' said Drusilla. 'How long are we going to stay here, Sap?'

'I hope to leave in good time to reach Corbin in daylight,' said Palfrey. 'There isn't much point in staying here, and Markham certainly wouldn't make us welcome guests. If things *do* turn out so that we're asked to stay, how do you feel about it?'

'I'll stay if necessary,' said Drusilla.

'But only if. I agree with you. I know one thing I mean to do,' went on Palfrey, getting up. 'Find out how Loretta is.'

They went downstairs. No one was about. Gerry had not said more than a few words since their return, and, according to Mrs. Bardle, he was back in bed, already suffering from a chill; the housekeeper explained that Gerry was never in good health. There was no sign, either, of his mother.

Palfrey picked up the telephone which Morne had used on the previous night. He had no difficulty in getting through to the sanatorium, and he was quickly reassured. Loretta Morne had passed a 'comfortable' night, and a post-operation X-ray showed that the crushed ribs were no longer likely to cause complications. The resident doctor at the sanatorium was dubious about her back, and Palfrey, knowing that it would be some days before anyone could judge the prospects of complete recovery, felt reasonably satisfied as he replaced the receiver.

Then he strolled into the music room. The curtain was drawn across the door, and at first glance everything seemed as he and Morne had left it.

He looked up at the minstrel gallery and stood staring, a cold chill in his blood. *The balustrade had been repaired.*

At first he could not believe it, and went closer. The balustrade was all in one piece; he could even see where the joins had been made. There were traces of sawdust on the floor, and one or two grains on the piano.

He swung round towards the inner room, startling Drusilla by his mood. He pulled the bell-rope by the fireplace savagely, went to the door and met a footman coming from the hall. 'Who mended the minstrel gallery?' he demanded abruptly.

'Why, Blackshaw, sir, I presume. The estate carpenter, sir.

'I want to see him at once,' said Palfrey.

After some minutes, footsteps sounded in the hall, and a short, compact man entered the room, a man with a browned, weather-beaten face and deep-set, dark blue eyes.

'This is Blackshaw, sir,' said the footman.

'Did you mend the minstrel gallery this morning, Blackshaw?'

'Yes.' There was no 'sir'. The man obviously resented being questioned by a guest.

'On whose instructions?'

'I had instructions in the usual way,' answered Blackshaw, with scarcely veiled insolence.

Palfrey looked at the footman. 'Ask the inspector of police to come in here at once, please.'

'Very good, sir.'

Blackshaw stood motionless, without removing his gaze from Palfrey's face. They waited for several minutes, but he did not once look away, nor did Palfrey look away from him. The man was as hostile and bleak as the moor outside. At last the police inspector arrived—a man named Hardy, big and solid, stolid of manner, a good-looking fellow in a dark way.

'You wanted to see me, Dr. Palfrey.'

'Yes. You have heard of Miss Loretta Morne's accident, I suppose?'

'A sad thing indeed, sir,' said Hardy.

'On my advice, Sir Rufus telephoned you last night to discuss it with you. There was evidence that the balcony of the minstrel gallery had been deliberately weakened at the place where Miss Loretta usually stood while listening to the piano. In my opinion, and in Sir Rufus's, there were indications of foul play. Sir Rufus locked the staircase door and put the key in his pocket. As you now know, he is missing. The estate carpenter tells me that he repaired the balcony after receiving instructions in the usual way. He will not explain further.'

Hardy fingered his chin. 'I *see,* sir.'

Blackshaw was still looking at Palfrey, but now there was a different expression in his eyes—a shocked one. The footman was standing, aghast, in the doorway. Hardy continued to finger his chin and look at Blackshaw, who turned to face him after a long while.

He said clearly: 'Sir Claude gave me my instructions, sir.'

'And is that usual?' asked Hardy.

'Yes.'

'Isn't it more usual for Sir Rufus to issue instructions?'

'The master seldom does, sir.'

'When were the instructions given?'

'A little after ten o'clock last night, sir.' Blackshaw turned and looked at Palfrey again, and there was now no hint of insolence; only that startled expression in his eyes. '*Was* Miss Loretta *murdered*?' he asked, and repeated: 'Murdered?'

'She isn't dead,' Palfrey told him, and the man's eyes lit up, 'but she may never walk again.'

Hardy said: 'You all understand, of course, that there is no proof that there was foul play. Dr. Palfrey was right to advise Sir Rufus and to tell me, but we cannot take anything as proved. Don't you agree, Dr. Palfrey?'

'It's unlikely that we shall prove anything now,' Palfrey growled, 'unless—— Blackshaw, where is the old wood?'

'It went on—on the kitchen fire.' Blackshaw's fingers were running up and down the seams of his corduroy trousers. 'That was my responsibility, sir. I saw no point in keeping it.'

'Did you notice the softness?'

Blackshaw hesitated. 'It *was* soft in parts, yes.'

'What would make it soft?'

'I didn't think about it,' said Blackshaw.

'Well, think about it now,' said Hardy. 'What would make old wood like that go soft, Blackshaw?'

'Water—might.'

'That would take a long time, wouldn't it?'

'Oh, yes, years,' said Blackshaw. 'Some spirits would. And some acids. Acids more likely. They would eat it away, sir. The rail was strong enough ten days ago. Once every month I look at it, never failing. There was nothing the matter ten days ago. It's old; it's treated with great care. If the wood went soft in that ten days——'

'It was no accident,' said Hardy softly. 'Is that what you mean?'

Blackshaw hesitated, and then said : 'That *is* what I mean.'

A movement at the door—and they turned, amazed. Morne had come in.

## THREE

## POST MORTEM

HARDY told Morne quietly what had happened. Morne listened without a word, but once he put his hand to his pocket, as if feeling for something. He drew it away, empty. When the story was over, he looked at Palfrey steadily and said with great deliberation: 'You saw me put the key into my pocket, did you not?'

'Yes.'

'It is not there now. Blackshaw, where did you get the key?'

'From its usual place, sir.'

'Is it there now?'

'I put it back,' said Blackshaw.

The key was on the hook from which Morne had taken it the previous night. Hardy took it with a polite murmur, and wrapped it in a handkerchief.

Morne looked at the footman. 'Ask Sir Claude to come here at once.'

'Markham is out, looking for you,' said Palfrey.

He thought that would bring about an explosion, but Morne kept his composure. He sent Blackshaw and the footman away. Palfrey told the story of the hunt again, more briefly than to Drusilla. Morne did not change his expression, even when he learned of the finding of Halsted's body. His silence, the steady gaze from his bloodshot eyes, created an atmosphere of great tension. He looked fit to drop, but stood there firmly until Palfrey had finished. Then he went to the doorway and called to the footman in the hall: 'Close this door, and allow no one in until I give you permission.' He turned back to the others and began to talk in harsh, clipped sentences, unfolding a story which gripped them from the first words . . .

Three months before, Morne's daughter had been driving her small car down Wenlock Hill—a hill so steep that many drivers preferred the alternative route—when her brakes had given way and she had crashed, escaping a fall over the cliff and certain death only by chance. A month afterwards, as she was riding along the edge of the same cliff, a gun had been fired close by, making her horse bolt. Loretta had been thrown, and

31

the horse had fallen over the cliff; again sheer chance had saved the girl.

No one knew who had fired the shot.

After the first accident she had been her normal self; after the second, she had become subdued, and had been reluctant to go out alone, although normally she was happy in her own company. Morne had questioned her; she had replied that she felt nervous, but assured him there was no reason for it. Absorbed in private matters, Morne had not given her attitude much thought.

Three weeks after the second accident she had gone away for three days. She had returned with a man of forty, fifteen years older than herself. She had brought him to Morne and told him that they were engaged. She brooked no argument; she seemed unhappy. She wanted her fiancé to stay at the house, but did not say why. Morne, believing that it was infatuation and would soon pass, had agreed. The man had been taken ill soon afterwards. Halsted had been called in, diagnosed pulmonary tuberculosis, and advised the man to go into a sanatorium immediately. The man, who called himself—Morne used those words—Frederick Garth, had refused. Halsted had urged him to change his mind; the sanatorium in the Wenlock Hills was renowned for its curative treatment. Garth had been obdurate, however. He rarely left his room, and he became so seriously ill that Halsted told Morne that he must have a second opinion. Morne had authorized him to consult whomever he liked. Two days before, Halsted had informed him that Palfrey was coming.

All this, Morne told them without a change of tone, looking alternately at Palfrey and Hardy, never at Drusilla. At that point he paused for the first time. He helped himself to another drink and stood back, holding it in front of him.

'You will perhaps blame me for accepting this situation. I blame myself. I am deeply involved, however, in work which I consider of great importance. I gave my home and my daughter less attention than I should have done. Yesterday morning I went into Corbin—the first time for six weeks that I have left the house. When I returned, I was told that Garth had left. My daughter seemed happier than I had known her for a long time. I was relieved. I assumed they had quarrelled and that he had gone because of that. I was fully satisfied with the development and asked no questions, even when my brother-in-law told me that an ambulance had called for Garth.

'At my request, my nephew, Gerald Markham, telephoned Dr. Halsted. As far as I knew at the time, Halsted cancelled his appointment with you, Dr. Palfrey. Later, Halsted telephoned a message which was taken by a servant; he had been delayed, but would arrive before six o'clock. It proved that Gerald had left a message, not spoken to Halsted himself. I assumed, however, that the message had been passed on to you, and was not greatly concerned. I was in my study at half past five last evening when Mrs. Bardle came to tell me of Loretta's fall. I was beside myself. I thought immediately that Halsted might arrive in time to help. I refused to see anyone else who might call; you doubtless heard me giving instructions. While you were helping with Loretta, I was thinking of the other accidents; I saw them as something more, something sinister. For the first time I considered the possibility of foul play. I did not discuss this, but when you told me your conclusions, Dr. Palfrey, I was in no further doubt. You know what followed.'

After a pause, Palfrey said: 'Yes.'

Morne raised his haggard face towards the ceiling.

'At three o'clock this morning I received a telephone message telling me that Loretta was dead. Everything—*everything* that has been good and happy in my life sprang from Loretta. I attempted to kill myself. My brother-in-law and an old servant restrained me. They left me in my room. I knew that one of them was outside my door. I could not stay there; I wanted nothing but death. I climbed out of the window and walked on to the moor. I went out intending to die. But morning came, and with it the sun, and I seemed to see Loretta shaking her head.' He broke off.

Palfrey said: 'Who gave you the message that your daughter was dead, Sir Rufus?'

'The sanatorium officials.'

'They did not. I inquired this morning,' Palfrey continued. 'She is comfortable. There is no great danger now.'

'She is—*alive*!' cried Morne. 'Loretta——' His eyes were blazing and his voice rang out; life seemed to pour back into him. 'Palfrey, this is true?'

'I spoke to the resident doctor,' Palfrey assured him. 'Your message was false.'

Morne walked slowly to a chair, sat down and covered his face with his hands. Hardy glanced at Palfrey and said: 'Is there somewhere we can talk, Doctor?' 'Yes,' said Palfrey. 'In my room,' and they went upstairs.

Hardy said: '*Some*one believed that if Morne thought his daughter dead, he would kill himself.'

'Yes,' said Palfrey. 'That was fiendishly clever. The Devil is in this business. Who was this Garth? Where is he now? Why was Halsted killed——?'

'We don't know that he was murdered yet,' objected Hardy. 'We must wait for the result of the *post mortem*. But there is one thing, Dr. Palfrey, that will greatly interest you—an unfinished letter to you, found in Halsted's pocket. Or, more correctly, in the lining. There was a hole in the lining and it had slipped through. It was the only thing left in the pockets—the wallet, watch, keys and everything were gone.'

Hardy held out a single sheet of paper which was wrinkled where it had been dried out. The ink had run badly, but the words were decipherable.

'. . . I particularly want you, Sap, because this is a most unholy business. "Unholy" isn't an exaggeration. Garth undoubtedly started with the usual symptoms. I think now that he might also be suffering from gradual poisoning. If so, I cannot tell what poison, myself.

'I am more worried than I can say about Loretta Morne. The girl is terribly frightened, but tries to cover it. It has to do with Garth. I feel sure of that.

'You will probably say that I should go to the police. If that is your opinion when you arrive, I shall do so at once. I would not ask you but for the work you have done abroad —I have read about that, of course. You seem——'

The letter stopped there.

Palfrey took another out of his wallet; the handwriting was the same, and he compared the dates; they were identical. The second letter, which he had actually received, was much less informative.

Hardy said: 'He probably decided that in the first he had said too much, Dr. Palfrey, and put the unfinished sheet into his pocket, wrote the second and forgot the first.'

'That's reasonable,' said Palfrey.

'Before you sent for me to talk to Blackshaw,' Hardy told him with an apologetic smile, 'I telephoned my headquarters and asked them what they could tell me about you! Halsted obviously thought you had particular qualifications for this business, and I wondered what they were. Now I know Halsted was quite right!'

'Good lord, no!' disclaimed Palfrey. 'There's all the difference in the world between spying and detecting, you know! But I must admit this business has got under my skin. What's your police surgeon like? Will he object if I'm present at the *post mortem?*'

'Not a bit,' said Hardy. 'He'll be glad to have you. I think I'll leave my man—he's a good chap—and come back with you.'

Instruments flashed in the electric light. Clements, the police surgeon, worked neatly and well, and did not talk. His face was grim. Palfrey thought that he was greatly affected by the fact that he was working on Halsted's body.

He himself certainly was. His thoughts went back to their early days—to Guy's, to Halsted's puckish good humour.

Clements bent closer to his work ; Palfrey sat on a high stool watching and thinking. At last Clements looked up. 'Well?'

'A narcotic,' Palfrey said.

'You wouldn't care to say what narcotic, would you?'

Palfrey went to the bench near the sink, tested, analysed. At last he looked up with a vacant smile.

'I'm no expert, of course. Some kind of morphine poisoning. Not laudanum and not opium as such,' Palfrey said. 'A mixture, and a new one. Halsted was worried by the symptoms of his patient Garth—or don't you know about that?'

'Hardy told me.'

'Well, we can tell him that Halsted either poisoned himself or was poisoned,' said Palfrey, 'and the thing he'll want to do first is to find out where Halsted had tea yesterday.'

'What are you going to do?'

'Finish my holiday,' said Palfrey, absently. 'This isn't my show at all, you know.'

But he felt that it was, and knew that he would not be able to forget it.

'I gathered that Hardy hopes you'll be here for a few days,' Clements told him as they parted, and Palfrey's heart leapt.

During the next three days, Hardy came several times to Palfrey's hotel and was eager to talk. He had not been able to trace Halsted's movements after he had left Corbin a few hours before his death, but his car had been found at the foot of a rock in the Wenlock Hills. There were no fingerprints except Halsted's. The night had been so dark and misty that there was little chance of finding anyone who had seen the car after it had left the pool on the moor. Hardy was able to say that the car had been driven to and from the pool, but the traces were lost on the road surface. It seemed likely that after Halsted had been left in the pool, his car had been driven close to Morne House, past the squat inn and to the Wenlocks, among the rocky valleys of which the driver had doubtless hoped that it would remain hidden for a long time.

Hardy admitted being disappointed in the results of his other inquiries.

'Who benefits if Morne dies?'

'His daughter.'

'And if she predeceases him?'

'His sisters, equally.'

'So Markham would stand to gain a great deal,' said Palfrey.

'Yes, but there's a serious snag in that line of country,' Hardy told him. 'Men don't commit murder for money when they've already got plenty. Morne and Markham haven't a great deal in common except wealth. Both are extremely wealthy. I can tell you this,' went on Hardy. 'The Markhams have always hoped that Gerald and Loretta would marry. The family has intermarried a great deal; there would be nothing unusual about it. Rumour—sorry that there's so much rumour in this!— has it that Loretta won't look at her cousin. She certainly shouldn't! A more vital creature than she it would be hard to find, and Gerald Markham is a weakling. No mind of his own, no desire to work; he wastes his time writing indifferent verse, composing bad music and playing the piano—he *can* play. I'll say that for him.'

Palfrey looked at him owlishly.

'You know a great deal about the Mornes, don't you?'

'Don't forget the Morne family is *the* family in Corshire,' Hardy objected. 'There isn't another that ranks with it—not even Dalby, who's Lord Lieutenant of the county.'

'Do they own much of the land?'

'Most of the land. Morne won't have anything done on it without his express consent. During the war, lead and tin mines were opened after being closed down for years.'

'Odd. Why did he close them?'

'He had no objection to them being worked by small private

36

companies, but refused to let them be worked by public companies before the war. The mines weren't particularly important, wages were low, and Morne wouldn't have it. There was plenty of other work; not more than a couple of hundred men were employed altogether in the mines on his estate. He made sure there was no hardship. Between ourselves, I've always liked him. He's been lonely since his wife died twenty years ago.'

'Curious business altogether. I told you about the pale face in my headlights, and the men who ran past the car, didn't I? Did you ever find out anything about it,' Palfrey asked.

'Not about the pale face,' said Hardy. 'Both Morne and Markham told me the same thing, and I've checked it with several of the servants. You did see lines of running men taking the hounds out for an airing. From where you were sitting, you couldn't see the hounds. It happens every night—— Why, what's the matter?' he demanded, as Palfrey sat up sharply.

'That might explain the scared face,' Palfrey said. 'Imagine a marauder in the grounds, suddenly aware that a pack of hounds was let loose. He would be scared and he would certainly run!' He settled back again. 'The trouble is that none of this helps at all to find who killed Halsted. *I'm* satisfied that he was murdered.'

'So am I, and I think the Coroner's jury will return a verdict of murder against some person unknown,' Hardy said. 'The inquest is in the morning. Will you be there?'

'Yes,' said Palfrey.

'You aren't exactly a free talker, are you?' said Hardy, with a reproachful stare. 'I have a feeling that there are deep thoughts in your mind.'

'You're the policeman; I'm here by chance.'

'You certainly aren't here by chance,' said Hardy. 'Halsted wanted your help. And *I* want your help, Palfrey.'

Palfrey sighed. 'I don't like this affair. I am not a detective. But if you ask me what I think is the most significant thing so far, I can only say one thing. Those bloodhounds followed *Morne*'s trail to the pool where Halsted's body was found, didn't they? People are prone to error, but bloodhounds know their master's scent. Morne went to that pool. I think, for what it's worth, Morne saw us when we found the body. Trees and rocks could have hid him from us; he might even have been up a tree.' He paused, and frowned at Hardy's astonished face. 'Are you glad that I opened up?'

## FOUR

# 'I WANT DR. PALFREY'

HARDY went off, shaken out of his calmness. Palfrey found Drusilla downstairs, sat down by her, and stretched out his long legs. 'I have told my piece to the persistent Hardy,' he said, 'and he gives me the impression that Corshire is shaken to its foundations.'

A page-boy came up. 'Telephone for you, Dr. Palfrey.'

'Thanks. No peace for the lazy!' He got up, and went to the telephone booth off the hall, expecting to hear Hardy's voice.

'Good afternoon, Dr. Palfrey. This is Ross, of the Wenlock Sanatorium. Miss Morne is asking for you.'

'I'm sorry. I didn't quite catch that.'

'She is asking for you,' repeated Ross. 'She came round for the first time this morning, stayed awake just long enough to say that she wanted to see you, and then went off again. She's now been awake for an hour, and all she says is that she wants Dr. Palfrey.'

'But she's never seen me in her life.'

'Well, she says the same thing over and over again: "I want Dr. Palfrey." She hasn't asked for her father or for anyone else; only for you.'

'Then I must try and come,' Palfrey said. 'How long will it take me to drive over?'

'An hour and a quarter by the moor, nearly two hours by the cliff road.'

'Cliff road for me,' said Palfrey. 'I don't want any more of that moor, if you understand me. Thanks. Er—what is Wenlock like for hotels? I don't know that I shall fancy driving back tonight.' He glanced at his watch. 'I shan't be there much before seven, shall I?'

'No, even if you start right away. I'll find you and your wife somewhere to stay; don't worry about that. Look for the "Dangerous Hill" sign about thirty miles out of Corbin. It'll be illuminated, but don't miss it.'

The first hour was a pleasant ride. Then darkness fell, and they came up a steep hill after passing a sign at a left-hand turning—not an illuminated sign. The engine of the Talbot laboured. The headlights suddenly seemed to strike a wall, a wall that looked like the road. Palfrey put on the brakes and the car stopped. All he could see on one side was rocks, on the other a void; in front of him was the road at that astonishingly steep incline, and so narrow that there looked hardly room for two cars to pass.

'What's on that side?' asked Drusilla, nervously.

'I don't know,' said Palfrey; but he did know. The edge of the road was also the edge of the cliffs, with a sheer drop into the sea. 'I doubt if we can try to get up it in the dark,' he said. 'I'll back down. There was a turning to the left, wasn't there?'

After travelling ten yards or so, he put the brakes on full. 'You'd better get out with the torch,' he said. 'Don't go near the right-hand side, just keep your torch-light on it. Sorry, sweet.'

'It's all right,' said Drusilla. She shone the torch, then came back, her face pale in the dim roof-light. 'You've about a yard and a half on the cliff side,' she said, 'and plenty of room on this side. If you can get nearer this side——'

The headlights shone on the jagged rocks of the cliff on their left. He drove close to them, and the wing scraped a rock. He straightened the wheels and eased off the brakes again. The car moved at a snail's pace. Drusilla was walking backwards all the time, shining her torch on to the rocks.

A car came along the road beneath them. It seemed far below, giving them some idea of the height they had climbed. It swung to the left of the road and disappeared.

'I've a quarter of a mile to go,' Palfrey muttered. He leaned out of the window and called: 'Are you all right, darling?'

'Ye-es!' called Drusilla.

He could see her legs and feet in the beam of light from the torch. The loud hum of the overworked engine drowned all other sound. Progress was painfully slow. Another car swung round the bend. It was still a long way beneath them. Palfrey continued for a dozen yards, on edge with the strain, scowling whenever he scraped a rock on the near side. Then Drusilla's light vanished.

He had no warning; the steady swing, showing her legs and feet, continued until the moment when the light went out. Palfrey jammed on the brakes, and kept looking over his shoulder, waiting for it to go on again. It did not.

He put on the hand-brake and opened the door.

''Silla!' There was no answer. In the deep hush which followed, he could hear the lapping of the waves on the rocks

**39**

below. *''Silla!'* He broke into a cold sweat and got out of the car.

*''Silla!'* The echo came back to him. It rolled round, deep, mocking. *''Silla! Silla Sil-la—la—la!'* It faded.

There was a movement behind him.

He swung round, but saw and heard nothing. Fancy was playing him tricks.

There *was* a sound! It came from behind him, and he turned again. He stood quite still, staring towards the rocks, able to see only the stones and boulders of the cliff-side.

*'Do you want to find your wife, Dr. Palfrey?'* It was a hoarse, whispering voice, coming out of the darkness. There was no sound after the voice stopped.

Palfrey found his voice. 'Yes.'

'Go back to Corbin and she will return by midnight,' the man said. 'I warn you not to be foolish, Palfrey. If you have a gun, don't use it. I shall not—— *Ah!'*

His voice ended on a high note of surprise, of pain. Palfrey saw nothing, but now he heard movement—a scrambling, struggling sound; rocks were moving down the cliffside, *men were struggling!* He moved forward, trying to see more clearly. He could hear heavy breathing, a gasp, a sharp sound and then a deafening roar, accompanied by a flash of flame. There was a gasp, a thud—and then only heavy breathing.

Palfrey climbed over the rock wall, and stood still. Every moment he expected that hoarse voice to come again, but it did not. The breathing grew easier. He took another step forward, but started when a man said: 'Hang around a minute, will you?' The new voice was startling enough in itself; the fact that it was American registered vaguely on Palfrey's mind.

'I'll shine a light,' the man said. 'Keep your distance a minute, Palfrey.' A light flashed out towards him. It shone into his face, lingered for a moment, then moved off. Palfrey, dazzled by the glare, heard the man say: 'Sorry. I don't recognize you. Is your name Palfrey?'

'Yes.'

'Fyson didn't seem to like you,' the man said. There was a hint of laughter in his voice. Palfrey warmed to him. 'Do you know Fyson?'

'No.'

'Take a look,' said the American. He shone the torch on the figure of a man who was lying unconscious with his head against a rock. 'Have you lost your wife?' asked the American.

40

'Yes, she vanished.'

'Right here, you mean?'

'Yes. Not long ago—not twenty minutes ago.'

'Then I should quit worrying,' said the American. 'She'll be around here some place. Are you really a doctor?'

'Look here, I want to find my wife,' said Palfrey. 'Shall we go into other things afterwards?' The American did not reply, and Palfrey moved forward. 'Yes, I am a doctor, and I was going to see a patient. The police in Corbin will verify that later.'

'I don't know that I want to see the police in Corbin or any place,' said the American, 'but I guess I'll take you at your word, Palfrey. Your wife just disappeared off the road, did she, somewhere around here?'

'Yes.'

'We'll see. Wait a minute, Fyson might do some good for once in his life—if he's alive—and produce a flashlight.' He bent down, and Palfrey could see his hands and face; the rest of his body was in shadow. The hands went through Fyson's pockets, and he gave a grunt of satisfaction. 'Here's one,' he said, and switched on a second torch. 'You go right, I'll go left.' He moved off.

The encounter had prevented Palfrey from giving all his thoughts to Drusilla; now his fears flooded back. He began to sweat, and now and again he wiped his forehead with the back of his hand.

'Palfrey,' called the American. 'She's here. There couldn't be two women on this damned hillside on the same night, could there? She's okay,' he added, as Palfrey began to stumble forward. He shone his torch, and Palfrey saw Drusilla sitting against a rock, her head lolling forward.

Drusilla's pulse was slow but steady; there was a smell of chloroform.

Palfrey looked up at the American. The two torches were resting on a ledge, and he could see his face. It was a berry-brown, merry face, with impudent blue eyes.

'Have a look at Fyson, will you? If he's dead, he's dead, and that's all about it, but if he's alive, I shall want you to do *me* a favour. Your wife will be all right here, I guess.'

Palfrey took off his coat and wrapped it round Drusilla's legs, then picked up his torch and looked about for the unconscious man. The American came with him. Palfrey knelt down, felt the man's pulse, and was surprised by the American's sharp voice: 'Is he dead?'

'No. It's probably concussion.'

'Sure. You bleed a lot from concussion.'

'The blood's from his torn scalp,' said Palfrey.

'That's grand,' the other went on. 'Now I guess I want you to help me carry him to your car and take him in that to my car—and then wish me good night.'

'Oh, do you?' said Palfrey.

'I know the police are your friends, but don't forget that you might not have found your wife without me, Palfrey. That's a turn that deserves another.' He repeated the words in a hoarse voice, startlingly like Fyson's. 'Don't worry,' he went on, in a normal voice. 'I've been practising that for six months. The day might come when I'll fool someone. What about it?'

Palfrey said: 'Where is your car?'

'At the foot of the hill.'

'Let's get him there,' said Palfrey. 'And get my wife to the car, too.'

At the American's insistence, they first took Fyson to his car. The man did not stir, but once he was sitting in a corner, with a large handkerchief round his head to keep the blood off the upholstery, the American insisted that he be given a shot of morphia.

'I don't want him to get away while we're collecting your wife,' he explained.

There was no harm in it, and Palfrey humoured him before they went back for Drusilla. She was beginning to come round, and talking wildly.

'But don't you see, Sap, everything turns on Loretta's fiancé. It must do.' Drusilla had never said that to him; she rarely tried to guide him; she was against him taking part in such affairs, hating them because of grim memories of being hunted in Europe. 'Of course it does. Everything turns on this man Garth, if you could only find him.'

The American's hand suddenly closed about Palfrey's wrist. In the dim light from inside the car, Palfrey saw the man's face, no longer merry and smiling, but grim and set. The American said, in a slow voice: 'Say, what's this about Garth? How do *you* know Garth? If you know Garth, you must know Fyson.'

'I don't know either of them.' Palfrey hesitated, then moved his hand suddenly, gripping the American's, and twisted slightly. The man gasped and stood transfixed.

Palfrey released him. 'Sorry. Showing off. Your grip isn't good.'

'Flying geese!' exclaimed the American. 'I didn't think you had it in you. I asked for that.'

'I'm in a hurry,' said Palfrey. 'Garth's fiancée is lying dangerously ill at a sanatorium not far from here, and is asking for me. If I hadn't taken the wrong road, I would be there by now.'

'That's a great pity,' said the American. 'Let's get to my car. I guess I want to hear your story pretty badly, Palfrey.'

'I hope to hear yours.'

The American knew of a wide stretch of road not far down, where Palfrey was able to reverse. Once that nerve-racking job was over, the rest was plain sailing. At the foot of the hill, the American's car was parked on a grass verge; it was a Packard with a roomy body.

'I'll come with you, I guess,' he said. 'It will mean tying Fyson up and leaving him where he can't be found, and leaving the car here. You'll have to bring me back tonight if I can't get a taxi.'

'I'll bring you if it's necessary,' promised Palfrey.

Together they lifted the unconscious man and carried him a little way up the side of the hill. There they left him behind a rock, bound and gagged.

'I wonder what Inspector Hardy would think if he could see me now,' said Palfrey.

'Maybe you can tell him one day,' said the American. They walked back to Palfrey's car. 'You're sure Fyson won't die on me?'

'He won't die. He's well wrapped up and sheltered from the wind. I can't guarantee that he won't be spirited away.'

They reached the car and, with a grin, the American held out his hand. 'You're with Mr. Nicholas Kyle,' he said.

'Good evening, Mr. Kyle,' Palfrey said, gravely. He began to talk. The man who called himself Nicholas Kyle smoked cigarette after cigarette, but did not interrupt. Palfrey omitted only his conclusions about Morne's visit to Mylem Pool, not seeing how that could affect Kyle's interest in the affair.

The lights of a town appeared as Palfrey concluded.

'Well, that's not bad,' admitted Kyle. 'It's a story I would be proud to own myself, Palfrey. Are we in Wenlock?'

'It looks very much like it.'

The sanatorium, Palfrey learned from a policeman on traffic

duty in the centre of the town, was up Hill Road as far as he could drive. The road ended at the sanatorium, which overlooked Wenlock Bay. The policeman was very helpful and talkative, but he kept looking at Kyle and now and again he glanced at Drusilla.

They drove on at last, and Kyle observed: 'I've been thinking about Fyson. He didn't want you to talk to this Loretta Morne.'

Palfrey shot him a quick, amused glance.

'Now, how did you guess that?'

'All right. Now, Fyson has friends. While he was keeping you and your wife away, his friends might have visited the sanatorium and seen this Loretta. It's eight o'clock now, so they've had time. Aren't you worried about Loretta?'

'Not yet. Fyson didn't know what time I would leave Corbin,' Palfrey pointed out. 'If they—his friends—thought they could do what they wanted at any given time, they would not have sent Fyson to hold me up, because it wouldn't have been necessary. Fyson stipulated midnight. As it's only about eight o'clock now, three hours can pass before anything is likely to happen.'

'I hope you're right,' said Kyle. 'I wouldn't be happy. I'm *not* happy. I ought to have thought of this before ; I could have telephoned a message from a call-box.' He sat quiet, but seemed on edge during the rest of the journey.

At last they reached a long building with a wide gateway over which, in neon letters, were the words: *Wenlock Sanatorium, Motorists quiet, please.*

Palfrey switched off the headlights.

'And I'm not worried, because the police have been within call of Loretta since it was known that there might be foul play,' he said. 'Will you wait for me?'

'Are you trusting me with your wife?'

Palfrey smiled and went through the gateway. He did not look back, but before he reached the first flight of steps leading to the Sanatorium, he wondered if he were wise to leave Drusilla with Kyle. The man was likeable and had put the Palfreys greatly in his debt ; but that did not mean that he was trustworthy. He went on, still slightly uneasy.

The policeman in the passage outside Loretta Morne's room was a burly fellow in uniform. He eyed Palfrey up and down, asked to see his identification papers, which contained a photograph, and pronounced himself satisfied. Palfrey said: 'I left

44

my wife asleep in my car, constable, and I'm a little worried about her. In this affair, unpleasant things happen. Could you keep an eye on her, do you think?'

'You needn't worry about *that*, sir.'

'No?' Palfrey showed surprise.

'The place is closely watched, sir.'

'*Is* it, by Jove!'

'You mustn't forget that Sir Rufus Morne is the uncrowned king of Corshire,' said Loretta Morne's physician, Dr. Ross, with a tinge of sarcasm in his tone. 'I can't say that I think such precautions are necessary, but the police do. My kitchen staff are kept busy running out to them with cups of tea!'

As Ross opened the door, it dawned on Palfrey that the police knew more, or suspected more, than they pretended.

Loretta was strapped up rigid beneath the bedclothes, with only a thin pillow. Her face was as white as the sheets, but her eyes were brilliant. Her face was drawn and she was obviously in pain. Palfrey felt sorry; in some curious way this girl mattered to him. She looked up at him and said: '*I want Dr. Palfrey.*'

Ross murmured: 'I'll leave you now, Doctor,' and went out. Rubber flooring muffled the sound of his footsteps.

'*I want Dr. Palfrey.*' Her voice was little more than a whisper. She stared at him and repeated the words, and he smiled at her and said: 'I am Dr. Palfrey.'

'*You* are?' Her eyes seemed to grow larger, and she looked at him searchingly for a long time. Palfrey heard a rustle of movement. He looked up, sharply, and saw a white screen and beneath it a pair of heavy boots. Another policeman, of course.

'Dr. Palfrey'—the man in the corner certainly could not hear her words—'you must answer me a question. Now.'

'I will try to,' said Palfrey.

What did it mean? What could she want to know from him? How had she ever come to know of his existence.

Her lips moved again. 'What'—he had to lean forward to catch her words—'what year did Dr. Halsted break—his front —teeth? What year did——' She stopped, as if she could not find the strength to go on, but her enormous eyes were staring at him.

Palfrey stared back. What year had Halsted broken his front teeth? It was ridiculous, she was wandering, she——

Realization dawned on him, and he remembered. Cricket, for Guy's; a flaming summer's day; a fast bowler who kicked

**45**

dangerously; Halsted in great form; an awkward one which rose higher; Halsted's bat flashing; a gasp from the bowler, and a spurt of blood from Halsted's mouth. What *year*?

Palfrey's last year at Guy's.

'It was at Blackheath in 1929,' he said, 'in a cricket match against——'

'You *are* Palfrey!' Her lips puckered; she was trying to smile. Her eyes closed with relief; she lay there for some time before she opened them again. She said: 'Look in the third post—of the minstrel gallery—from the door. The third post—of the minstrel gallery——'

Palfrey murmured: 'Yes, I will. The third post from the door.' His mind was racing, so many things dawned upon him in those few seconds. She had confided in Halsted; Halsted had sent for him because of it; Halsted had been murdered because someone had learned that she had given him her confidence. Halsted had told her of that half-forgotten incident, so that she could be certain that she was talking to the real Palfrey. Perhaps, at that very time, Halsted had been afraid that he would die.

The third post——

Had the third or the fourth post been taken away after the 'accident'? Would he find it intact, or had it been destroyed? A message, an explanation, a clue which she considered of vital importance, one of the reasons for her fears and for giving Garth shelter, was hidden in that post.

'Thank you,' she said, and a few moments afterwards she was asleep.

'Well?' Ross's voice startled him. On the spur of the moment, Palfrey said: 'She gave me a message for her father.'

'Did she say why she gave it to *you*?'

An answer sprang to his mind at once. 'Yes, Halsted had mentioned me to her.' He was suddenly annoyed by the bright blue eyes of the doctor. 'It is confidential, of course,' he said. 'I must get out to Morne House at once.'

'Oh, yes, yes. Of course,' said Ross. He coloured, as if he knew that he had been rebuked. 'I will cancel the reservation I made for you at the Esplanade Hotel. Unless your wife will be staying in Wenlock?'

'I think she'd better,' said Palfrey. 'It's been very good of you, Dr. Ross.' Most decidedly, he disliked the man.

Ross accompanied him along the rubber-floored passages in

silence until they reached the hall. Then he asked whether Palfrey would like a snack.

'I don't think so, thanks.' Immediately he had spoken, Palfrey realized he was hungry. He changed his mind, and smiled apologetically. 'Well, if it could be ready in five minutes or so.'

'Yes, I'm sure it can. Perhaps you would rather have something to take with you.'

'That's even better,' said Palfrey.

'I'll give the instructions myself,' said Ross, and turned away. Palfrey lit a cigarette, glanced towards a bulky man who was sitting in an armchair in the hall, with a newspaper in front of his face. There was something familiar about him. Palfrey stared. The paper moved, and Inspector Hardy smiled up at him.

'Why, hallo!' exclaimed Palfrey. 'You've been quick!'

'As a matter of fact, you've been slow,' said Hardy. 'I started out half an hour after you and got here first! Have you seen her?'

'Yes.' Palfrey lowered his voice and told the Corbin man exactly what Loretta had told him. He also gave his conclusions, voiced his questions, and waited, confident that Hardy would take a sensible view.

'I think perhaps you'd better go out there by yourself,' said Hardy, at last. 'At least, without me, although I shall be on pins until I know that the third post is still standing. Of course, if you have any trouble in getting whatever is hidden there, I'll step in, but I've a feeling that you'll get more out of Morne than I ever shall. And, in any case, I've left two men at Morne House,' he added, with his deep chuckle. 'Ah, here come your sandwiches.' He heaved himself up from his chair. 'Now, how can I make myself useful?'

'In several ways,' said Palfrey. 'You can take my wife to her hotel and get a maid to put her to bed.' He laughed at Hardy's expression. 'No, she's not drunk. She had a fall which upset her, but she's all right. Then you can arrange for a car to follow mine across the moor, preferably with an armed man inside it.'

'What trouble *have* you met tonight?' asked Hardy.

'I took the wrong road, went up the steep hill and was shot at while coming down,' Palfrey told him. There were limits to what he need tell Hardy, and he was anxious not to betray Kyle. Later, he might have to give information about the man, but for the moment he had convinced Hardy that he was being frank. 'That was to try to stop me from coming to see Miss

47

Morne,' he went on. 'The man outside lent me a hand and made himself generally useful. I brought him along and am going to give him the best dinner in Wenlock. I'll have to leave you to arrange that, too, but I don't think he will mind. Try to find him a whole bottle of whisky!'

'I *see,*' said Hardy. 'So you were shot at. I saw headlights up the hill as I turned the corner. I thought it funny, but I was in such a hurry to get after you that I took no notice. I—*now* I know why the lights were off at the sign at that corner,' he added, his voice rising. 'I couldn't understand it. The light was there even during the war.'

'Oh, the trap was nicely laid and I obligingly walked into it,' confessed Palfrey.

Ross came up again, with a Thermos flask and a bakelite cup. Palfrey was effusive in his thanks. Outside, a man stirred from the side of the steps and said 'Good evening, sir' to Hardy. Palfrey concealed a smile, and walked down the steps, looking towards his car. Drusilla was still asleep, with her mouth open. Kyle must have slumped down in his seat, for Palfrey could not see him.

A moment later he missed a step. Kyle wasn't there.

'Your friend doesn't seem to want that dinner,' remarked Hardy, dryly. 'Be frank with me, Palfrey. Ought I to look for him?'

'That's up to you,' said Palfrey. 'I wouldn't, personally. Everything else apart, I would think it a waste of time.'

He helped to get a befuddled Drusilla from his own car to Hardy's and drove off in a very puzzled frame of mind.


FIVE

THE THIRD POST

THE night was clear, without a trace of mist, and the road was good. Palfrey drove fast. Next to him sat one of Hardy's men, dark and sombre. The detective officer had already had his supper, but he accepted when Palfrey suggested a drink. He opened the Thermos flask carefully, poured a little into the bakelite cup and said: 'I'll have the cap.'

'Thanks,' said Palfrey. He took the cup with his left hand

48

and sipped. 'Lord, that's hot!' He nearly spilt the tea as he snatched the cup away. 'I'll wait until it's cooled down.'

Two hundred yards behind them the headlights of the second police car swayed along the road and were reflected in Palfrey's driving mirror. Hardy had taken extreme precautions, and Palfrey pondered over the situation ruefully. At one time he had thought that Hardy was a slow-moving, slow-thinking fellow, eager for the slightest help from Palfrey. Instead, Hardy was deep, and knew much more about the affair than he had revealed. The accident and the murder could not be the first incidents. The man next to him sipped the hot tea noisily. They were out of the hills now, and on the moors. The car behind him was keeping pace, sometimes drawing closer so that the lights reflected from the mirror and dazzled Palfrey.

'I'll pour some tea out for you and hold it while it cools,' offered his companion.

'Thanks very much.'

Palfrey turned a corner, saw a flat stretch of road in front of him and opened out. A few minutes should see them at Morne House, and he had to be prepared with an excuse for his return visit.

Something wet fell on his leg, and he glanced round, sharply.

'Look out,' he said, 'it's spilling.'

His companion did not move; he was sitting back with the cap of the flask in his hand tilted over. Suddenly the man slumped forward and dropped the cup. Palfrey looked sideways at his companion. 'Wake up,' he said, but there was no conviction in his voice.

This was not natural sleep; the man was drugged.

A picture of Ross's flashing smile appeared in Palfrey's mind's eye.

There was no point in stopping to see if he could help his companion; that would be much easier inside the house. He trod more heavily on the accelerator, and as he did so he saw a yellow flicker of lights on his left.

The flares of Morne House were on, so someone of the household was out that night. He saw the squat inn, on the right this time, turned and drove very fast towards the lighted house. The dancing flares shone on the dark stone walls and the huge bears; the whole had a satanic look and sent a shiver down his spine.

He pulled the car up outside the front door and pressed his horn urgently. The other car was some way off now; he had gained half a mile. He helped his companion out, as the great door opened.

Palfrey had no stomach pump, and he was not certain what drug had been used, but he gave orders crisply, and a footman hurried off. The police were still sitting outside in their car; Palfrey called them in and explained briefly. Mrs. Bardle came up, the policemen took their colleague to a bedroom, where he was to be given an emetic, watched closely, and kept warm with blankets and hot-water bottles.

Palfrey lit a cigarette and stood smoking, reflecting that he had acted in a high-handed fashion, taking complete charge and issuing orders; but Mrs. Bardle had not hesitated to obey him, and it had all been necessary.

Mrs. Bardle came back: a thin, angular woman with sharp features and fine, bold eyes.

'Do you wish to see Sir Rufus, sir?'

'I would like to, yes,' said Palfrey.

'If you will wait just one moment, sir, I will see whether he is downstairs.'

Palfrey's mind raced. Since the policeman's collapse, he had forgotten that he needed a convincing reason for his return.

Morne suddenly appeared in the doorway, like a great bull. No, thought Palfrey, like a bear. He wore a dinner jacket and looked well-groomed and composed. He held out his hand.

'I am very glad to see you again, Dr. Palfrey.'

'Thanks,' smiled Palfrey. 'I've just come from Wenlock. I saw your daughter. Progress *is* good. Better than we had any right to expect.'

Morne said: 'You are always a bearer of good tidings!'

'My good fortune,' dissembled Palfrey. 'Not always a peaceful messenger, I'm afraid. I've had two upsets tonight. One on the road from Corbin to Wenlock, another from Wenlock here. Details will bore you, but the facts are there.' He no longer looked diffident, and his voice was incisive.

'I don't quite understand you,' said Morne; 'but come along and have a drink.' He rested a hand on Palfrey's shoulder, a gesture Palfrey thought was uncharacteristic, and led the way into the other room. No one else was there.

Palfrey explained. He spoke quietly and Morne looked at him with keen interest.

'I had intended only to satisfy myself about your daughter's condition before I returned to London,' Palfrey told him. 'The

50

attempt to stop me from seeing her made me decide to see you again.'

Morne said, as if puzzled: 'Why should it, Dr. Palfrey?'

'All these things happened after my first visit. I gave you information about your daughter's accident which brought the police here. Someone did not like it, Morne. Someone did attempt to murder your daughter, and it's reasonable to assume that the same person resented my interference and tried to stop it.'

'You realize you are suggesting a member of my household caused the accident to my daughter, don't you?' asked Morne, in a very soft voice.

'Yes. It's right that you should know what I think.'

After a long pause, Morne said: 'Dr. Palfrey, by your prompt handling of the situation when you arrived here on Monday evening, I think you saved my daughter's life. I am, therefore, for ever in your debt. You have placed me under a further obligation by your frankness and by the trouble you have taken to come here tonight. I hope you will not place yourself in any further danger.'

'Now what does he mean?' asked Palfrey of himself. 'I don't quite understand you,' he said aloud.

'I mean that I hope you will not venture out again tonight,' said Morne.

'Oh,' said Palfrey, and relaxed again. 'I was rather hoping that I need not. It means that three extra policemen——'

'Mrs. Bardle has told me they are here, and I have given instructions for them to be looked after,' Morne assured him.

'You're very good,' said Palfrey. 'Now, if I may use the telephone, I'll let my wife know that I'm not going back tonight.'

Palfrey got out of bed and contemplated the grey ash in the grate. He had been so tired that he had not wanted to stay up until the house was silent, and Hardy's man had raised no objection to calling him, saying that he was on duty all night. He had said also that the Markhams were out but that Morne's sister Rachel had been in her room all the evening.

Palfrey dressed quickly. At last he went into the passage, and found the policeman sitting on an upright chair near the landing.

'How's your friend who was drugged?'

'Sleeping naturally, sir.'

51

'Good!' Palfrey moved off, down the stairs. If he found anything in that third post, Hardy would undoubtedly insist that it be given up. Yet the girl would not have taken such precautions had she wanted the police to know.

Palfrey took out his torch—Fyson's torch!—and walked to the gallery door. The curtain was half drawn, and he could see the lower steps. His slippers made no sound as he went up, shining the torch. It was piercingly cold, and he was excited—not nervous, but excited. Repressing his eagerness earlier in the evening had sharpened it. He was tensely anxious lest the third post had been removed.

He reached the gallery and approached the balustrade, still shining his torch. One post—two—three——

The repair was beyond the third and beyond the fourth post!

He went to the third and shone the torch upon it. Nothing seemed unusual; the hand-carved wood was dark with oil and gleamed dully in the light. Bears surrounded it, tiny carvings exquisitely done. He touched them one after the other, but nothing happened. There must be a way of opening the post; it was almost certainly hollow; Loretta must have meant that. He leaned over the balustrade to examine the front. He touched the first bear-head, twisted and turned it; it was loose! With increasing excitement he concentrated on it, leaning right over, one hand holding the torch, the other exploring. He pulled at the head, and it moved outwards.

The torch shone into a narrow cavity. He put the torch into his pocket and gripped the balustrade, so as to lean further over, and explored again.

*Someone gripped his ankles!*

His hand slipped from the balustrade **and he** felt himself being heaved over.

He kicked out. The grip was too firm to be shifted, but he gained a moment's respite. He grabbed the post. He could see and hear nothing, but the pressure was increasing. A sudden heave and a gasp and he was over. The jolt on his shoulder and his wrist made him cry out, but he managed to hold; it was a matter of life and death to hold on. He hung, swaying.

Suddenly a torch light shot out, carving a straight line through the darkness. He could not see who was holding it, but he felt a hand brush against his fingers; his assailant meant to make him fall.

He hung straight, but a sharp pain at his knuckles made him wince. He drew in his breath and let go, bending his knees, trying to judge the distance to the floor. He struck it with his toes, lurched forward and fell. His head struck something which slithered along the floor.

The light of the torch went out.

And then another light came on, much brighter, one of the chandeliers. He heard a rustle of movements, several heavy, booming footsteps, followed by the sharp sound of someone running up the staircase. Hardy's man, he thought. A door slammed. The footsteps now sounded hollow; Hardy's man was on the balcony.

He looked up and saw a stranger looking down, a man dressed in a light grey suit and smiling a droll smile.

'"Flat burglary as ever was committed",' quoth the man.

Palfrey gaped. 'What?'

'Othello,' declared the man. 'Shakespeare.' He had a long, narrow face with a long chin and a humorous mouth, large dark eyes and curly hair.

Palfrey got up and felt for a cigarette. The man stood smiling down at him. Palfrey shifted his gaze and looked towards the third post. There was an open slit there, as he had left it.

'Did the beggar get it?'

'No. I did.'

'I hope that's a good sign,' said Palfrey. 'Are you coming down or shall I come up?'

'I will come down. The great Dr. Palfrey must be put to no inconvenience. True, King Rufus might think differently if he knew that the great Dr. Palfrey was "by night a stealthy, creeping thing, a marauder with ill-intent", but——'

Palfrey said: '"An honourable burglary, if you will, for naught I did for gain, but all in honour."'

'Nicely turned!' The man laughed lightly and, to Palfrey's astonishment, started to climb over the balcony. 'If you can, I can.' The other climbed over, lowered himself, hung at full length and dropped. He did not fall, but staggered against the piano.

'Am I entitled to ask you what you were doing here?'

'Well, I don't have to ask you. I know what you were doing,' said the other. 'I do wonder if this is the best place for a heart-to-heart talk. Shall we go to your room?'

'We may as well.'

It was Palfrey's companion who opened the bedroom door and, when they were inside, promptly turned the key in the lock. So the key was back again.

'I keep pausing to wonder who you are,' said Palfrey.

'Oh, yes. Remiss of me. A nephew of King Rufus. Only son of his second sister, whom you have met, I believe. Rachel, a sister of Rufus. Don't let that worry you,' went on the stranger. 'I am not on good terms with any of the family. By name I am Bruce, for my father was a Scotsman and a McDonald at that. You are burning with curiosity to know how I came to be in the gallery tonight, aren't you?'

'Yes.'

'I spied a stranger,' said McDonald.

'Meaning me?'

'Good Lord, no! You aren't a stranger. You are Public Hero No. 1 at Morne House. I fancy he wore a mask or grease paint, or something. He knows the place pretty well, because he was coming out of the priest hole in the West passage. My room is near there. In fact, I could hear movement in the priest hole and was looking out of my door.'

'How long ago was this?' asked Palfrey.

'About one o'clock. I had finished a session with Gerry, who is always a trial, and was solacing myself with a mild dose of Old Bill when I heard the rustling and rumbling. So out I popped. This fellow went straight to the minstrel gallery and waited there. I also waited. Then you came along. Breathtaking, wasn't it?'

'You were slow,' said Palfrey.

'Oh, no. I wanted to catch you with the goods,' said Mc-Donald. 'How did you come to know of that hiding-place? As far as I knew, only two people had ever discovered it.'

'You and your cousin,' said Palfrey. 'She told me.' He explained at some length, including the broken teeth of Halsted's youth. McDonald listened wide-eyed, then said:

'That's like Loretta! This little packet that I've got in my pocket ought to be interesting, don't you think?' He put his hand to his pocket and kept it there. 'Before we open it, oughtn't we to come to some kind of understanding?'

'How do you mean?'

'Loretta's behaviour makes it pretty clear that she was anxious that the police should learn nothing of this,' said Mc-Donald. 'Of course, in some circumstances, we might have to tell the police, but not as a matter of routine. Is that understood?'

'Yes,' said Palfrey.

'Good!' said McDonald, and took the papers out.

54

## SIX

## THE PAPERS

THERE were three papers in all; two were folded and white, the third was rolled and looked like thin tracing paper, with a blue tint. McDonald handed one of the white pieces to Palfrey and unfolded the other himself. Palfrey glanced down at a set of figures; nothing else but figures in two columns, which seemed to mean nothing at all. They were not totalled, there was no word of explanation, nor was there anything in the way of a key.

'What's yours?' asked McDonald, and handed his to Palfrey.

The second paper was a list of numbers, 1 to 26, and opposite each was a letter of the alphabet. The first line of letters ran straight from A to Z, the others were jumbled.

McDonald looked up, his eyes bright.

'Message and code,' he said.

The sheet of tracing paper was a foot wide and some eighteen inches long. As it opened, Palfrey looked eagerly for the drawing. McDonald was equally expectant. When it was nearly unrolled, they glanced up and met each other's gaze.

'It can't be blank!' protested McDonald.

Palfrey pulled. 'It is,' he said. Then he suggested: 'Invisible ink?'

'Not on tracing paper, surely. The glaze won't take it.'

'I'm no expert,' said Palfrey, 'but I think we'll find, eventually, that there is something on the sheet and that it relates in some way to the two lists. I don't see that we can do ourselves much good by worrying over it tonight.'

'Well, who's going to keep these things safe for the night? Others might know we've been wandering about, you know.'

'Yes. I'd taken it for granted that we would make copies of the figures and letters and have one apiece,' said Palfrey. 'The sheet of tracing paper is a different kettle of fish.'

'Keep the thing under your pillow.'

'So you'll allow me to have it?'

'I have a feeling that you're more qualified than I,' said McDonald. He was making a copy of the letters and figures. 'We ought to say a great deal more than we have, of course, but you'll be here in the morning, won't you?'

'I don't want to leave it too late. I'm going to Wenlock.'

'Then I'll come with you. I can pop in to see Loretta. Good night!'

Palfrey opened the door. He looked along the passage and was surprised to find the guard missing. McDonald hurried down the stairs, remarkably light on his feet. Palfrey waved to him and turned back to his room, but he had not reached it when he heard his name called in a sibilant hiss. He hurried back to the landing. Looking over the great staircase, he saw McDonald kneeling over a huddled figure close to the fireplace. He hurried down.

'Two of 'em,' said McDonald. 'This one's all right, I think. Just knocked out.' He pointed to the shadowy corner by the fireplace, and Palfrey saw a second policeman.

Neither man was badly hurt. After ten minutes both were conscious and one was talking freely, defending himself desperately. He had not seen or heard anyone; he had just been knocked over the head on the way to the minstrel gallery, after Palfrey. One man was to stay within sight of Palfrey's room, to make sure no one went inside if Palfrey were out, the other was to dog Palfrey's footsteps. Hardy had forgotten nothing, but the silent prowler at Morne House had outmatched them both.

'I'll find out who it was,' growled one of Hardy's men.

Palfrey said sharply: 'Not yet. I don't want it known that I was prowling tonight. Nurse your heads and report to the inspector as soon as you can, but don't give anything away here. You're Sergeant Whittle, aren't you?'

'Yes, sir.'

'Will you do as I ask?'

'I suppose it *is* best,' said Whittle, reluctantly. 'It's not much use us being here as far as I can see. You have to be born in the place to know every door and passage.'

'Never did man speak truer words,' declared McDonald. 'Give it up, except for one thing. Look after Dr. Palfrey!'

Not even the bright sun of next morning could rid the moor of its aspect of utter desolation.

A mile beyond the gateway, Palfrey glanced over his shoulder and looked back at Morne House. It was taller than he had realized, dark and forbidding, and it seemed to absorb the rays of the sun, getting no light from them.

An A.A. box stood at some cross-roads, at the foot of a hill which led towards the main Wenlock Range. The range looked bright and friendly in the sun ; nothing suggested the brooding menace of the cliff. Had the cliff incident happened only last night?

Palfrey was on edge now to see Drusilla. But first he must ring Hardy. He talked of Ross.

'Oh, yes,' said Hardy. 'I'm on to that poisoning, of course, but I ought to say that Ross has a first-class reputation.'

'How did you get on to it?' asked Palfrey, sharply.

'Whittle's reported,' said Hardy. 'The man drank your tea ; obviously you were to go to sleep while driving. You needn't worry about it. I'll tell you everything I find out when I see you. Unless you're still thinking of returning to London today,' Hardy added, slyly.

'It will have to be tomorrow,' said Palfrey.

'Splendid! By the way, I telephoned your wife a couple of hours ago. She's fully recovered.'

'Thanks very much,' said Palfrey, gratefully.

When he rejoined McDonald, Palfrey explained to him how he came to be at Morne House. 'Now it's my turn to put a question,' he finished. 'Did you know there was trouble brewing?'

'I had no idea,' said McDonald. 'I've been abroad, you know. Navy. I'm on long leave now. I arrived in London ten days ago, dropped Loretta a line and asked her when she was coming to Town. The next I knew was Loretta's accident. I came down immediately, and heard the whole story.'

They were on the top of the hill, looking down into Wenlock, which was at its best in the midday sun. Over the town, the twin towers of the seventeenth-century abbey watched with the benevolence of benign, unquestioned authority. Out of the wooded grounds, now bare of leaves, peeped the roofs of houses, red, green, blue and soft yellow ; all seemed to face the bay. Out to sea, brown sails fully spread, a fishing fleet was moving slowly homewards. To the north, the gaunt edges of the cliffs gave the only sombre note.

'Before the flare-up last night there was a family pow-wow,' McDonald went on. 'Rufus, my mother and Dinah—you know Dinah, don't you?—on the one side, and Uncle Claude and Gerry on the other. I was neutral. Uncle Claude and Gerry stuck to the theory that Loretta's fall was an accident and that Halsted's death had nothing to do with his coming visit to the house. Rufus led the faction which believed it was murder. The upshot was that Rufus said he had faith in *your* judgment and hoped you would stay in the district long enough to help to find the solution. Must you go back to London?'

'Yes,' said Palfrey. He was silent for a long time and conscious of McDonald's steady gaze. 'But I needn't stay there long.'

'I hope you'll come back,' said McDonald. 'Turn right here, then down the hill and turn left—that's if you want the Esplanade Hotel first.'

'I do, thanks.'

'There was some talk about this fellow Garth,' McDonald went on. 'I haven't placed him yet. Once I knew that he was bedridden practically all the time he stayed at the house, I didn't greatly worry. What *I* want to do is to find the swine who tried to murder Loretta. Does Garth come into it much?'

'As Loretta's fiancé——'

'*What!*' The exclamation came so violently that Palfrey was really startled.

'Didn't you know that?' he asked.

'It's damned nonsense.'

'Your Uncle Rufus told me of it himself,' said Palfrey.

'Do you mean to say he allowed Loretta to become engaged to a man he didn't know? A stranger? A—— No. Palfrey, I'll never believe it! It doesn't make sense,' said McDonald. 'I can't believe that Rufus——'

He broke off, and, after turning into a main road, with the bay immediately in front of them and tall hotels rising into the sky, Palfrey murmured: 'Unless pressure was brought on Sir Rufus to agree.'

'I'd just thought of that,' said McDonald, slowly. 'But it doesn't add up, Palfrey. Rufus and I don't get along, but I can't believe that he has ever done anything which would lay him open to blackmail. He's killed my affection for him, but not my respect. As a matter of fact, he's the nearest thing to a perfect human being I'm ever likely to meet. His life is a model.'

'In spite of which, he accepted Garth as Loretta's husband-to-be,' said Palfrey.

McDonald said nothing. Palfrey reached the promenade, called in Wenlock the Esplanade, and, on McDonald's instructions, turned left. The Esplanade Hotel was a double-turreted, white building set in small but pleasant grounds and standing on a corner. Palfrey pulled up. 'I'll wait here,' said McDonald, and took out a pipe.

'Right-ho,' said Palfrey, and turned to go into the hotel. As he did so, something struck him on the shoulder, not heavily, but enough to alarm him. He swung round. He saw a man disappearing round the corner and heard something fall to the ground. He ran to the corner, but the man was out of sight.

Slowly he turned and looked round. On the pavement lay a ball of paper.

McDonald got out of the car quickly as Palfrey examined the missile. It was, in fact, a stone wrapped in paper. He opened the paper and smoothed it out, and was beginning to read when Drusilla came out of the gateway and called: 'Sap, what's happened?'

He raised his head and smiled warmly. Drusilla looked at her lovely best, hatless, wearing a green woollen dress, her eyes sparkling with gladness at seeing him.

'Hallo, my sweet! Nothing to worry about.' He gripped her hand. 'Someone threw a stone, and about the stone was a piece of paper, and this is what it says,' declared Palfrey, looking at the paper again. ' "*Meet me at the green cottage with the parrot in the window in Cheddar Gorge. Say Monday, 2.30 p.m. N.K.*" '

'N.K.,' repeated Drusilla, blankly. 'Do you know him?'

The American's merry face appeared in Palfrey's mind's eye.

'I know him slightly,' admitted Palfrey. 'The man has an eye for the spectacular.'

'Why should he want you to meet him anywhere?' asked Drusilla.

'Perhaps he has taken to me,' said Palfrey dryly. 'I'll tell you the long, long story soon, my sweet.' He looked at McDonald and said gravely: 'This is Bruce McDonald, a nephew of Sir Rufus Morne. You should be good friends. He saved me from breaking my neck last night. He can tell you everything while I go and see Hardy,' he declared. 'I—— Oh, confound it! Hardy is in Corbin.'

'He telephoned to say that he would be here for lunch,' said Drusilla.

Hardy arrived at half past one, but he was not alone. With him was a big, blond man of middle-age, a handsome giant of a fellow, with wavy hair, a big bushy moustache, and the bluest of blue eyes; a man to like at sight.

The Palfreys and McDonald were waiting in the lounge when they arrived. Hardy looked somewhat put out when he saw McDonald.

59

'I knew you would not mind me bringing Colonel Cartwright along,' he said to Palfrey. 'He is our Chief Constable.'

'Oh. Delighted,' murmured Palfrey, shaking hands. 'My wife —Mr. McDonald. The head waiter tells me that at your request they've laid a table in a separate room for us.'

'I thought we could talk more freely in private,' said Hardy, and glanced at McDonald.

'Not my show,' McDonald said, quickly.

'I hope you'll stay,' said Palfrey.

'No, thanks. I'll be available afterwards, if you want me,' said McDonald. He smiled and went off, and Palfrey tactfully did not insist. McDonald, undoubtedly, had quickly sensed that he was not wanted.

Cartwright took command. He had, of course, been in close touch with the case from the moment it had broken, and Hardy had passed on everything that Palfrey had reported. Cartwright made it clear that he warmly appreciated Palfrey's interest and his guidance. They felt fortunate, he said, that Palfrey had been called to Morne House. *Did* Palfrey believe that there was bad feeling there?

'I mean among the members of the household.'

'I wouldn't say so,' said Palfrey. 'There is strain. No one has given me any hint that he or she thinks the murderer can be identified, if that's what you mean.'

'That is interesting,' said Cartwright. 'Most interesting. Have you drawn any further conclusions, Palfrey?'

'No. I feel now as I did before. There is evil lurking in that house. One senses it. There's danger, too, and a keen dislike of prowling strangers.' He told Hardy and Cartwright of the attempt to toss him over the balcony.

Hardy said, after a pause: 'Could it have been McDonald?'

'No. I heard footsteps on the gallery and also on the stairs at one and the same time. I also heard a door close. This morning, McDonald showed me the door—it's in a corner of the gallery, covered by a tapestry. I would never have noticed it, although anyone could have found it by moving the tapestry aside. No, whoever attacked me, it wasn't McDonald. It wasn't necessarily a member of the family. And the place is so vast. I have seen a few of the servants, but there may be dozens I haven't met. One could live at Morne House for a month and be unaware of others living under the same roof.' He rolled a piece of bread between his fingers, and went on: 'I doubt whether I am telling you anything new. Your man Whittle was right last night, Hardy, when he said that he would want an army to cover that place properly.'

'Yet it must be covered,' said Cartwright.

Palfrey eyed him brightly. 'Why? Because of the suspected attempt to murder Loretta Morne? Hardly justification, I fancy, for leaving men there indefinitely. Murder would be a different matter. Unless I am wrong about the law, you've no right to have men living there at the moment. Have you?'

'None at all.'

'And the man who softened that wood might have come in from the outside,' Palfrey said. 'Or it might have been the fellow Garth. Nothing known about Garth, I suppose?'

'Nothing,' said Cartwright.

'Awkward situation,' said Palfrey. 'Switch over to Halsted, and what have you? Reasonable evidence, but evidence which might not hold in a court of law, that Rufus Morne visited the pool where Halsted's body was found. I drew conclusions, but they need not be the right ones.'

Cartwright said slowly: 'I think you were right, Palfrey. Those bloodhounds would have left the pool and continued the trail if Morne had not been about there when you arrived. It's curious that he pretended to be surprised that a body had been recovered from the pool.'

'Curious, but not damning,' answered Palfrey. 'Now, Colonel, cards on the table! Last night you had the sanatorium *very* thoroughly guarded. You took other precautions which might have been thought excessive. You say that Morne House *must* be covered. None of these things really square up with the situation as I know it. Mind you, I've no right to ask for an explanation, but what I notice, other people might also notice.'

'I'm not so sure that they would,' said Cartwright, with a pleasant smile. 'I don't think it will surprise you if I say that we have been watching Morne House, from a distance, for some months. You've got the details more clearly than I have, Hardy; you tell them.'

'Very good, sir,' said Hardy. He looked at Palfrey with a friendly smile, and went on: 'Three months ago to the day, Dr. Palfrey, an unidentified man was found dead at the foot of Wenlock Cliff. That particular cliff is near the spot where you had your misadventure last night. There is an inlet, though the sea doesn't often go right up it, and beneath are rocks on which a man would smash to his death.' Hardy hesitated, then went on with a frown: 'There was no evidence of foul play. An open

61

verdict was returned. Three weeks afterwards, quite by accident, we learned that on the same day and about the same time, Miss Loretta Morne had been driving her car when the brakes failed and she narrowly avoided death.'

'Oh,' said Palfrey.

'A week after we learned that,' went on Hardy, 'Sir Rufus went on horseback to the cliff. He was seen there talking to a man. That evening, a man's body was found at the foot of the cliffs. This time there was evidence of foul play—our man Clements and Sir Bertram Miles, who came down to examine the body, agreed that some wounds had been inflicted *before* the fall. We interviewed Morne, of course. He admitted seeing a man, not necessarily the dead man, and also admitted speaking to him. Morne said that the man he spoke to was a stranger who happened to be on the cliff. We couldn't disprove that.

'Then followed the second accident to Miss Morne,' went on Hardy, 'the one when her horse fell over the cliff not far away from the same spot and nearly sent her to her death. We have been making inquiries, and learned that Miss Morne had been somewhat abnormal—not her usual self. You realize, don't you, the difficulty of getting information from such a place and from such people?'

'Yes,' said Palfrey.

'Then came Halsted's death and your own adventures,' broke in Cartwright. 'I told Hardy to take *every* precaution. It seemed to me that Miss Morne was in grave danger, even at the sanatorium. Her persistent requests to see you suggested that she was going to confide in you, as she had undoubtedly confided in Halsted. We did not want the same thing to happen to you as it did to Halsted, and so we went to extremes last night. I was appalled when I heard about the tea.'

Palfrey smiled. 'So was I!'

'There was a little morphine in it,' Hardy said.

'Have you seen Ross?'

Hardy laughed. 'He's almost beside himself!'

'I hope he is,' said Palfrey grimly.

'But there's no proof that he put it in or that it was put in at the sanatorium,' Hardy reminded him. 'It was in the back of your car while we were shifting Mrs. Palfrey to mine. Then, if you remember, we all stopped at the Wenlock police station and left the cars outside while I arranged for your escort. What about that stranger you picked up?'

Palfrey explained. He talked for some time, and, when he

had finished, Hardy and Cartwright had many questions for him. The only thing that he kept back was the suggestion for a rendezvous at Cheddar Gorge.

Only on one matter were the police difficult, and he did not blame them. Knowing that Kyle was going to return for Fyson, Palfrey should have reported at the first opportunity, Cartwright said.

'The man Fyson would be an invaluable witness,' put in Hardy.

'As well as Kyle,' added Cartwright.

'Look here,' said Palfrey, reasoningly. 'Had Kyle got my wife and me out of the scrape and left us at the foot of the hill, nothing could have prevented him from getting safely away. He put himself in my hands. I played fair. I've no doubt I shall meet him again. When I do, I'll be under no obligation to him, nor he to me.'

'Why should you meet him again?'

'He will want to know what else I can tell him.'

'It isn't by any means certain,' complained Cartwright.

'And there is another thing,' urged Palfrey. 'Kyle has his wits about him. If I had tricked him last night, I think he would have got away. He might not have reached Fyson and he might have lost his car, but he would have been very angry and either cut me off his visiting list or been unpleasant. I don't think it would serve your purpose to have him off my visiting list.'

'There may be something in that,' admitted Cartwright.

'I hope you'll come to agree that I was right,' said Palfrey. 'I think Kyle unimportant compared with the papers which I got from the minstrel gallery,' he went on, and took the papers from his pocket and handed them to Cartwright.

The Chief Constable's eyes brightened. He and Hardy turned their attention to the papers. They were as mystified as Palfrey and McDonald had been.

'We'll have to get the experts on it. I think you'd better take it to London, Hardy, and see the Yard people. We'll have to have them down now; we can't keep it entirely to ourselves, more's the pity.'

'It's time——' began Hardy.

Then, out of the corner of his eye, Palfrey caught sight of a man outside, a man who was tossing something into the room. It was small and dark, skimmed the top of the window, and fell on the table. Palfrey pushed Drusilla off her chair. Hardy made a grab at the thing, but it gave a furious hiss and he backed away. Cartwright ducked. There was a flash, a subdued explosion, and then flames spread everywhere.

## SEVEN

## THE COTTAGE WITH THE PARROT

A PAPER fluttered down in front of Palfrey's face. One corner was ablaze. He put out a hand and snatched at it, put that fire out, screwed the paper up and pushed it into his pocket as he scrambled to his feet. The smoke was thick and harsh, the flames were more subdued now, except those on the floor, where they had caught the carpet.

'Those papers!' cried Cartwright, in a muffled voice. 'Damn the flames! Hardy, look for those papers!'

'I am!' called Hardy.

'I've got 'em,' called Palfrey. 'Let's get out.' He raised his voice, calling 'Fire'. The door was flung open. The draught fanned the flames, someone shouted, a man rushed in, took Drusilla by the arm and dragged her out. Cartwright was furthest from the door, but moved swiftly. With Hardy and Palfrey, he was jammed in the doorway, and in front of them a man was standing holding a fire-extinguisher.

'Mind! Out of the way!' Cartwright cried. 'Mind!'

They got through into the passage, and the man squirted a foul-smelling chemical on to the flames. Someone else rushed in in great alarm.

McDonald, who had taken Drusilla out of the room, appeared by Palfrey's side.

'*Did* you get the papers?' Cartwright demanded, smoothing down his hair, which was singed on one side. He made way for another man with a fire-extinguisher, but smoke was driving them further from the room.

'I got the only one that matters,' said Palfrey. 'You've still got your copies, Mac, haven't you?'

'Safely in my pocket.'

Palfrey took out the tracing paper, and Cartwright said in alarm: 'It's burned!'

'Only at the tip, like my fingers,' said Palfrey, 'but we shouldn't grumble about that. I fancy someone saw you holding it up against the window, Colonel, and acted on impulse. Nice people. Fire bombs to hand, morphine available as required, chloroform on tap, not to mention a so far unidentified poison which killed Halsted.' He opened the paper out, to smooth it, but stopped and stared down.

'There's something on it!' exclaimed Drusilla.

'Yes,' said Palfrey, in a smug voice. 'The heat brought it out. The simple things!' He smoothed the paper out and, while people pushed past them and a testy manager complained that they were in the way, they looked at the drawing. It was like the road plan, with short, straight lines leading off from a main line which went from north to south; they knew that because of the only other mark on the paper, the drawing of a compass. 'Well, we oughtn't to grumble,' added Palfrey. 'What we ought to have done was to get outside and find the customer who started the show. No luck, I suppose?'

'Hardy didn't lose any time,' said Cartwright.

Hardy came back with a negative report. The fire-raiser had been seen from the main dining-room window, but no one could remember what he looked like. He had gone across the garden, through the small orchard and, presumably, into the town. Hardy said that he would have the whole force out looking for him that afternoon.

'Well,' said Palfrey, 'this looks like our fade-out.'

'*Are* you going back to London?' asked Cartwright.

'Yes. I must for a day or two.'

It was not difficult to arrange for a colleague to take over his appointments for the following week. Over the week-end, Palfrey saw two or three patients whom he was anxious to treat personally, and thus eased his conscience. He was more excited than he allowed Drusilla to see. She, too, was filled with excitement which she tried not to show.

On the Saturday evening he telephoned Hardy, who expressed himself delighted to hear from him. How was progress, asked Palfrey? There wasn't any progress. Nothing else had happened, nothing had come from the tracing and nothing from the code and cypher. It completely puzzled the cypher experts, in spite of its apparent simplicity. A man in London was still working on it, but was of the opinion that they had not got the key on the two sheets of paper. An inspector from Scotland Yard was in Corbin now, but had made no headway. Hardy said that he was a very good fellow, a better man could not have been sent, but he also understood the difficulties of dealing with Morne and Morne House.

Hardy supposed that Palfrey had not changed his mind.

'You don't seriously think that I could do more than you and a Yard man,' said Palfrey.

'But I do, Palfrey. I wouldn't think so, normally, but with Morne I'm quite sure. He doesn't often take a liking to anyone, you know ; his attitude towards you is quite exceptional. Understandable, of course, but exceptional.'

'I see,' said Palfrey, mildly. 'Well, I'm weakening. Don't be too surprised if I look in some time on Tuesday.'

'I shall expect you,' Hardy declared.

'If he goes on like this, I shall need a new size in hats,' said Palfrey to Drusilla.

Hardy replaced the telephone in his office, studied his shoes for a few moments, then got up, put on his hat and coat, and drove to Cartwright's home, which was on the outskirts of Corbin.

'I'm *still* not sure about Palfrey, sir,' he said, after greetings had been exchanged. 'He said that he might come down on Tuesday. What I can't make up my mind about is whether he really came down here because Halsted sent for him, or whether he was already interested in the business. It's all very well to say that Z.5 has been disbanded since the war. I daresay it has. But Palfrey was a prominent agent, and he might be used by Intelligence now.'

'Had you thought of that before Morne gave you the idea?' asked Cartwright.

'I suppose I hadn't,' admitted Hardy, 'but I've got the bee in my bonnet now. I don't mind admitting that I shall feel annoyed if he *is* working for Intelligence. We had more than enough of that kind of thing during the war, didn't we?'

Cartwright nodded.

'They'd come down, poke about, arouse suspicion and get into trouble, and when they'd gone we'd be told they had been sent by the London people. They might at least tell us in advance who they *are*. I don't ask to be taken into their confidence, but unnecessary secrecy gets under my skin.'

'Obviously,' said Cartwright.

Hardy laughed self-consciously. 'Sorry if I'm putting it rather strongly, sir. But I do feel strongly. It's on our beat, when all's said and done. I suppose it was excusable in wartime, but surely it isn't in peace.'

'I don't disagree with you,' admitted Cartwright. 'What I do say is that nothing will shift the people in Whitehall. They're as immovable as Wenlock Cliff! You're right, of course; they did come down here a great deal during the war. That wasn't surprising; we know that Huns landed from U-boats somewhere near the cliff.'

'We never found who helped them to get away,' said Hardy.

'So that's worrying you, is it?'

'Yes, sir, it is,' said Hardy. 'When you come to think about it, there isn't a better place than Morne House for hiding a man for a few days. It's my opinion that Garth had some pull over Morne and found sanctuary by exerting pressure. Miss Loretta knew it, and fell in with it. *If* Morne had anything to do with sheltering spies, that would be a strong enough hold, wouldn't it?'

'It's all surmise,' objected Cartwright.

'I know, sir, but it would explain a great deal. It would also explain Palfrey being sent down here by Intelligence. Isn't there *any* way you can find out what Palfrey is doing?'

'I don't know of a way,' admitted Cartwright. 'You've told our friend from Scotland Yard about this, I suppose.'

'Oh, yes, I've told Wriggleswade,' said Hardy. 'He's of the same mind as I am, sir. Intelligence gets a bit above itself. If I had my way *now*——' He broke off.

'What would you do?' asked Cartwright.

'I'd have Palfrey watched,' said Hardy, and looked appealingly at his chief. 'I've even got the man in mind—young Rundell. He doesn't miss much. What do you think about it, sir?'

After a pause, Cartwright said: 'Yes, I'm rather taken by it. Is Rundell free now?'

'He reported back from leave this morning. He wasn't due until Monday; he's mustard keen.'

'Well,' said Cartwright, and smoothed his blond moustache. 'We *ought* to tell Wriggleswade.'

'But wouldn't that spoil it?' asked Hardy. 'I suppose we couldn't do it without, but—well, sir, you could leave it to me to tell him and I could leave it to you. That wouldn't do for long, I know, but only the time between now and Tuesday matters. Directly Palfrey gets into Corshire we can tell Wriggleswade. If we tell him now, he'll suggest a Yard man keeping an eye on Palfrey, or else he'll pooh-pooh the very idea. He's a bit inclined to throw his weight about, you know.'

'Oh, yes, but he's not a bad fellow,' said Cartwright. 'All right, talk to Rundell.'

Detective-Sergeant Rundell, of the Corshire C.I.D., left for London on the Sunday morning, fully briefed, determined and convinced that he had been given the chance of a lifetime. It would require exemplary patience and might be trying, but he was confident.

He felt bewildered when, on the Monday afternoon a little after two o'clock, Palfrey and his wife drove into Cheddar Village, parked the Talbot and walked towards the Gorge. While they were parking, Rundell took the opportunity to send a telegram to Hardy.

Palfrey locked the door of the car and turned with Drusilla towards the Gorge. It was a bright, sunny day and there was a surprising number of people taking the same road. One party of schoolchildren made a crocodile fifty yards long on the happy trek to the wonders of the caves—wonders announced on notice-boards and in shop-windows and by a hoarse-voiced man who stood at a corner, showing sightseers the way.

'Did you see the snub-nosed chap?' Palfrey asked Drusilla. 'That nose was in London, not far behind us when we stopped for lunch, and this very minute has gone into the post office.'

'So we've been followed,' said Drusilla. 'Do you know who it is?'

'I haven't the faintest notion. Stranger to me. Dark hair, dark jowl, a bit of Corshire about him, I shouldn't wonder. I always knew that my treatment of Kyle got under Hardy's skin.'

'That wasn't surprising,' said Drusilla.

'No. I wonder if Mac's here yet?'

'He's probably been waiting since dawn,' said Drusilla.

McDonald, on being told of their decision, had expressed himself delighted. It had been agreed that he should go on ahead and meet them at the cottage with a parrot in the window. McDonald seemed to enjoy the prospect of a mysterious journey and encounter with the American.

'There's a green cottage,' said Drusilla, her voice rising.

'One green cottage, two green cottages,' murmured Palfrey, looking towards the left of the road. In front of them were the great cliffs of the gorge rising like bulky, forbidding sentinels,

68

dark grey and light intermingling, some scrub and grass on the lower slopes, but the higher bleak and bare.

The cottages stood close together a little way ahead of them. Outside was a notice-board offering eggs and bacon and chips for 3s. 6d. There was a small queue outside the door.

'There it is!' exclaimed Drusilla, and moved her arm as if to point.

Palfrey held it by her side.

'Don't forget Snub-nose,' he said. 'But you're right, begob, there's a parrot.'

They passed the window where the parrot was squatting. It was the cottage which offered bacon and eggs and chips, and there was no chance of getting in immediately. Palfrey glanced at his watch; they had ten minutes to spare.

'What shall we do?' asked Drusilla. 'We must be here at half past two.'

'The truth is that I'm worried about Snub. I don't mind being followed, but I don't want him to see where we go, and there isn't much chance of losing him here. We could go for a long walk, but that would make us too late, and—— Oh-ho!' He broke off, with a gleam in his eyes. 'It's a simple matter, really. Most things are. The caves. Crowded with sightseers. See the queue waiting to go in—not a large one. We will tag ourselves on the end of it. I believe it's dark inside.'

'They have lights.'

'Not everywhere, surely.'

They joined the queue. It was longer than he had thought, for the cave entrance was up steps and the steps were lined with people.

'It's twenty-five past two,' said Drusilla.

'And Snub has joined the queue,' said Palfrey. 'He's seven people removed. Hallo, we're moving!'

Coins were rattling in the pay-box. A guide was calling out into the road: 'Hurry up, now. The next tour is about to start.'

Palfrey put down a two-shilling piece and hurried with the rest of the crowd through a narrow entrance, dimly lighted, at the beginning of the cave. A guide was regimenting the people and giving instructions.

'Is Snub here?'

'Just coming in, and looking anxious,' said Palfrey. 'He'll look more anxious in a moment. Isn't it lovely and dark in front?'

'You needn't worry about the darkness,' said the guide. 'I'll switch the lights on as we go through. It wouldn't do to keep them on all the time, you see, except a few pilot lights. It'd spoil the effect.'

A single dim light cast a diffused glow. The crowd, nearly sixty strong, was gathering about the guide. Some distance ahead there was another glimmer of light. The guide, with the natural showman's gift, went on talking. Palfrey looked round and could see heads outlined against the roof, but could recognize no one.

'Take off your hat,' he whispered to Drusilla.

She obeyed without question; Palfrey removed his.

'We'll see the first show and then duck for it,' said Palfrey. 'If I read this fellow aright, he'll switch the light off when we've finished this one, and get us all worked up and eerie; he knows his job. That will be our best chance, I think.'

Drusilla felt for his hand. Palfrey squeezed.

'*Now,* ladies and gentlemen——' said the guide.

Palfrey edged towards the far side, to put as many people between himself and Snub as he could. Drusilla still clutched his hand. People were too interested to worry; several were moving about to get a better position, and his own movements were not noticeable. He looked at Drusilla. The light was concentrated on *The Fonts,* famous stalagmite basins, and was not bright enough for him to see her clearly, and she was close by him; Snub, some distance away, could not possibly pick them out. He squeezed Drusilla's fingers, and whispered: 'This is it.'

The light went out.

There was still a dim light, but they could not see a yard in front of them. The guide was moving, people were shuffling, it was eerie and fascinating. The air was cold.

Palfrey reached the wall, felt along it, and tip-toed along, with Drusilla close, stumbling over feet, trying to accustom himself to the darkness. It was not easy, nor would it be easy for Snub.

Palfrey bumped into the wall. Then he saw a glimmer of light and a moment later they were in sight of the entrance. He kept to the side, so that if Snub were suspicious and followed them he could not see them outlined against the light. Half-way along, he paused. There was no sound of footsteps.

'Snub is enjoying himself,' murmured Palfrey. 'We're all right now.'

They were breathless when they reached the green cottage. There was one welcome sight: the queue had gone. Palfrey

70

glanced at his watch and saw that it was nearly a quarter to three. In spite of his assurance to Drusilla, he was worried in case Kyle had become impatient.

They went in, and saw McDonald sitting in a corner, drinking tea and reading a newspaper. He glanced up and winked. Palfrey winked back.

'*What-ho!*' squawked the parrot. '*Time for tea!*'

'Oh, hallo,' said Palfrey. 'There doesn't seem to be much room here, old lady.'

There was no room at all, but a woman came bustling through a doorway and said that there was room in the garden, if they would like it.

A few large coloured umbrellas, faded by weather, were dotted about among garden chairs and tables. It was cold enough, but half a dozen couples and a small party had dared the weather, and the sun was shining straight into the garden.

In the far corner sat a man, alone, almost bald, with a nut-cracker face.

He looked up and saw Palfrey.

He frowned.

It was only the slightest knitting of his brow, and might have been accidental, but Palfrey took its meaning. This was Kyle, but he did not want to be recognized yet. Palfrey led Drusilla to a table from which he could watch the man, and, when they were seated, explained.

'I suppose it means he's watched,' said Drusilla.

'Yes. Not an easy job to spot the villain.'

In the cave there had been an element of amusement at getting rid of Snub. All that was changed. The man Palfrey had met on Wenlock Hill had been a merry soul, akin to McDonald. This man looked ill-tempered, solitary, as hard as his weather-beaten face. He was in the middle-thirties, Palfrey judged.

The woman came up with a loaded tray, walking up the steps as if they were gentle slopes. She made a bee-line for the Palfreys.

As she turned away after serving their meal—

'*Hey, missus!*' the nut-cracker man spoke, and Palfrey frowned, for his accent was not American but broad Lanca-shire. 'Hey, missus,' he repeated for all those present to hear. 'When tha' cooms oop again bring us another dish of tea.'

'Yes, sir, thank you.'

The woman went off ; the man went on eating. Palfrey picked up his knife and fork. 'We'd better start eating,' he told Drusilla.

71

'*Is* that Kyle?'

'I'm not sure. I've only seen him in darkness before. See if anyone is paying him much attention, will you?'

He looked one side of the garden, Drusilla the other. The large party chattered, couples leaned forward and spoke in whispers.

Except one couple.

A man and woman, youngish people, dressed in town clothes, the woman rather smart, the man neat and dapper, were sitting over their bacon, egg and chips. They did not speak. Now and again they looked towards the nut-cracker man, as if they, too, were trying to decide whether they knew him. The woman was good-looking in a bold way; she wore too much lipstick and rouge, and her hair was rolled in a golden net. The man was of different quality. He had dark, sleek hair, heavily oiled and brushed straight back from a high forehead. There was something foreign about his sallow face.

Nut-cracker got up.

As he moved towards the steps, the other couple got up and put a ten-shilling note on their table. Nut-cracker went down the steps, walking like an old man. The others followed him. It was too deliberate to be accidental; they were following him.

The Palfreys got up.

'Stay with Mac,' Palfrey whispered, and hurried ahead of Drusilla.

McDonald looked up as Palfrey went out in the wake of the others. Palfrey jerked his head back towards Drusilla, and mouthed the words 'Take care of her'. He did not know whether McDonald understood him.

Out in the road, Kyle was walking up the gorge. The others followed him as far as the cave which the Palfreys had visited. Then the girl, after a word from the man, left him and walked up the steps towards the cave. Palfrey hung back, for he could see at a greater distance now. The sallow man went on, and Palfrey saw that he had his hand in his pocket.

Kyle did not change his pace and the sallow man kept up with him. Palfrey did not know whether to keep well behind or to hurry and force an issue. There was something frightening in this slow, deliberate chase; for it *was* a chase.

The sallow man called out, abruptly: 'Kyle!'

Kyle did not answer or stop.

'*Kyle!*' The sallow man gained a little. Palfrey quickened his step.

No one else was about. There were no cars. The three men seemed to be alone in the vastness of the gorge. The only sound was their footsteps. The sallow man did not once look round, although he must have known that he was being followed. The three of them went on, the sallow man gaining on Kyle.

Kyle stopped, moved towards the side, and sat down on a boulder.

There was another, larger, boulder between Palfrey and the sallow man, and Palfrey crouched behind it, his hat in his hand. For the first time the foreigner looked round. He seemed satisfied that they were alone. He went up to Kyle and spoke, but Palfrey could not hear the words.

Another car came up the gorge, a Packard with a big body. Palfrey remembered Kyle's Packard, and then he saw the driver, a man, with a woman sitting next to him. Palfrey hardly noticed the woman; his eyes were fixed on the man, whom he could see quite clearly, for the car was slowing down. He looked exactly like the 'Kyle' of the green cottage!

The sallow man continued to talk. The Packard drew level with them, then stopped with a squeal of brakes.

The sallow man turned . . .

The 'Kyle' to whom he had been talking got up and hit him!

It was a powerful blow to the stomach, and the foreigner had no chance to protect himself. He doubled up. The door of the Packard opened, the motorist 'Kyle' leaned out, and the two men between them bundled the foreigner into the back of the car. A woman shouted! Palfrey, half-turning, saw the foreigner's girl-friend running desperately towards the scene, and running behind her was the man with the snub nose.

Another car came humming up the gorge.

The Packard door slammed. The foreigner was inside, with the two 'Kyles' and the woman. The fair-haired woman was screaming *"Stop him! Stop him!"* A passing cyclist stared in astonishment, braked hard, and nearly came off. Brakes squealed behind Palfrey. He looked round and saw Snub on the running board of a small car which he had presumably commandeered. He uttered the word 'Police', as the car flashed past in the wake of the Packard, but the Packard had disappeared. Palfrey did not think the small car was fast enough to catch it.

The woman with peroxided hair stood shaking her fists no longer shouting. Suddenly she turned round. She was sobbing and gasping, but she ran down the gorge and Palfrey followed

her at a smart pace. As she drew level with the caves, Palfrey
saw McDonald and Drusilla approaching. They were staring at
the frantic woman, and so were most of the other people in this
more populous part of the gorge. Palfrey beckoned, and
Drusilla hurried towards him.

'Follow her, will you?' Palfrey said urgently. 'Not out of the
village. Messages to the Cliff Hotel.'

'Yes,' said Drusilla. She turned at once and went hurrying
after the frantic woman, while McDonald stood undecided.
Palfrey joined him.

'This is Drusilla's job,' he said. 'We can't go everywhere the
woman can.'

'What's been happening?'

'As daring a piece of kidnapping as I'm ever likely to see,'
said Palfrey and laughed in sheer admiration. 'It was perfectly
done. By two Kyles.'

'*Two* Kyles.'

'Yes. And Snub's gone haring after,' said Palfrey. 'Sorry,' he
added. 'I'm not quite myself.' He looked after Drusilla, now
nearly out of sight, and added: 'I suppose it was wise to let her
go alone.'

EIGHT

TRUNK CALL

THE woman turned neither right nor left until she reached the
end of the road, where she hurried to a telephone kiosk. The
door closed slowly behind her. Drusilla could hear her voice,
but not the words. She seemed to be shouting at the operator.
Then she opened the bag again, looked through her purse,
dropped it and cried so that Drusilla could hear:

'I haven't got anything smaller than a two-shilling piece. I
*must* get through!'

Something was said. She shouted again, then pushed open
the door with her foot. Drusilla, taking risks, was nearest her.
'Here, *can* you give me change for two shillings, please? I've
got an urgent call!' It was a coarse voice, loud and agitated.

Drusilla had a shilling and some sixpences. The woman
grabbed them and dropped the two-shilling piece she was hold-

ing out in exchange. She gasped, turned back and said: 'I've got it! I've got it!' A pause. 'Yes, Mayfair 01341. *Yes!*'

'Mayfair 01341,' repeated Drusilla to herself. The woman took her foot away and the door closed. Drusilla repeated the number over and over again as she watched the woman, who tapped her foot against the glass door, sighed with exasperation, and then suddenly stiffened. Her voice sounded clearly: '*He* can't be out!'

She argued volubly, but did not get her call. At last she came out of the kiosk, and Drusilla slipped in after her. Out of the corner of her eye, she could see Palfrey on one side of the street and McDonald on the other; McDonald was nearer the woman, who walked on a short distance to a waiting bus. She walked up and down in front of the bus, which was marked 'Bristol', then seemed to make a sudden decision and climbed in.

McDonald sauntered over and followed her.

Drusilla left the kiosk and joined Palfrey. He was standing behind a doorway, and could not be seen from the bus.

'She isn't likely to notice anything, but we'd better not take chances,' Palfrey said. 'Any luck, darling?'

'Mayfair 01341, but no reply,' said Drusilla.

'Good work!'

'Not exactly good,' said Drusilla. 'She's demented, Sap. What happened?'

Palfrey told her as they strolled back up the road towards the cottages. Then he espied a number of people sitting at little tables, as if at tea, high on the bank above them. A flight of wooden steps led up there, with a sign inviting custom.

'We can watch the road without being seen up there,' Palfrey said. 'Can you manage more tea?'

'I'll swim in it to help,' said Drusilla.

There were few people in the tea-room, which had a corrugated iron roof and rows of garden tables and chairs. The Palfreys sat opposite each other near the road, and had to get very close to the edge in order to see everyone there.

Keeping an eye on the road, Palfrey told Drusilla all that had happened.

'Which one *was* Kyle?' she asked, fascinated.

'I can't say,' admitted Palfrey. 'I saw them together for a few seconds, and they weren't quite so much alike then. I fancy the car-driver was the real Kyle; the other fellow was a little stiff in his movements even when they were bundling the foreigner into the car. That's two,' he added.

'Two what?'

'Captives of Kyle,' answered Palfrey. 'First Fyson and then this customer. I wonder where Kyle keeps them.'

'Hardy would say that you take that much too lightly,' Drusilla remarked.

'Yes, wouldn't he! The point is that Fyson was *not* a nice man, and I didn't like the look of the sallow customer. Did you?'

'Not a bit,' admitted Drusilla.

'So my sympathies are still with Kyle,' said Palfrey, 'but I hope we see him before long. By to-morrow we shall have to tell Hardy the whole story. No evasions this time. At least he can't blame us for what happened.'

'I'm all for telling him,' said Drusilla, 'but why must you?'

'Our Snub. A Corshire man, I feel pretty sure, and when he jumped on to the small car he yelled *"Police,"* so Hardy proved he is a dark horse by having us watched in London. There are a lot of things I'm prepared to take,' went on Palfrey, 'but being suspected by the police isn't one of them. Hallo, there's Snub!'

Snub was getting out of a car further up the gorge. The Palfreys watched him as he walked past the caves, past them and then towards the telephone kiosk near the bus terminus. He was there for some time. 'Making his report to Hardy, I suppose,' murmured Palfrey.

It was now after half-past four, and Palfrey began to despair of seeing Kyle again that day. It was a most unsatisfactory situation. The only result of their exertions was the Mayfair telephone number and the possibility that McDonald had found where the fair-haired woman lived. McDonald, however, being unpractised in such affairs, might easily lose her.

'We'd better take a walk,' said Palfrey. 'I don't want to leave until after dark.'

They paid their bill and went down the flight of steps. As they reached the road they heard a car coming from the top end of the gorge. Palfrey glanced towards it, conscious of the grandeur of the gorge itself. The tops were now covered in mist, and he shivered slightly ; he no longer liked mist. Then his eyes brightened, and he exclaimed: 'There's the Packard!'

'It's travelling fast,' said Drusilla.

'Surely it's not being chased!'

76

The car came hurtling towards them. The road was almost clear, now, and a few people pressed against the sides as the car flashed by. Twenty yards from the green cottage it began to slow down. Then the driver jammed on the brakes. It was a woman. She was dark, sleek and had a humorous mouth. A Tyrolean hat sat jauntily on her dark hair which hung down to her shoulders in a glossy page-boy bob.

Kyle, or a man who looked like Kyle, was by her side.

He opened the door while the car was still moving, jumped out, blew a kiss, and the car moved off again. It disappeared at speed.

Kyle stood looking about him. Perhaps because the Palfreys were so near, he did not see them at once. He was not the man whom they had seen in the garden of the cottage. He was younger and rather taller, and his face was broader, though it, too, looked rather like a nut-cracker, and was berry-brown.

His grey eyes were narrowed until he saw them. Then he beamed.

'Well, well! If it isn't Dr. Palfrey!' He strode across the road. 'I'm glad you made it, Palfrey, I was afraid you would be too shocked to stay around.' He looked at Drusilla and grinned. 'Chloroform certainly didn't suit you, Mrs. Palfrey. You look much better without a red nose.'

Drusilla laughed.

'But I mean it,' said Kyle. 'Are you two hungry?'

'We've drunk enough tea to float a battleship,' said Palfrey.

'That's too bad. I haven't eaten since breakfast, and then it wasn't much of a breakfast. Will you object to watching me eat?' He did not wait for an answer, but took an arm of each and went into the cottage.

The woman came in, took Kyle's order and pressed the Palfreys to have a cup of tea with him. Drusilla wavered. 'Sure, bring some tea,' said Kyle. He turned his silvery grey eyes on Drusilla and went on: 'I thought the English could always take a bowl of tea.'

They were alone in the room now, and Palfrey decided that it was time Kyle stopped fooling.

'The English are a patient race,' he said, 'but there are limits to their patience. Were you here at half past two?'

'No. That was a friend of mine. Not bad make-up, was it?'

'Not bad,' admitted Palfrey.

Kyle said: 'Let me get it off my chest, Palfrey. When I sent for you I didn't expect to have any trouble today. Then I learned that I was known to be staying down here. The Frenchie was on my tail. I didn't want to make trouble for you. I persuaded my friend to take my place. I told him to give you the ice if you arrived—and I had an idea you would arrive,' went on Kyle, with a chuckle. 'Then Susie and I looked after Frenchie.'

'Very clear,' murmured Palfrey.

'I'll make it clear soon. The woman might be in any moment. They give you service here.' Almost on his words she came in with a huge plateful. When she had gone, Drusilla poured out the tea.

'Well?' said Palfrey snappishly.

'I know, you're curious. All right,' said Kyle. 'Susie and I and one or two friends have been chasing Fyson's bunch for a long while. A *very* long while. We don't know them all. We know Fyson and Frenchie and Rose—that's Frenchie's girl. And that reminds me,' went on Kyle, 'what happened to Rose?'

'She went to Bristol,' said Palfrey. 'At least, she got on the Bristol bus.'

'*Did* she then! That's a new one. I've only known her in London. Maybe she's in a show there.'

'A show?' asked Drusilla.

'Sure, she's a Footlight Fanny,' said Kyle. 'Chorus. Getting sinewy in the leg, too ; they'll soon put her in the back row. But she can dance. I'm sorry for her, but she should pick her company better than she does. If Frenchie felt that way, he would break her neck and leave her cold and be necking some-one else the same night. I've known Frenchie longer than I've known any of them,' said Kyle, and his eyes glittered. 'It's no secret that I don't like that guy.'

'Well, he's probably got the stomach-ache now,' said Palfrey. 'Where is he?'

Kyle grinned. 'He's gone to bye-byes!' He raised an eyebrow when he saw Drusilla's expression. 'No, Mrs. Palfrey, I do not mean that he's been killed. Susie and I don't do that kind of thing except in emergency. Like the other night,' he went on. 'I would have killed Fyson if he'd given any more trouble, but that would have been in self-defence, wouldn't it? Not to mention Mrs. Palfrey's defence!'

Palfrey said: 'What we owed you for the other night has been repaid, Kyle.'

Kyle's expression changed. In a flash, he looked bleak, wary, dangerous. He said: 'What does that crack mean, Palfrey?'

Palfrey said: 'I don't like people who kidnap Frenchmen in Cheddar Gorge and spirit away people from the cliff-side— unless they've got a good reason. Unless I know the reason, too.'

'I'm trying to tell you, aren't I?'

'You're wondering how little will serve to satisfy me,' said Palfrey. 'A little won't.'

'Tell me something first. How much have you told the police?'

'Everything, except the rendezvous here. As I was followed by the police, that didn't make a great deal of difference,' said Palfrey. 'Snub, the broken-nosed man who followed you, had been following me. He's probably still in Cheddar. I saw him telephoning a report to his Inspector after he came back.'

'I get it,' said Kyle, rubbing his tuft of hair. 'All right, Palfrey, we know where we stand. That Fyson trick was to stop you getting to see Loretta Morne. Fyson won't talk more than that, I've tried all I know to make him, but he won't say anything else. But it was enough for a start. He didn't want you to see Loretta. Why?'

Palfrey said: 'Loretta had something to give me.'

'What?'

Palfrey laughed. 'Shall we leave that until later?'

Kyle looked at him speculatively. Then abruptly: 'Was it a map, Palfrey?'

Drusilla's expression gave it away.

'So it was a map. I'll give a lot for that map.'

'The police have it,' said Palfrey.

'That's too bad,' drawled Kyle. 'You made a mistake there. Was it the original map?'

'It only showed up on the paper when it was heated.'

'Then it was a copy,' said Kyle, with some relief. 'It wasn't the original; maybe Fyson's friends still have that. Palfrey, you want to know what I'm after. I can't go any further than saying that I want that map. It's important. It's worth plenty. To get that map, Fyson and Frenchie and their friends have gone to a lot of trouble, and I've put myself out quite a bit.' He learned forward and bared his right forearm. From just above the wrist almost to the elbow was a long, thin scar. 'I got that in the process, Palfrey. A present from Frenchie. That's how badly I want it.'

'Why?'

'For business reasons,' said Kyle, emphasising the 'business'.

'That isn't good enough,' said Palfrey.

'It will have to be,' Kyle retorted.

'Then I can't help you.' Palfrey was abrupt.

Kyle said: 'Palfrey, I'm not my own master. I've written asking how much I can tell you. I haven't got the answer yet. I can say this: that map is dynamite.' He laughed, a sudden, unexpected sound. 'It's more than dynamite! And it's dangerous to a lot of people, a lot of decent folk who live a good life and don't know what's coming to them one day if I don't get that map *and* all the copies. Fyson's friends have a copy of the map, but I don't think they know the place it refers to. I know that if Fyson's friends find the place there will be a lot of trouble for those decent folk.'

'Very touching,' murmured Palfrey.

Kyle snapped: 'I'm serious.'

'So am I. Who are Fyson's friends?'

'Tell me that and you'll tell me plenty,' said Kyle. He relaxed again. 'I've been trying to find out for months. I know Fyson, Rose and Frenchie and two others. They aren't big shots. They just do what they're told. There are plenty of people like that, Palfrey. They're controlled by a guy whose name I don't know, but I do know they're scared of him. *He's* dynamite, too. Maybe it's Morne. I wouldn't know.'

The little tea-room was cold. Outside it was growing dark and rain began to spatter sharply against the window.

The woman came in. 'Would you like anything else?' she asked. Obviously she was anxious to close the café.

Kyle took out his wallet, put two pound notes on the table, looked up at her with a bright smile, and said: 'Sure. A fire. And maybe supper, later on.'

She hesitated. 'Well, sir——'

'It needn't be in this room,' Kyle said.

'There *is* a fire in the sitting-room, sir, upstairs.'

'That's fine,' said Kyle.

The parlour was small, crowded with furniture and ornaments, and pleasantly warm. Drusilla sat on a horse-hair sofa and put up her legs. Kyle pushed the sofa in front of the fire, and he and Palfrey sat in saddle-back armchairs on either side. The woman replenished the fire, then left them alone.

A car passed outside, they could hear the wheels splashing. Rain beat on the windows, which rattled unexpectedly under a sudden gust of wind.

'Sure,' said Kyle. 'It might be Rufus Morne.'

80

'Is that a guess?'

'A pretty wild guess,' Kyle admitted, very serious now. Drusilla looked at him and wished he would smile, showing the flash of his white teeth. 'I make it only because his daughter told you where to find the copy of that map. I have been wondering why she wanted to tell you. She might know what Morne's up to. She might *think* she knows. She might prefer someone to find out. What do you know about this Loretta, Palfrey?'

'That she's been nearly murdered three times,' said Palfrey.

'Maybe by her father,' Kyle said.

Palfrey had a quick vivid mental picture of Morne, standing with his back to the fire, haggard of face, bedraggled after his wandering on the moor. A tormented soul.

'Why, did she have this fellow Garth staying with her?' demanded Kyle, abruptly.

'Who *is* Garth?' asked Drusilla.

'One of Fyson's friends,' said Kyle, and laughed mirthlessly. 'Not the leader, Palfrey, but more important than Fyson or Frenchie. I don't know whether that's his real name, but I do know he's a scientist, Palfrey.'

Palfrey said: ' "Scientist" is a loose term.'

'Loose? I guess so. He's a physicist. He's been working on something—I don't know what.'

He *did* know; Palfrey felt sure of that. Kyle knew he knew much more than he had yet told them, and he would not talk more freely yet. To try to make him would be a waste of time.

Kyle said: 'I hunted Garth out of the place where he lived, Palfrey. I hunted him out of his laboratory. I've chased him all over England and in parts of Europe. I've made his life hell, and I will again. But I've never caught up with him. I've never found out what he's working on. I got this far and lost him.'

'This far?'

'He was in Cheddar for a week at least,' said Kyle; 'and since he's been gone, Frenchie and Fyson have been down here. I thought they'd got Garth hidden here some place until I went after Fyson one day and we fetched up on Wenlock cliffs. That was the night you came along. You told me there had been a Garth at Morne House. I guess it was the same man.'

'He was there for some weeks.'

'After I'd got hold of Fyson, Susie told me that Frenchie was still around here. So I came back. Frenchie was looking for me, of course; he thought he'd got me this afternoon.' Kyle laughed.

'Why did Susie drive off?' asked Drusilla.

'The police will be looking for the Packard,' Kyle said, dryly. 'I wanted to see you or I wouldn't have come back through the gorge. She drove off so they wouldn't realise I was here. I want Garth, and they *say* he left Morne House the day Loretta was hurt. I don't know much more about that house, Palfrey, but it wouldn't surprise me if they're still hiding Garth there. Did anyone see the ambulance that was supposed to take him away?'

Palfrey said: 'Yes. The police know there was an ambulance there that morning.'

'Garth needn't have been in it,' said Kyle. 'Don't you agree?'

'Oh, that's possible,' admitted Palfrey.

'That's what I want you to do,' said Kyle. 'Find out if Garth is still there.' He grinned crookedly, but his eyes were wary. 'It's not so much to ask, Palfrey. I don't want you to do anything about the guy. Just find out if he's at Morne House, and let me know. I'll do the rest.'

'Not without telling the police,' Palfrey declared.

'I can't work with the police, Palfrey.'

'I can't work against them.'

'I'm not a criminal,' Kyle said. 'I'm working for a man who wants to put things right.' He was very earnest now. 'Maybe I haven't acted according to the law with Fyson and Frenchie, but they won't be hurt.' His eyes lit up. 'Listen to me, Palfrey. When I've got Garth, I'll turn Fyson and Frenchie over to the police, with plenty of evidence to make a case against them. More than enough evidence. I won't wait until I've got Garth, I'll turn them over when you tell me if Garth is at Morne House. Can we agree on that?'

Palfrey smiled. 'Fyson and Frenchie have been kidnapped, Kyle. You kidnapped them. That's a criminal offence. I can't condone it.'

'You're hard,' said Kyle, 'but I'm offering to set them free. Or as near free as they'll get for a long time. I wouldn't do that if I thought the police would let them go. *You'll* be doing nothing wrong. Will he, Mrs. Palfrey? You'll be making sure that Fyson and Frenchie get humane treatment.'

'Where are they now?' asked Drusilla lightly, a shade too lightly, but it nearly worked, for Kyle said:

82

'They're in——' He broke off and grinned. 'That was neat, Mrs. Palfrey! They're in a safe place, I guess, and being well looked after.'

Palfrey sipped his drink. 'We're wasting time,' he said, 'I can't do anything to help you without first telling the police. They may agree that it's worth trying. If they do, they'll be looking for you as well as Garth. You'll have more risks, but you'll have a chance.'

Kyle said thoughtfully: 'That's worth thinking about.' There was a long pause. Then abruptly: 'Okay. Tell the police!'

'That's more like it,' said Palfrey.

'You'll do nothing to help them to get me, will you?'

Palfrey laughed. 'There isn't much I can do, is there? After tonight, you'll be washed up in the gorge, of course ; they'll keep this place watched closely, and I shall have to give them a description of you.'

'You're hard,' said Kyle.

Someone knocked on the street door.

Kyle got up and opened the door of the room. They could hear the woman walking through the café to open the street door. A man's voice sounded. The woman said: 'I really don't know.' The man spoke again, and his words were audible this time. 'Is *any*one here, please? The man is tall, rather thin——'

Drusilla exclaimed: 'That's Mac!'

Palfrey got up, Kyle turned round sharply. 'Who's Mac?'

'Bruce McDonald,' Palfrey said. 'He followed Rose this afternoon.'

'*Did* he!' said Kyle. 'Who is he?'

'A friend.'

'A police friend?'

'Confound you, no!' Palfrey went out on to the narrow landing and called down. 'We're here, Mac!'

'So they *are* your friends,' said the woman. 'Let me take your coat, sir. You're drenched.'

'Thanks, but I haven't time,' said McDonald.

'We'll come down,' said Palfrey. He led the way down the dimly lighted stairs.

'Let me have a word in private with my friends, will you?' he asked the woman.

She said: 'I've *nearly* got supper ready, sir,' to Kyle.

'That's fine,' said Kyle. 'Maybe I'll have to ask you to keep it hot.' He led her out firmly, and the others stood in the little front room, among the empty chairs and tables set for the next day's meals. McDonald was obviously eager to tell his story, but glanced doubtfully at Kyle.

'I'm in this,' said Kyle. Palfrey nodded.

'Right!' said McDonald. 'I followed the girl to Bristol, Palfrey. She went to a rooming-house at the back of the *Theatre Royal,* stayed for a while and then came away with a man. They got on the first bus back to Cheddar: it arrived half an hour ago. They walked up the gorge and—vanished!'

Palfrey echoed: 'Vanished?'

'Yes, into the side of the cliff. I *think* I heard them go up some steps, but I couldn't swear to that. I did find a flight of steps, but I thought you might be waiting here, and——' Kyle was already putting on his raincoat.

'We're going for a walk,' he said. He went to the doorway and called out: 'Sorry, honey, we've got a little job to do, but we'll be right back for the supper.' He was looking at Drusilla, and added: 'Can you lend my lady friend a mackintosh?'

Palfrey said: 'You'll stay and keep warm, 'Silla, won't you?'

'I'd rather have a mac,' said Drusilla. 'But if she can't lend me one, I'll get my coat wet.'

Kyle laughed. The woman found a mackintosh which was rather short, but Drusilla managed to pull it on over her fur coat.

Soon they were out on the road. The rain was teeming down, and occasionally a fierce gust of wind drove down the gorge, so powerful that they had to stand still and battle against it. During the lulls, Kyle asked questions and McDonald answered in monosyllables.

'The only steps I know lead to Gough's Caves,' Kyle said. 'We're about there now. The couple just vanished, did they?'

'Yes.'

'Gough's Caves,' murmured Kyle. A gust of wind howled down the gorge and took his breath away. They all stood still. As the wind died down, the headlights of a car travelling down the gorge picked them out, and Kyle muttered to himself. The car served them a good turn, for its headlights showed some steps leading to the caves, not far ahead of them.

They reached the steps and Kyle stopped.

'What's it to be?' he asked.

For a moment no one answered. The wind howled and died away again ; and then they heard a scream.

It was not imagination; all four of them heard it and started and looked at one another. It came again, high-pitched, seemingly from a long way off, and ended abruptly. There was silence; for a moment even the wind was hushed.

Drusilla said in a shaky voice: 'It came from—the cave.'

'Let's go!' exclaimed Kyle.

He led the way up the steps. Palfrey took Drusilla's arm, let McDonald go in front, and whispered: 'I've got to find out what that was. I'm not taking you inside. Will you give us twenty minutes? Well, say half an hour. Then fetch the police.'

Drusilla said: 'I suppose I'd better.'

Palfrey squeezed her hand. 'It's the best we can do,' he thought. Kyle would not agree with it, of course, but then Kyle need not know.

They reached the top of the steps and then they heard a car splashing down the gorge. Curiously, all the traffic seemed to come down, none went up. They sprang towards the wall of the pay-box, to be out of sight. The headlamps shone a bright glow which spread about the windows of the souvenir shop, on the signs, even as far as the entrance of the cave itself. There was an iron trellis grill across the entrance, and outside the grill there was plenty of room for Drusilla to shelter from the wind and rain.

The car passed.

'Okay,' said Kyle and stepped forward. 'Don't show a light, any of you.' He was holding a lighted torch in his hand. A dim red glow showed where it shone through his fingers. That was all they could see of it; only his fingers were visible, then a few inches of the iron trellis gate. He pulled at it, but it did not open.

'That's a pity,' he said, 'but it shouldn't take long.'

A moment later metal clinked on metal. Now they could just see the fingers of his other hand, holding what looked like a narrow piece of steel. It glinted as he twisted. The scraping of metal against metal continued until there was a sharp click.

'You see, I'm not so bad,' he said, and there was a chuckle in his voice. 'Palfrey, I'm prepared to go alone.'

'No,' said Palfrey.

'You add to the risks, you know. I don't want to lead you into trouble.'

'I'll come with you,' said Palfrey. 'Eh, Mac?'

'I'm in this,' McDonald said promptly.

'You make it hard,' sighed Kyle. 'On my own, I wouldn't

have a care in the world, but with you—— Mrs. Palfrey, will you stick around here? It's dry enough. If we haven't shown up in reasonable time, you'd better fetch help.'

'That's a good idea,' said Palfrey eagerly.

'But if the police come, *I* want a break,' said Kyle.

'Fair enough,' agreed Palfrey.

'Here we go,' said Kyle, and began to open the gate. Only a faint hissing sound came from it. 'We're through,' whispered Kyle. 'We'll have to manage without a light for a bit, Palfrey.'

'Yes. Straight on for fifty yards, and then the floor slopes.'

'I've been in here too,' said Kyle.

Drusilla stayed outside the gate. Palfrey's hand touched hers, but they did not speak. It would be almost unendurable for her to wait there for long.

Inside, the silence was eerie, and darkness frightening. They began to move forward. Soon there was a soft and gentle sound. Palfrey heard it and stiffened, listening. Water was falling—they were near *The Fonts*!

They stood straining their ears. The gentle sound, hardly a sound at all, was coming from their right.

'We should go left then,' Palfrey said. They groped about for a few minutes, all holding hands. They could see nothing at all, and could not be sure they were not walking in circles.

McDonald suddenly pitched forward, wrenched his hand away from Palfrey, fell and gasped.

'Quiet!' hissed Kyle.

'S-sorry,' stammered McDonald. 'I—I kicked against something.' He was kneeling down now; Palfrey could tell that from the direction of his voice. McDonald was breathing very quickly. He was scared. He said with a catch in his voice: 'It's a body.'


NINE

## DEAD ROSE — AND GARTH

'ALL right,' whispered Kyle. 'So it's a body.'

There was a savage note in his voice. He shone the torch towards the floor, allowing only a sliver of light between his fingers. The beam lit up something black. Rose had worn a black coat. The light travelled further along, past her hand, which lay limp on the gravel, up to her shoulder, then on to her head. Her face was white. Her hair shone gold where the light touched it. Her throat gleamed red——

'Oh, my God!' gasped McDonald.

Kyle said nothing. Palfrey said: 'Keep the light steady, Kyle.' He went nearer to the girl, sought her hand and felt for the pulse; it was still. 'It's no use,' Palfrey said. 'We'll have to fetch the police.'

'Then minutes won't make any difference,' said Kyle in a reedy voice. After a moment's pause, he added in a sharper voice: 'What's that?' He shone the torch downward. It lit upon a piece of cord close to the wall. The cord was moving slightly. 'We-ell,' breathed Kyle, 'that's how they find their way. It should be easy now.'

Palfrey made up his mind then. 'Mac, will you go back to Drusilla, send her for the police and wait at the entrance yourself?'

'I'm quite game to stay here.'

'I know you are. But I'd rather you went.'

'All right,' said McDonald. He bent down and gripped the cord. 'Don't go too far in, will you?'

He went off, his shuffling footsteps sounding clearly. The cord, which Palfrey was holding, quivered with his grip. Kyle put out his torch and said:

'I suppose you were right. I'll lead the way.'

'Right-ho,' said Palfrey.

Both of them held the cord. They went more quickly than before, but still carefully, for they did not want to make a noise. Suddenly, they reached a corner. Kyle turned, murmuring a warning to Palfrey to go slow. Then he stopped abruptly.

'What is it?' Palfrey's voice was sharp.

'A light,' said Kyle, softly. 'Plenty far off.' He went on, and Palfrey turned the corner. The light, in the roof, spread a faint glow about the smooth rocks. They quickened their pace. A faint murmuring sound reached them. *Men were talking!*

The light grew brighter as they went along. The voices were echoing about the caves.

A man was saying: 'Well, I think we ought to get out while we can.' It was an ordinary English voice. 'We'll leave him. it's the only thing to do.'

'We've *got* to get him away!'

The first speaker swore. There was a moment of silence. Kyle was peering round a corner. Palfrey looked over his shoulder. He saw that Kyle had a gun in his hand, and it gave him a measure of confidence.

The silence lengthened.

Kyle moved a little further forward, and Palfrey was able to see the man who was lying on a blanket, at full length. A living skeleton—for he *was* alive, his lips were moving slightly as he breathed through his mouth. Apart from that, he looked like a dead man.

Two men were sitting on garden chairs, staring at each other. One was short and very thin, the other taller, plump, and dressed in a huge teddybear coat. A diamond ring on his finger scintillated in the light—the multi-coloured light which came from the other side of the cavern.

Iron railings and a flight of steps divided the first part of the cavern in two. Beyond, on one side, were the three men. On the other an incredible sight met the eye. It looked like a tiny village, snow-covered roofs and lights shone from them. Palfrey stared at it, and then, out of the dimness of the past, memory served him. He had seen this before, a village, a snow village—*Swiss Village*, that was it. The 'buildings' were reflections of the stalactites in the roof of the cave. The 'village' was water, a smooth shallow sheet of water, protected, he could see, by glass.

The small man said: 'We've got to get him away.'

'*I'll* get him away,' said Kyle and stepped forward.

The two men jumped up; one chair crashed, the little man backed to the wall and thrust his hand towards his pocket. 'That's enough!' snapped Kyle, but the little man ignored him and his hand disappeared. Kyle said 'All right', and fired.

The roar of the shot was like thunder. The roof seemed to shake. Palfrey shot a swift glance upwards, expecting to see something fall. Echoes were rolling round, near and far away, but nothing happened to the cave, only to the little man. He took his hand away. Blood was spilling from it. He staggered back against the wall and raised his wounded arm.

Kyle bounded up the steps.

'That'll do for you,' he said, and with a movement almost too quick for Palfrey to follow, he put his hand into the fellow's pocket and took out an automatic. 'Catch, Palfrey!' he called, and made as if to throw the gun. He did not throw it, however, but grinned at Palfrey's expression and handed it to him. 'You'll feel safer with that,' he said. 'Sol, I would like to take you with me too, but I've got enough on my hands.' He was speaking to the fat man.

'Ky—Kyle, I——'

'I know, I know. You're a good guy really. You've mixed with the wrong people. Like Garth.' He said to Palfrey: 'I'm going to get Garth away. Don't be foolish enough to try to stop me. I *want* the guy.'

'Carry him down the steps,' said Palfrey, in a strained voice. 'Just carry him down the steps, and let him die in your arms.'

Kyle said: 'That lie won't work!'

'If you move him, you'll kill him.'

Kyle stood undecided. He shot a swift glance at the plump man, who stood terrified, with his hands level with his chest. The little fellow had not uttered a word; he was feeling his right forearm and looking down stupidly at the dripping blood.

'He won't be fit to talk for weeks, even if he lives,' Palfrey said. 'Do you want the other men?'

'I know all they can tell me.'

'Then get out,' said Palfrey. 'The police won't be long. It's your only chance. Garth is worthless; he'll be worthless to anyone for a long time. There's a slim hope of saving him, but it's so slim I wouldn't like to risk a penny on it.'

*Suddenly the light went out.*

Darkness fell upon them like a blanket. Time seemed to stand still. Then came a movement, a savage oath, a bump. 'Stop him!' cried Kyle. Palfrey felt something brush past him. Then a vivid flash of light showed the little man running, the plump man turning, and Kyle grabbing at the little man's coat. The flash was gone before Palfrey saw anything else, and another thunderous roar boomed and beat about his ears. He did not know whether anyone else was hurt, but he knew the shot had come from the foot of the steps. Another shot, and this time the flash was further away. He heard the roar, followed, close to him, by the sound of a bullet hitting the rock. Kyle bellowed: '*Watch Garth!*'

Watch Garth; the fool, did he think Garth could move?

*Watch Garth!* One of these men would try to deal a death blow. Palfrey stepped forward as a torch flashed out close to his

89

feet. It shone on Garth. Palfrey kicked at it. He caught the hand which held it, and the torch fell, but did not go out. The man with the light sprang up and leapt at Garth. Palfrey closed with him. A small man, wiry, slippery, twisting and turning, writhing in Palfrey's grip——

Something pricked Palfrey's arm. A knife!

Dead Rose . . . her throat cut. . . .

Palfrey tried to bring up his knee, but the man was too close.

He felt the prick of the knife again, beneath his right ear. He got one hand up, clutched, felt the fingers and grasped the wrist. If only he could find the spot! When he had been showing off to Kyle, it had been easy enough. He found it, twisted, and the man squealed and dropped the knife.

The torch rolled over a ledge and went out. The man was limp in Palfrey's grip. Would he remain like that or was he foxing? He wasn't foxing. Then another torch shone out, and Kyle said: 'Are you all right, Palfrey?'

'Yes.'

'That's fine.' The beam travelled over the floor of the cave, picking out some of the colours. It fell upon Garth's face and stopped. Garth was still breathing. 'I'll be seeing you,' said Kyle, and he turned the torch towards the steps, went down and walked away.

His footsteps faded. Only the heavy breathing of his prisoner sounded above Palfrey's breathing. They seemed to stand like that for an age, and then there were other sounds, the sounds of several people approaching. A light went on not far away, and a man called out: 'Are you there? Are you there, Sap?' That was McDonald. '*Sap!*' That was Drusilla.

'All safe,' called Palfrey.

On the following morning, a little after eleven o'clock, Palfrey was in the Chief Constable's office at the Corbin Police Headquarters.

The police had been uncommunicative. He wanted to know what had happened to Kyle.

Cartwright said: 'Why didn't you tell us about Cheddar Gorge, Dr. Palfrey?'

'I wanted to give Kyle a chance of talking freely,' said Palfrey, 'and I thought he would sheer off if he knew the police were at hand. Has he talked yet?'

Cartwright said: 'You are in a better position to know that, aren't you?'

Palfrey's smile broadened. 'So he got away?' In spite of the two frowning faces opposite him, he laughed. 'It was a good effort, you must admit.'

'I do *not* find it amusing,' said Cartwright.

He leaned forward on his desk, and said slowly: 'Dr. Palfrey, you may have the best of motives in behaving so oddly. You may have the *fullest* authority. I do not know. I do ask you to realize that we have been extremely patient. You should tell us the *whole* truth.'

'My statement does,' said Palfrey. He was puzzled. What did the man mean by 'You may have the fullest authority'? Didn't he know that Palfrey had no authority at all, and was feeling more than a little uncomfortable about it?

Hardy said abruptly: 'Why two departments can't work together, *I* don't know.'

'Departments?' echoed Palfrey. 'What——' He paused, and understanding dawned upon him. His first reaction was one of sheer astonishment. 'Departments!' he repeated. 'If you mean Z.5, I haven't worked for Z.5 for a long time.' If they had thought him an Intelligence man, it explained why they had given him so much rope. It meant, also, they had not believed that an ordinary private individual would carry on as he had. It would not be easy to justify himself. Cartwright might get nasty. Hardy's tolerance might have been inspired *only* by his belief that a different Government department was involved.

'Is this *true*?' asked Cartwright, and his eyes seemed to bulge.

'Gospel truth,' said Palfrey. 'All my own work. An excuse, perhaps; I *have* been rather used to doing whatever wanted doing and asking about it afterwards. A bad habit in a private citizen, of course. I'm sorry. I do see——'

Hardy snorted and then he began to laugh. Cartwright also saw the funny side. Palfrey smiled, warily at first, then broadly; then he, too, chimed in with a laugh—of relief. These were good fellows, open to reason, but—*why* had they suspected that Intelligence was concerned in this affair?

Palfrey lounged on the bed and Drusilla sat in the hotel arm-chair, looking at Palfrey and listening to the rain. It had rained steadily since the previous night, and Corbin was covered by a mist that was really cloud. The hotel was quiet, for it was the middle of the afternoon.

'Well, what are we to do?' asked Palfrey. 'No further formal request for assistance yet, you understand ; the matter has been left in abeyance. On the whole, I suppose they have fair reason to be satisfied. That Mayfair telephone number, the house where Rose had been staying——'

'Was she on the stage?'

'Yes. In a musical at the Hippodrome in Bristol,' said Palfrey. 'I've no doubt the police are pretty busy among the cast, but I don't see that they're going to make much progress. The man who had that final shot at Garth, and whom I managed to hold, killed Rose. The knife that was used was found in his pocket, with his finger-prints on it. The man Sol was eager to give corroborative evidence, apparently. The fellow Kyle shot isn't a talker, but with the knife, the prints and Sol, the case is clear.'

'Have they found out anything else?'

'A little. Garth has been in the caves since he left Morne House. Apparently the caves have been used for some time as a hiding-place for loot. There are several unexplored caves—I believe the word is 'undeveloped'—leading off the main arches. They're rarely inspected. Garth was hidden there, and the murderer and the man Kyle shot visited him from time to time. So did Frenchie and Rose, I gather. After Frenchie was taken away, Rose went haring to see Sol and brought him back with her. Sol was the man through whom the others received their instructions from our mystery man.'

'Has he talked?' asked Drusilla.

'Hardy says he doesn't seem to know very much. The police probably won't confide in me altogether, you know, but I think in this case Hardy's telling the truth.

'The manager of the cave is very upset,' Palfrey went on. 'He's been here today. He can't be blamed. These people were clever and careful, and hid their traces well. Now we,' he said thoughtfully, 'have a pretty problem on our hands: what to do next?'

'What *can* we do?'

'I don't know. The Morne angle is an obvious one. Kyle will probably try to get in touch with us again. And there's at least a possibility that I shall be asked to give an opinion on Garth. Small wonder Halsted wanted me to see him. The man's just wasted away. It might be cancer, of course, but Halsted would have recognized that. I'm hoping he *will* recover, but the report from the hospital is pretty grim.'

Drusilla said: 'I wonder how Loretta is.'

'The same thought sprang to my mind. And who put the stuff in my tea? I think——' The telephone bell rang. Palfrey answered the call.

'This is Susan Lee.'

'Oh, Susan Lee. I don't think I have had the pleasure——'

Drusilla jumped up. *'Susie!'* she exclaimed, and Palfrey had a quick mental vision of the girl who had driven the Packard down the gorge, let Kyle out, and driven off again.

'Oh, so it's you, is it?' he growled.

'I would very much like to talk to you, Dr. Palfrey. I'm speaking from the telephone near the hotel exchange. . . . Yes, in the lounge. Shall I come up or will you come down?'

Palfrey said: 'I'll come down. At least, my wife will. You had better, for the moment, be a friend of my wife.' He rang off, with her laugh echoing in his ears.

'My dear, sweet, simple, innocent husband,' said Drusilla, 'your friend Nicholas Kyle has kidnapped two people under your own dewy eyes, he travels armed wherever he goes, he leads a gang of law-breakers which is at least three strong, has treated you as if you were dirt beneath his feet—*and*, my precious darling, he is wanted by the police. There is a price upon his head. You have been dealt with by two forgiving gentlemen whose leniency is a thing to marvel at, but, as you once said, you don't want to wither away behind prison bars. *You* didn't come here to see Susan Lee or whatever she calls herself. You didn't ask her to come. She has come herself, doubtless because Kyle has told her that you will probably be fool enough to see her first before telling the police about it, but——'

'Instead, you'll see her first,' said Palfrey. 'While I telephone Hardy.'

'All right,' said Drusilla. She went out with such alacrity that Palfrey looked owlishly at the closed door. Drusilla was as anxious as he to know what Susan Lee had to say. But she was right. He lifted the telephone and gave Hardy's number.

After five minutes he put out his cigarette and went downstairs to the small lounge. He could hear Drusilla talking; she stopped, and the other woman spoke. Hers was a pleasant voice

93

with a faint American accent. Palfrey opened the door and walked in, then came to an abrupt halt and stared at Susan Lee—or the girl who called herself Susan Lee. She was not dark; she was fair. Her hair was not in a page-boy bob, but piled up Edwardian fashion, and most attractively, with a small hat perched on one side.

*Was* she the same girl? He could see no likeness. The length of the face, perhaps, was there, but her cheeks were fuller than he remembered, and he could have sworn that her eyes were dark, not this china blue with their brimming laughter.

'Quick change,' said Palfrey.

'Oh, not very quick. You haven't seen me since yesterday evening, you know.'

'*Did* I see you?'

'Well, I saw you,' declared Susan Lee, 'skulking behind a rock on the left-hand side of the gorge while Frenchie was talking to Old Nick.'

'Old Nick?'

'Yes. We have to have names for them both,' said Susan Lee. 'Nick is just Nick, and nothing else would suit him, but when our Lancashire friend comes on the scene we call him Old Nick.'

'Apt, I shouldn't wonder.'

'Oh, he's a dear,' declared Susan Lee. 'You'll think so too when you know him better. He doesn't look like Nick in real life, of course. But he's about the same height, and he's nearly bald, and when he takes out his teeth his cheeks sink in, rather like Nick's. It doesn't take a lot to make him look more like Nick, you see. We aren't wizards. It's just ordinary make-up.'

Palfrey sat down beside her.

'Why are we so favoured, Miss Lee?'

'I come to warn you, Cæsar, not to tempt you,' said Susan.

'So you've come to warn me, have you?' He paused. 'Odd line you used then. Not quite as originally written. Why misquote Shakespeare?'

'I thought it would make you jump,' said Susan. For the first time she looked serious, although her eyes were still smiling. 'This man, McDonald,' she went on. 'How well do you know him?'

'Not particularly well.'

'Why didn't you tell Nick that he came straight from the House of Morne? That wasn't fair, was it?'

94

'Fair?' mumbled Palfrey. 'I don't know. He served a turn. A very good turn. We would never have found where they were hiding in the caves, but for Mac.'

Susan said gently: 'Nick is an expert at his job, you know. Even his enemies admit that. For weeks he has haunted Cheddar Gorge, trying to find out where these people were hiding, and he failed. Don't you think it was curious that an amateur like McDonald found the hiding-place at the first go?'

Drusilla leaned forward.

'Rose was beside herself, and not careful,' she reminded her.

'Rose was, perhaps,' said Susan, 'but she had been to fetch Sol Krotmann, and Sol isn't the fat fool that he looks. In fact, he had been to the caves before, in broad daylight, and disappeared as if off the face of the earth. Why, on a dark and windy night, did he lose his head and show an amateur the way?'

'It's a point,' said Palfrey.

'It's a very strong point,' Susan assured him. 'Especially as McDonald is a Morne.'

'Well, only half Morne.'

'I think McDonald *knew* where they were,' declared Susan. 'Shall I tell you something else, Doctor? This morning, Nick and I have been very busy, looking up files of the *Corshire News* and finding pictures of the Mornes. Then Nick, who has even more nerve than I have, asked if he could buy prints of the photographs. It was easy, because the Mornes are well in the news again.'

She opened her bag and took out several photographs, so large that they caught at the sides of the bag and she had some difficulty in taking them out. Silently, she handed them to Palfrey. The top one was of Morne. McDonald followed, then Gerald Markham, his father, his mother and McDonald's mother. 'All the Mornes,' said Susan. 'Are they good photographs?'

'Remarkably good.'

'What about McDonald and Gerald Markham?'

'Yes. Good enough.'

'*Both* have been seen in Cheddar Gorge during the last week,' Susan told him serenely. 'I don't mean yesterday, either. Did McDonald tell you that it wasn't his first recent visit to the gorge?'

'I don't remember.'

'You mean that he didn't,' said Susan. 'Of course he didn't. But don't you think it would be worth knowing *why* McDonald and his cousin are so interested in Cheddar Gorge?'

'Possibly,' admitted Palfrey, cautiously.

'You hate admitting that you've been fooled, don't you?' asked Susan, gently. 'I can sympathize. May I have those photographs back? . . . Thank you.' She pushed them into her bag. 'Of course, if you decide to try to find out why McDonald behaved like that, and care to pass the answer on to Nick or me, we'll be delighted, but obviously we can't strike a bargain.'

'No. What else?'

'Nothing else,' said Susan Lee. She stood up and smoothed down her skirt. She was a refreshing creature—not lovely, as Drusilla, but with the light of the sun in her eyes and in her hair, quick and graceful in her movements. She held out her hand to Drusilla. 'Good-bye. Thank you for being so sweet.' She turned to Palfrey. He hesitated. She took his hand and squeezed it, and her laughter bubbled up. 'You needn't feel conscience-smitten, she said. If the police *do* detain me, it won't be your fault, because I walked into here with my eyes open. And Nick's eyes. They see much more.' She turned and went out.

Drusilla shot a startled glance at Palfrey. They hurried to the door. Hardy was too sound to allow anything to go amiss, and the girl had no chance of getting out. She was entering the hall, and two men—including Detective-Sergeant Rundell—moved from their chairs and approached her. Another man hurried past Palfrey; he had obviously been watching the lounge. Serenely, Susan walked on. Rundell touched her arm. She paused and looked round, as if surprised.

'Yes?' She was haughty.

'I would like you to come with me, please,' said Rundell.

'I *beg* your pardon.' Susan threw back her shoulders indignantly, and at the same time glanced towards Palfrey. *She winked.* Then she wrenched herself free. Outside, someone shouted.

The shout was followed by another. Rundell glanced uneasily towards the door and at the same time stretched out his hand again. Then something was tossed into the hall from outside, and burst in front of Palfrey's eyes. Smoke rose up, billowing out as if from a great fire. One moment there was only a small oblong thing, the size of an egg, on the floor, and the next

96

moment Susan's legs were hidden in smoke. Palfrey just had time to see her move from Rundell, and Rundell stagger back as if she had pushed him; then the smoke filled the middle of the hall.

There was pandemonium inside and outside. Hardy's voice was raised: 'Guard the door! Guard the door!' Footsteps thundered; someone *laughed*.

'That's Kyle!' snapped Palfrey. 'Come on!'

He grabbed Drusilla's arm, rushed with her into the small lounge and through the french window. He dashed round the hotel towards a side gate, reached the street and ran towards the corner, with Drusilla close behind him. Smoke was spreading swiftly, enveloping the hotel.

A car sounded near at hand; Palfrey caught a glimpse of the front of the car looming out of the dense cloud of smoke. Palfrey could not see what else happened, for the smoke thickened.

At last they reached a clearer space. Palfrey looked at Drusilla and saw she was smiling, as if convulsed by secret laughter. She caught his eye. Kyle's laugh seemed to echo about them, but Kyle and his Susie were a long way off by then.

The incident made Hardy really angry, which was understandable enough. It also angered Cartwright, and Wriggleswade was beside himself with mortification. It transpired that he had been in charge of the party of policemen who had surrounded the hotel to make sure that Susan Lee could not escape. Hardy had deferred to him, and Hardy's only consolation was the fact that he had left the arrangements to Wriggleswade. All these things Palfrey learned when he saw Hardy and Cartwright at the Chief Constable's office about half past six that evening.

Hardy was still covered with soot; Drusilla and Palfrey had changed. Wriggleswade was having a bath, Hardy said, and his tone inferred that he hoped the man would drown.

'Well, we ought to admit that it was quite a notion,' said Palfrey, mildly. 'My wife and I were trying to imagine how on earth the girl could get out of that jam, and we were as surprised as anyone. No one was hurt, I hope?'

'No,' growled Hardy.

'You see, Kyle wouldn't go too far,' murmured Palfrey.

'Unlike you, Dr. Palfrey,' said Hardy, a dangerous glint in his eyes, 'I do *not* enjoy the spectacle of the police being made fools of, and an insolent American behaving as if he were in Chicago instead of in England.'

'Oh, Chicago isn't bad,' said Palfrey.

'We must get on with the job,' interrupted Cartwright. 'What did the woman have to say to you, Palfrey?'

Palfrey said: 'Not a great deal, but what there was should interest you.'

He told the story faithfully, not without some misgivings.

Cartwright said that obviously McDonald and Gerald Markham must be questioned. Murder had been committed. There was *prima facie* evidence that one of the men now under detention had killed Rose—whose other name, it proved, was Lindsay—and it had been generally assumed that the crime had been committed at the time of the scream. It was possible, however, that it had been committed before that. The accused man flatly denied knowing anything about it.

'Well, you'd expect him to,' said Palfrey. 'Are you suggesting that McDonald might have gone into the cave, killed her, come out and fetched us, and——'

'Isn't it possible?' asked Cartwright.

'No,' said Palfrey. 'Most decidedly not. That would have meant that the girl had been dead for nearly an hour when I reached her. She hadn't. There was little or no surface coating of the blood, and in the temperature of the caves it would have had at least a coating. The body was too warm, too. That isn't opinionative; that's medical evidence.'

'Do I take it that you are advising us *not* to question McDonald and Gerald Markham?' asked Cartwright.

'I am not advising you,' said Palfrey. 'I can only tell you the facts within my province as a doctor.' He picked up his hat. 'Anything else?' he asked.

'Yes,' said Cartwright, speaking heavily. 'There is one other thing, Dr. Palfrey. When you worked for Intelligence Z.5, from whom did you receive orders?'

Palfrey said: 'That's no secret. The Marquis of Brett.'

'And is he still the leader of Z.5?'

'Technically. I don't think it's working now. Why all this? You're not still harping on that idea, are you?'

Cartwright said: 'Perhaps you will tell me that you did not know that the Marquis of Brett is staying at Wanling Lodge.'

Palfrey stared. 'I don't even know where Wanling Lodge is.'

'It is three miles out of Corbin,' said Cartwright, 'the home of Mr. William Jefferson.' He stood up. 'I think you might have been more frank with us, Dr. Palfrey.'

Palfrey felt a surge of furious anger. 'I am *not* working for the Marquis of Brett or for any Government department.'

At the hotel, where cleaners were working in the hall and the grounds, they found a letter waiting for them. Mr. William Jefferson requested the presence of Dr. and Mrs. Palfrey at dinner that night . . .

Jefferson was a short, bald-headed man, wealthy, quiet and mellow; a man of influence behind the scenes, a banker, a philanthropist, a friend of kings. After dinner he led the others to a small room where liqueurs and brandy were served, and then unobtrusively left them.

Brett cracked a nut. 'What's troubling you, Palfrey?' he asked.

'You,' said Palfrey, angry now with himself and yet still feeling justified. 'You should have given us some warning. After a lot of trouble, I convinced Cartwright and Hardy that I was here in my private capacity. When they learned you were here, they didn't believe me. I don't blame them.'

'What is really worrying Sap is the suspicion of McDonald,' Drusilla said. 'He liked McDonald; we both did.' She had told Brett and Jefferson about that, for the conversation in the dining-room had been mainly about the Morne affair. 'And there's something else too,' she went on, smiling at her husband. 'He feels like a fish out of water. There's nothing he would like better than to plunge into this particular pool, but he can't. He isn't used to police restrictions.'

'I want you to work on the Morne affair,' said Brett.

'So that *is* the game,' murmured Palfrey. His heart was suddenly lighter. Brett would not be interested in the Mornes because of a murder or two; he was too highly placed in Government circles for that. Brett was the man who had conceived the idea of setting representatives of the United Nations to work together in a spy organisation called, for convenience, Z.5, and had controlled that organisation. And Brett was interested in the Mornes.

'I was afraid of that,' said Drusilla, but she was smiling.

Brett spread his hands out before the fire. 'I don't think I need beat about the bush, Sap. It was the police capture of

Garth—yes, yes, I know how that came about—which started things moving in London. It sounded an alarm.'

'Why?' asked Palfrey.

'Because Garth was at one time one of our atom bomb experts.'

There was silence in the room, a tense, electric silence.

'Garth was in America during the first trials,' said Brett, very softly. 'He had been working on it for years, at the same time as Rutherford at Cambridge. He was brilliant. I knew him slightly then, and I've seen him this afternoon. Why do you think they have done that to him?'

'Is it—starvation?'

'You should know better than I. They have reduced him to a living skeleton. And that man, for some weeks, had the hospitality of Morne House.'

'Yes,' said Palfrey.

Brett said: 'Garth worked on similar lines to the others, but believed that the manufacture could be done on a much smaller scale. Others agreed with him, but to find the method would have taken too long. The present American method was adopted. Garth helped with that. Whether he continued with his own experiments I don't know. I think it likely that he did.'

He paused; the others did not speak.

'Other things will occur to you at once,' said Brett. 'In Corshire there is uranium. Where it is known, it is closely controlled; the Government has taken over the mines. But there may be undiscovered deposits.'

'Morne has mines on his estate,' said Palfrey.

'Mines which he has closed down,' Brett said. 'And Morne sheltered Garth. We understood that Garth was ill. He was for some time in a nursing home. Immediately we heard the story which came from the Corshire police to Scotland Yard we visited the nursing home. There was a man there masquerading as Garth but most definitely *not* Garth. Not even like him. I have seen this man myself. He has admitted that the impersonation has been going on for seven months. He was paid handsomely for it; he was a sick man suffering from tuberculosis. The man who paid him is now under arrest—a man named Krotmann.'

'Plump, frightened Sol!'

'Garth, then, was taken somewhere else. No one knows where. No one knows what he has been doing. No one knows whether he was working of his own free will or under pressure when this thing started. Possibly he felt a grievance against those who decided not to adopt his suggestions; possibly he decided to continue his experiments along his own lines and afterwards found himself under pressure. Undoubtedly he *has* been under severe pressure for the last few weeks—months, probably.' Brett stopped, and looked at the inelegant, lounging figure of Palfrey. 'We've got to find out *everything*, Sap.'

# Book Two

## THE SHADOW

### TEN

## EVERYTHING ON THE TABLE

BRETT had gone back to London; the Palfreys were still at the Corbin hotel.

Hardy and Cartwright had been told, that morning, that Palfrey was now working for Intelligence. They had not been told why. Instructions from Brett and a higher authority had been firm; absolute secrecy was vital.

Those prisoners who were at Corbin were being taken over by the Special Branch for questioning. Agents whom Palfrey knew were on their way to Corbin. A furnished house had been rented for their headquarters, although officially Palfrey was still staying at the hotel.

'Well, our particular job is the Morne angle,' Palfrey said. 'And also McDonald. What time is he coming?'

'He said he'd be here in time for lunch,' said Drusilla.

McDonald, who had been to see Loretta the previous day, had gone from the sanatorium to Morne House. In view of his frequent declarations that he disliked the house and the people in it, his jaunt was surprising, but Palfrey wanted to keep an open mind about McDonald. Had the suspicion risen up only on account of his following Rose to the caves, Palfrey would have discounted it, but if he *had* been in Cheddar before . . .

Above all things, Palfrey wanted to see Kyle.

The telephone-bell rang. Drusilla lifted the receiver. Palfrey saw her change of expression and jumped up.

'Yes,' she said. 'Yes, Mac. At once.' She replaced the receiver and said: 'Morne's been attacked and hurt.'

'*Morne!*' exclaimed Palfrey. 'Badly enough for the hospital?'

'No, he's at home. He's asking for you.'

'A Morne habit,' said Palfrey. 'Give Hardy a ring and tell him we're going out there at once. At least, I am.' He went to

102

the dressing-table and took an automatic from the bottom drawer. Drusilla was saying 'Yes, we're going at once' into the telephone. Palfrey smiled at the 'we'. Yet he wished this had come a little later, when Brett's men could have followed him across the moors. Hardy's men would be faithful, but were they up to the standard required for this business?

There was a chance that McDonald had lied, of course; he might have planned to get them out on the moor. But it wasn't easy to check up on that. Drusilla put a call in to Morne House while Palfrey fetched the car from the garage, and first a servant, then Mrs. Bardle, told her that Sir Rufus was in bed after an accident.

The police car picked them up in the High Street, and Palfrey drove at speed through the narrow streets, with the dark clouds still massed above his head and the rain teeming down. The police car, a powerful one, was driven at equal speed. Out in the open, before they reached the moor, the rain hit the windscreen and bounced off with hissing fury, slowing down the windscreen wipers. Presently they came within sight of the moor. At this spot they were nearer the sea than on any other part of the road. In the far distance, the sky was bright, and suddenly the sun came out and shone upon Wenlock Cliff.

'Happy augury,' murmured Palfrey.

Over the moor the road was for the most part straight and level. They passed through two villages, built of dark stone, in the dour but not unattractive Corshire way. In a third village there was a sharp left-hand turn on the far side. A few hundred yards before it,' Palfrey said: 'That's odd, sweet. No police car.'

Drusilla looked round. Palfrey was right; there was no sign of the car.

They slowed down to less than fifteen miles an hour, and looked back repeatedly, but the police car did not emerge from the narrow High Street, and there was no sound of another engine. Palfrey drew in to the side of the road and listened intently.

'When did you last see them?' asked Drusilla.

'As we turned into the village,' said Palfrey. 'We'd better go back.'

'And run into trouble,' said Drusilla.

'We can't leave them,' Palfrey declared, uneasily. 'And we can't be sure that we won't run into trouble further along.' He turned the car towards the village and put on a burst of speed, slowing down only when they approached the first cottage. At a bend in the road, Palfrey braked quickly.

A crowd nearly fifty strong had gathered about the wreckage of the police car. Palfrey got out of the car and pushed his way towards the front. He was still uneasy ; odd things could happen in crowds. Then he forgot everything but the sight in front of him. The three men from the police car were stretched out on the pavement ; two of them were terribly injured. The nose of the car was smashed completely where it had struck the stone wall of a cottage ; the wall had suffered hardly at all.

Was this an accident? Had the police driver put on too much speed? Or had the crash been deliberately caused?

Palfrey joined a doctor who was attending to the men, explained who he was, and set to work to help. There was little he could do. Soon an old ambulance appeared from a side turning, and Palfrey spoke to the village policeman.

'I just don't know what happened, sir,' the man said. 'Some say they were travelling too fast, and it's a bad bend here, sir. *Some* say they heard an explosion first. As if the engine blew up, sir.'

'I think the quicker you let the chief inspector know, and have him out here, the better,' said Palfrey. 'I shouldn't touch the car until he's had a chance to examine it.'

'No, sir. Traffic will have to be diverted.'

'Do you have much traffic across here?'

'Not very much,' said the policeman, 'especially at this time of the year.'

'Has there been any this morning?'

'None that's stopped,' he was told. 'Mr. Gerald drove through half an hour ago with Mr. McDonald.' He seemed to take it for granted that everyone would know who they were, and certainly did not know that he had given Palfrey another sharp jolt. 'Going into Corbin, sir.'

They must have driven very fast if they had passed through the village about half an hour before and not met Palfrey on the road. He was sure that he had not seen them. They might have taken another road, of course. It was sheer conjecture that they had been heading for Corbin. He searched the engine and the car, remembering that someone 'thought' they had heard an explosion. Nothing which might cause one was hidden in the Talbot.

'I think we'll have a spot of speed,' he said, as he climbed into the car.

104

The road was flat and straight. On they went, thinking of the crash behind them, wondering what might lie ahead.

Suddenly Drusilla said: 'Don't forget that humpbacked bridge.'

'Bridge?' echoed Palfrey. 'Oh, yes, I remember.' He scanned the road and saw, in the distance, the muddy stream which meandered through the moor.

The bridge came into sight, and Palfrey slowed down. On one side was a copse of trees, and as he drew nearer he thought he saw something beneath the trees. It looked like a car. He kept one hand on the wheel and dropped his other to his coat pocket and his automatic. Yes, it *was* a car. He reached the bridge, travelling very fast, and the Talbot lurched. As it did so, the car behind the trees backed into the road, making it impossible for them to pass. Palfrey put on the brakes.

A man came strolling from the trees—Kyle. Susan Lee, who had been driving the car, got out and followed him. She was still the fair-haired, laughing, smartly dressed woman whom Palfrey had met at the hotel. Palfrey sat still, unsmiling, with the automatic in his pocket. Drusilla whispered: 'Now we'll see what they really want.'

'Good morning,' greeted Kyle cheerfully. 'Sorry to put a scare into you, but I wanted a chat, and the police don't make that easy.'

'How did you know we would be driving out here?'

'We didn't know,' said Kyle. 'We recognized your car from a distance. I'm good at recognizing cars. I'd recognize my Packard anywhere if I saw it; I'm now reduced to an Austin!'

Palfrey said: 'A police car was following me. It crashed. I think someone caused the crash. Two men will probably die.'

'Oh,' said Kyle, heavily. Susan's eyes were no longer laughing. 'I'm sorry about that, Palfrey, but don't get the idea that we had anything to do with it. We've been one side or the other of these trees all morning; we haven't moved more than fifty yards since sun-up. Isn't that so, Sue?'

'Yes,' said Susan.

'Why are you here?' asked Palfrey.

'We want to talk to McDonald,' said Kyle, 'then we'll vamoose. I don't like this moor. It makes me feel conspicuous. It wouldn't surprise me if we could be seen from Morne House, and I don't like the feeling of being watched, but there are some things I've just got to have, and a line on McDonald is one of them.'

'I see,' said Palfrey. Why did he find it difficult to disbelieve this man? There was a curious streak of honesty in him ; something innate, something which made him likeable whatever the circumstances.

'A four-hour vigil is too long to waste. Or are you in a hurry?'

'A great hurry,' said Palfrey.

'That's too bad. Now don't get me wrong, Palfrey,' went on Kyle, dropping his hand to his pocket. 'If I show a gun, it doesn't mean I want to hurt either of you. It simply means that I want to see McDonald and I wouldn't trust you to go along and do nothing about it. I don't want to show a gun,' he added earnestly. 'Be friendly.'

Palfrey said: 'Why didn't you tell me why you wanted Garth, Kyle? Why didn't you tell me who he is?'

'Oh,' said Kyle. 'So you're on to that.' He kept his hand at his pocket, but his expression had changed, and Susan Lee seemed to grow tense. 'Who told you so soon?'

'The Marquis of Brett,' said Palfrey.

If Kyle knew what Palfrey had done in the past, he would know much about Brett, and would be able to judge the implications of that statement. Palfrey did not think it greatly mattered if Kyle knew for whom he and Drusilla were working ; the man knew the truth about Garth, that was the vital knowledge.

'So he did,' said Kyle, and there was a gleam in his eyes again. 'Did he commission you, Palfrey?'

'Yes.'

'Then that's another reason why we should get together! You won't be tied down by the police,' said Kyle. 'And I've a clear bill with you, Palfrey.'

'A clear bill of what?'

'Don't you remember me telling you about my employer?' asked Kyle. 'I referred to him the question of keeping you informed, and the answer has come through. You're okay. You wouln't have been okay if you had still been tagging along behind the police.' He took his hand away from his pocket. 'Maybe you're not in so much of a hurry now.'

Palfrey said, feeling much easier in his mind: 'I am. Morne has been hurt, and wants to see me.'

After a pause, Kyle observed. 'That family certainly sends for you when it's in trouble. Who told you he had been hurt?'

'McDonald.'

'And you still trust that guy!' marvelled Kyle.

'Drusilla telephoned back——'

'Now, listen,' said Kyle. 'In a house like that it would be easy for anyone to confirm a lie, Palfrey. I wouldn't like to go into Morne House on McDonald's say-so.'

'Well, I'm going,' said Palfrey, flatly.

'After that police car was smashed up?'

'Yes.'

'Palfrey, I hand it to you,' drawled Kyle. 'Okay, you can go. Will you handle McDonald?'

'Yes.'

'And share the news?'

'If you can convince me that it's necessary, yes.'

Kyle grinned. 'I can convince you. How long do you reckon you'll be inside?'

'I don't know.'

'Are more police coming out to lend you a hand?'

'They'll send some, I expect,' said Palfrey.

'We'll hang around until they arrive,' said Kyle. 'There's a hollow way over there where we can park the car and watch the house. If we see anything that looks like trouble, we'll be on our way. When the police arrive, we'll vamoose. When will you send word to me?'

'I don't know where to send it.'

'Try the *Rose and Crown* in Wenlock,' said Kyle, 'and ask for Pettigrew.'

The Palfreys drove off. A few minutes afterwards, glancing to the right, they saw Kyle's car bouncing over the moor towards the hollow from which he had said he could see Morne House. The interview had done much to satisfy Palfrey about the man.

The House of the Bears. . . .

The gates were open. As the car pulled up, the front door opened and squat, dark Markham stood on the threshold.

'You've taken your time coming,' he barked.

'We lost no time for the sake of it,' said Palfrey, sharply. The man succeeded in putting his back up at sight. 'Is Morne badly hurt?'

'I don't know.'

'Have you had another doctor?'

'Not yet.'

'Are the police still here?'

'Two useless idiots,' declared Markham. 'Don't waste time in

107

asking pointless questions, Palfrey.' He led the way towards the stairs. His wife came hurrying from the landing. 'Look after Mrs. Palfrey, Dinah,' said Markham, and he and Palfrey went on alone. They turned a corner, and Markham opened the first door. 'I think he's been poisoned,' he said. 'I gave him an emetic.'

Palfrey snapped: 'And you didn't send for the nearest doctor?'

'You were as near as any of them,' said Markham. 'He's better now. He's broken his ankle, too, I think.'

Rufus Morne was lying on, not in, the bed. The left leg of his trousers was turned up, his foot was bare, swollen and discoloured. There was a bowl of water and a towel on the floor, and the room smelt faintly of antiseptics. Morne's red head was raised on pillows and, although pale, he did not really look seriously ill.

Palfrey sat down by the side of the bed and took his wrist. 'What's been happening to you?'

'It is inexplicable,' Morne said. He ignored Markham, who stood by the foot of the bed. 'I was perfectly fit and well first thing this morning. I went for my morning ride. I returned for breakfast. Only after I had been working in my study afterwards did I begin to feel ill.'

'Symptoms?' asked Palfrey.

'My heart beat so quickly,' said Rufus. 'I felt on the verge of collapse, Palfrey. I got up and tried to go downstairs, but could not walk properly, and fell. That was when I hurt my ankle.'

'I see,' said Palfrey. He opened the shirt and busied himself with the stethoscope. 'You seem all right there,' he said, after a pause.

'I am much better,' said Morne.

'Good!' Palfrey looked at his eyes, his tongue, the palms of his hands. There was no sign of any particular poison, no sign of illness; only the ankle seemed likely to give any trouble.

'You'll certainly have to stay in bed,' Palfrey said, 'or at least keep that foot off the ground. And an X-ray would be wise.'

They put Morne in the shooting brake. As they were about to leave, Hardy and another policeman arrived post-haste. A few words of explanation satisfied him. Palfrey was glad that the chief inspector would be there with Drusilla. Markham stayed behind with his wife; there was no sign of Mrs. McDonald that morning.

They reached the town without incident. The sanatorium had been warned to expect Morne, and Ross was on the doorstep to greet them. In his bright smile there was a touch of nervousness, Palfrey thought, and when Morne had been taken to the X-ray room, Ross said abruptly: 'I hope you didn't share the police suspicions, Dr. Palfrey?'

'Suspicions of what?' asked Palfrey.

'The poison in your tea.'

Palfrey smiled. 'My dear chap, if you'd wanted to poison me, you wouldn't have made it so obvious.'

'Oh,' said Ross, as if that answer surprised him. Then he smiled broadly. 'I'm very glad you feel like that, Dr. Palfrey! I was greatly worried, I assure you. I felt that it was a reflection on this establishment.' He did not seem very sure of himself in spite of his words, and he added quickly: 'Would you like to see Miss Morne?'

Loretta was still lying stiff and encased, but her eyes were open and she had lost something of the drawn, haggard look she had worn before. She recognized Ross but not Palfrey. When Ross uttered Palfrey's name, she turned her eyes towards him quickly.

Palfrey glanced towards the corner, where now a policewoman was sitting.

Loretta's hand moved slowly towards him. He touched it and she smiled up at him. 'Did you get those things?' she asked.

'Yes,' said Palfrey.

'Did you understand them?' Her voice was very low. The policewoman's chair creaked, as if she were straining forward to catch the words.

'I'm still studying them,' Palfrey said.

'Have you found—the mine?'

Swift excitement surged through Palfrey. Of course! The drawing on the tracing paper represented the plan of a mine!

'No,' he said, 'not yet.'

'You must,' she said.

'I am trying,' he assured her. 'Does anyone else know, Miss Morne?'

A change came over her, and she said slowly but very firmly: 'I cannot tell you.' She closed her eyes, and he could see that she was determined not to say anything more. She stirred when he removed his hand, but did not open her eyes.

He went over to the corner.

'Did you get that?'

'Not all of it, sir,' said the woman sitting there. 'Wasn't there something about a mine?'

'Yes.' He gave her the gist of the statement, and added: 'I shall be seeing Chief Inspector Hardy very soon, so I'll tell him. But make sure that your message goes to Corbin at once. You'd better give it to Colonel Cartwright himself.'

There was a tap at the door, and Ross appeared. Sir Rufus was out of the X-ray room now, and was being wheeled along to see his daughter. He looked at Palfrey cheerfully enough, and did not seem perturbed by his plight.

'How is she?' he asked.

'Sleeping,' said Palfrey.

This was the first time he had seen Morne with his daughter. He decided to stay. Ross went off, and the policewoman also went out. Palfrey sent away the push-chair attendant, took the chair himself and pushed Morne towards the bed. Then Palfrey went to the window, pretending to look out, but watching Morne all the time. For a few seconds the man's face showed only concern. Then he smiled, eased himself forward and touched Loretta's hand. He held it for a moment, and she stirred. Morne took his hand away and looked at Palfrey.

'Thank you,' he said.

The man was passionately fond of his daughter, there could be no doubt of that.

Half an hour later, Palfrey was looking at the hastily prepared X-ray plates. There was no fracture and no serious dislocation; Morne had only sprained his ankle.

But what had caused the fainting fit and the giddiness? Halsted could have told them so much. As it was, he might have a record of his professional visits to Morne. The record would say if there were any symptoms of a weak heart. There was none.

Back at Morne House, Markham and Morne said they did not know where Gerry and McDonald had gone. McDonald had received a telephone call soon after speaking to Palfrey, and said that he must go in to Corbin immediately. Gerry had wanted to do some shopping. It was odd that they had chosen to go immediately after Morne's accident, and Hardy seized on that point, but could make nothing of it.

McDonald's mother, Drusilla told Palfrey, was in her room. She was remarkably shy of company. Something seemed to have given Dinah Markham a new lease of life, and she talked lightly and brightly. Drusilla mentioned this to Palfrey when

110

they were alone for a few minutes before tea. Hardy was going to leave immediately afterwards. He had told them that there was no sign that the accident on the road had been arranged; it might, perhaps, have been caused by a blow-out. But clearly he was not satisfied.

'Can we stay here?' Drusilla asked Palfrey.

'I can't even make up my mind whether I want to,' said Palfrey, and then laughed at Drusilla's expression. 'I think we had better visit the *Rose and Crown*, don't you?'

'Well, if we're going, let's go before it gets quite dark,' said Drusilla. 'I don't fancy driving across the moor by night.'

Palfrey went upstairs to see Morne, who welcomed him with his unfailing courtesy. For a few minutes, Palfrey chatted brightly. There was no need for him to stay, the ankle would soon recover if he rested it, and——

Morne said quickly: 'I shall be most disappointed if you do leave, Dr. Palfrey. I feel that if there is a repetition of the attack which I had this morning, I *might* not recover so quickly unless you are at hand. I hope you *will* stay, at least for the night.'

Suddenly, across the quiet, without warning, came the roar of an explosion which shook the room.

ELEVEN

## THE TOWN WHICH SHOOK

THE roar did not die away. . . .

It grew louder, deafening them. It continued for what seemed an age, and when at last it rumbled into silence, there came another sound, a gentle hiss, which grew until it whined about them. The curtains blew violently. Doors slammed. A great puff of wind sent flames leaping into the room with a billow of smoke, then sucked furiously up the chimney again.

The hissing died away, and there was silence.

Morne gasped: 'What was that?'

'I'll find out,' said Palfrey.

He hurried out of the room, feeling as if he had just finished an exhausting race. His body was trembling, he felt cold, and his forehead was damp. Movement helped him, and, as he turned into the passage towards a crying sound, he was more himself.

Two or three servants were standing at the top of the stairs. They turned their pale faces towards Palfrey, who hurried past them. The wailing, a dreadful, tormented sound, was coming from the small room between the hall and the music gallery. There was something uncanny about it, an eeriness in keeping with the great house.

Mrs. Bardle came hurrying out of the inner room.

'Who is it?' asked Palfrey, sharply.

'Lady Dinah, sir,' Mrs. Bardle hurried past him and he went into the inner room. There, Drusilla was standing helplessly by the fireplace while Rachel McDonald tried to quieten Dinah. Had the woman's mind been turned?

Rachel McDonald seemed not to notice Palfrey. Her acquiline face was set. She was a magnificent woman, a feminine Rufus Morne. Suddenly she took her sister's shoulders and shook her, and kept on until her sister's head nodded helplessly to and fro. Palfrey felt that this was not wholly because she wanted to quieten her sister; there was something stronger, some deep passion which showed itself in her pallor and the vigour of her movements.

Palfrey stepped forward. The woman was quieter now; the screams had turned to moans.

'I think that's enough,' said Palfrey.

Rachel looked at him sharply. His eyes met hers. She stopped, then took her hands away. Dinah collapsed into a chair, her head upon her chest.

'She'll be all right now. You'll get her to bed, won't you?'

'Mrs. Bardle has gone to prepare her bed.'

'That's splendid,' said Palfrey. 'It's easy to understand, I suppose,' he murmured. 'That was a bang, wasn't it?'

'Yes,' said Rachel.

'Somewhere on the moor, I suppose.'

Mrs. Bardle came in. She helped Drusilla to raise Dinah, who had not the strength to walk. Palfrey touched Drusilla's arm, then lifted the helpless woman and carried her towards the stairs. For a moment, Rachel's eyes were on him, showing faint surprise at his strength.

Mrs. Bardle, hurrying ahead of him, stood by the open door of Dinah's room. The bed was turned down and a maid was putting in hot-water bottles. Palfrey nodded approvingly, and laid the woman on a small settee drawn up near the fire.

112

'Sap, what was it?' Drusilla asked, as he went downstairs again.

'The big noise? I don't know.'

As he told Morne what had happened, his mind was busy with the explosion. Had it been out on the moor or further away? Was there an experimental station, once operated by Garth, near Morne House? Had the explosion been in the mine which Loretta had mentioned?

Was it an atomic or nuclear explosion?

The very thought chilled him. If it had been, then it must have been a long way from Morne House, and there was no telling how widespread the damage might be.

Morne was saying: 'I am not surprised, Dr. Palfrey; my sister has been very much on edge since the accident.'

'Naturally,' smiled Palfrey. But had she? Earlier that day, at least, she had been much more calm and composed; he and Drusilla had commented on it.

'I suppose you have no idea what caused the explosion,' said Morne.

Was that as guileless as it sounded? Was Morne trying to find out whether Palfrey knew what Garth had been doing?

'None at all,' Palfrey said, 'but I'd like to find out more about it. I'll have a word with Hardy.'

Outside, it was dark and bitterly cold. The flares had not yet been lighted, although McDonald and Gerry were still out. As Palfrey reached the foot of the steps, with Drusilla shivering by his side, the first flare was lit. A man standing on a ladder plunged a small torch into one of the bowls of oil. The flames shot up, filling the night with garish light.

Palfrey called: 'Hardy! Are you about?' There was no answer, and he raised his voice: '*Hardy!*'

This time there was an answer from somewhere far off. A torch shone upon the figure of a man who was hurrying towards the house.

'Get your coat,' Palfrey said to Drusilla. 'There's no point in catching cold.' He hurried towards the man, and recognized Sergeant Whittle. Perhaps the red, dancing flames gave his face that haggard look.

'What is it?' Palfrey demanded, as the man drew up.

'The—the inspector, sir. And the others——' Whittle could hardly speak, and his teeth were chattering. 'They—they're *blind,* sir!'

'Blind!' echoed Palfrey.

113

'After that—after that dreadful flash,' Whittle said, and he began to mutter to himself, as if it had turned his mind also. 'I must get help. I must get help.'

Palfrey gripped his shoulder. 'Where are they?'

'Just—just about the gate, sir.' Whittle hurried off, staggering. Drusilla came hurrying down. She had brought Palfrey's coat and made him put it on. They hurried towards the gateway, and, as they did so, a fresh light appeared—the headlights of a car turning from the main road.

They shone on Hardy and two other men who were standing up, and a fourth who was lying on the ground. It was bizarre. Hardy was looking *away* from the headlights and away from the Palfreys; he was peering into the darkness, trying to *see*.

The car slowed down, and Palfrey saw Gerald Markham's fair hair.

'Hardy!' Palfrey called, and the man turned towards him, hesitatingly. Palfrey reached him. 'All right, old chap,' he said. 'You'll be all right.'

'I can't'—Hardy's voice was thick—'I can't see.'

'What was it?' asked Palfrey. 'The flash?'

'Yes,' said Hardy. 'Ghastly.'

McDonald's voice sounded from behind Palfrey.

'What's the trouble? Can I help?'

'Yes,' said Palfrey. 'You can take them into the house. The flash dazzled them.' 'Dazzled' seemed tragically inadequate, but he could think of nothing better. 'What happened to this chap?' he asked, and bent down by the side of the man on the ground.

Hardy said: 'Whittle said the—the blast knocked him against the wall. He banged his head.'

'Then that's not serious either,' said Palfrey.

This false cheerfulness increased his own depression. He could only hope that it helped the others.

'Where's Gerry?' asked Palfrey, a little later.

'Flat out, I shouldn't wonder. That explosion floored him. It nearly floored me,' added McDonald, with a growl.

'Where were you?'

'Out near the bridge,' said McDonald.

'Whatever it was, it was pretty powerful.'

'Dr. Palfrey makes an understatement,' said McDonald, with a dry laugh. 'I thought the earth was going to open up and swallow us, car and all. We were in the dip just past the bridge. The worst of the blast went over us.'

'Which direction was the flash?' asked Palfrey.

114

McDonald said, heavily: 'Wenlock, I'm afraid.'

'Oh,' said Palfrey. He finished his drink. 'I'd better go and see those fellows,' he added, and hurried away. He felt he should not have left Hardy and his men on their own.

He reached the room where they had been taken, and found Mrs. Bardle and Whittle in charge. Whittle was more himself, although no longer ponderous or antagonistic. He had been badly frightened ; his own sight had suffered for a few minutes, but he could see normally now.

'The others will do, soon,' said Palfrey, after he had looked at Hardy's eyes. That *must* be true, although he did not feel competent to judge. 'How are you feeling, Hardy?'

The inspector was sitting back in an easy chair, his eyes still damp from bathing.

'I'm all right in myself,' said Hardy. His voice was stronger, and he was making a conscious effort to regain his composure. 'I've no doubt this other business will go.' He leaned forward, pressing his hand against his forehead. 'My head's aching pretty badly,' he said. 'I can still hear that roar . . .'

'The *earth* seemed to shake,' Whittle said.

'I fancy it was an underground explosion,' Palfrey said, speaking as casually as he could. 'It wouldn't surprise me if a store of explosives in one of the mines blew up. The mines on the estate were used for munition dumps at one time, weren't they?'

'Well, I'm damned!' exclaimed Hardy. 'I hadn't thought of that. You're probably right. It makes our little job here seem small beer.'

'You won't feel like that in the morning,' said Palfrey.

'What worries me is what's going to happen here,' said Hardy. 'We're no use.'

McDonald and Drusilla were still downstairs, and McDonald was in a restive mood.

'What I'd like to do is go into Wenlock and see what has happened there,' he said.

'I'm with you,' admitted Palfrey, ''but we can't leave this place yet.'

'Why not?'

'I think an attempt was made earlier to murder Morne,' Palfrey said.

McDonald tossed down his drink. 'I see. So one of us did it.'

'Someone who was here this morning did it,' said Palfrey. 'It might have been a stranger.'

115

McDonald said: 'No strangers have been in here, Palfrey; the police have watched and so have the servants. If there were an attempt to kill Morne, someone living here did it. What is going to happen if we *do* stay here? With Hardy and the police helpless, what can we do against an assailant who might strike out of the dark. I don't suppose I've got a clean bill. Since Hardy questioned Gerry and me, I've felt that I was under suspicion, although the Lord knows that isn't justified.'

Palfrey said: 'The police must question everyone. Surely you can see that. You puzzled them, you know.'

'Why?'

Palfrey said: 'Because you didn't tell them and you didn't tell me that you and Gerry had been to Cheddar Gorge before I took you there.'

McDonald's expression did not alter. He stopped pacing the room, then lowered himself into a chair, without once removing his gaze from Palfrey.

Palfrey had not intended to bring out the challenge then. If McDonald were responsible for anything that had happened, a worse moment could not have been chosen.

McDonald said: 'I hope you'll believe what I'm going to tell you. Gerry and I followed Loretta to the Gorge.'

'When and why?'

McDonald said: 'I think I've made it clear before that I am fond of Loretta. So is Gerry. Whatever else we quarrel about, we have that in common. The day I got back from the Far East I found a message from him at my club. He said (*a*) that Loretta was worried about something, and told me of her "accidents", and (*b*) that he knew she went out alone sometimes and he thought that she was being blackmailed. At all events, she had borrowed money from him, a thing she had never done in her life before. Proud, our Loretta! Not wealthy in her own right, and King Rufus had clear ideas about the amount of money that a young girl should have. Not that she has ever had to manage on little or nothing, but she could not stand a drain of a thousand pounds, shall we say. It was a thousand that she borrowed from Gerry.'

He paused, and Palfrey nodded.

'Gerry and I got together and decided that we would try to find out where she went. Natural enough, I hope you'll agree. I came down as far as Bath a few days afterwards. Gerry telephoned to say that Loretta had left the house again and was heading for Bristol. I met him at the Grand Hotel, by appointment. She was still in the city. She had been,' added McDonald, 'to the Theatre Royal.'

'Oh,' said Palfrey. 'Rose Lindsay stayed near there.'

'Let's keep to the sequence of events,' said McDonald. 'Gerry and I hurried off and waited near the place. She came out of the side door. She had a taxi waiting, and so had we. She went to Cheddar Gorge and we followed her. Once we were there, she lost herself. Just like that,' added McDonald. 'She was in a crowd, and she vanished. She didn't turn up again for several hours. Then we saw her in the taxi, heading again for Bristol. We had a puncture on the road and lost her. We caught up with her here. Interesting story, isn't it?'

'Very,' said Palfrey.

'Well, that was that,' declared McDonald. 'Mystery without an explanation. Loretta isn't one who takes kindly to being questioned. Gerry did, in fact, question her. She let him have a piece of her mind, and that closed the subject. Her line was: "If I want to go to Cheddar Gorge I shall go to Cheddar Gorge and I shan't ask your permission." Characteristic of Loretta. The truth, if Gerry read it aright—and I think he did—was that she was frightened to death for fear of the reason for her trip becoming known. She had good reason to be frightened, hadn't she?'

Palfrey nodded.

'Well, we couldn't question Loretta any further,' went on McDonald. 'Neither Gerry nor I were very happy about it. I had several things to do at the Admiralty and had to go back to London, leaving Gerry here to hold a watching brief. He did, but not very successfully. I came down as soon as I heard about her third accident. I didn't want the police or you to know that I thought Loretta was being blackmailed, and so I held my tongue—intending, if I may say so, to talk whenever it seemed necessary.' He brooded for some time, then added slowly: 'How did you know that I'd been to the Gorge before?'

'Kyle told me,' said Palfrey.

'I'm surprised that you believed him.'

'The police checked up. It wasn't difficult to prove.'

'So that's why Hardy thought it was worth questioning us! He didn't give anything away. Why have you, Palfrey?'

'I prefer to know my friends from my enemies, especially here tonight,' said Palfrey.

'Meaning I've passed?'

Palfrey smiled. 'I've got to take a chance on you. Tonight

117

Morne's room must be watched, and no one must get in there. We've got to count the police out, apart from Whittle. What about Gerry?'

McDonald shrugged. 'A broken reed.'

'Why?'

'The explosion shook him to bits. So it's up to Whittle and me,' declared McDonald. 'And that cuts out any chance of going into Wenlock tonight. I would like to know what the situation is.'

'We could telephone Ross,' said Palfrey. But when he tried, the telephone was dead.

'So we really are cut off,' McDonald said, in a thin voice. 'This is going to be a nice night.'

Hardy's sight had not improved, but two of the three men also blinded by the flash were now able to see objects placed close before their eyes. The police were therefore in much brighter mood. Hardy was able to talk freely. Palfrey did not tell him of McDonald's story, but did suggest a vigil shared by Whittle, McDonald and himself. Hardy raised no objections and, thought Palfrey, seemed relieved.

Now Palfrey was on duty in the passage outside Morne's room, in the middle of the night.

A clock struck three. In one hour he was to call McDonald. Was McDonald reliable?

The chimes died down, and the house was silent. Palfrey imagined he could hear creaking steps and rustling movements.

There was a shadow on the wall opposite the stairs ; *a moving* shadow of a man or woman.

He dropped his right hand to his pocket and clutched his gun. Whoever was there was still coming upwards. Palfrey could hear nothing. He backed as far as the door of the room where McDonald and Whittle were resting. As he opened it, McDonald whispered: 'Is that you, Palfrey?'

'Yes. Wake Whittle. Get up.' Palfrey turned away from the door and peered along the passage. He could still see the shadow, longer and less distinct now.

A figure turned into the passage, came as far as Morne's door, stopped there, and tried the handle. The door was locked.

Palfrey took a step forward, the gun in his hand. He opened his lips, and as he did so a scream came from the direction of the hall, so ear-splitting that it made Palfrey flinch and turn cold. The creature at the door turned, swift as thought, and then

118

Whittle made a mistake. *'What's that?'* he whispered.

The figure at the door moved, not slowly this time, but racing towards the end of the passage. Palfrey raised his gun, aimed low, and fired.

*Nothing happened.*

But he had loaded the gun in Corbin; he knew it was loaded. He tried again, there was only a faint click. Then McDonald tore past him and the figure reached the corner. Whittle lumbered by. Footsteps sounded on the stairs, there were startled voices, a thump. Then a door banged; it sounded like the front door. There were footsteps outside now, on the flagstones of the courtyard.

But it was pitch dark. As Palfrey reached the door, he thought that it would be hopeless to find the man—surely only a man could have run like that—and it would be unwise to venture out too far. McDonald was already out of sight, and Whittle was disappearing. The footman was still by the door, and his voice quavered. 'Doctor—Doctor——'

Then Ruegg appeared in the doorway.

'Can you come here at once, Dr. Palfrey, please?'

Palfrey went towards him, remembering the scream.

The light was on in the minstrel gallery.

There, beneath the balcony, lay Dinah Markham; her neck was broken.

Drusilla was sitting up in bed, smoking. Palfrey sat in an easy-chair near the foot of the bed, warming himself in front of the fire which Ruegg had rekindled.

It wanted an hour to dawn.

McDonald and Whittle had found no trace of the man who had tried to get into Morne's room. No one admitted knowing who had emptied Palfrey's gun, and the bullets had not been found. No one admitted seeing Dinah Markham leave her room. No one had heard anything until that scream, which had awakened Ruegg and another footman who, at Morne's orders, had slept in an ante-room that night.

Markham was distraught; *too* distraught to be genuine, thought Palfrey. He had reasoned with and tried to soothe the man, and eventually Markham had been persuaded to go to bed, after taking a sedative. Gerry had reacted oddly; he had not said a word, had just stood and stared, dry-eyed, at the broken body. He looked as if he had been paralysed by the sudden tragedy.

Had Dinah been thrown over? Or had she jumped? She had been so unnerved by the explosion that suicide had to be considered.

Her body had been taken back to her room. Mrs. Bardle and Rachel had stayed there. The house was now in fact a house of death.

Hardy, awakened, had at first not realized that he could now *see*. He had jumped out of bed, giving orders, then suddenly stopped, and cried: *'My eyes are all right!'* Afterwards, his vision had dimmed again, but Palfrey believed there would be no lasting ill-effect. Hardy had taken charge, marshalled the servants, given his instructions, taken over Palfrey's self-imposed responsibilities. Now Palfrey sat pondering the question of who could have had access to his gun. He had not taken it out of his pocket, but he *had* taken off his coat when he had gone to bed for a spell of duty.

He had heard no one enter the room.

As a result, that stealthy figure had escaped unhurt.

He did not accept it as proved that the man had forced an entry; it could have been Markham or Gerry or even Rachel McDonald. Any one of them could have run into the courtyard and got back into the house by a window or door left open for that purpose.

'Hopeless,' thought Palfrey, in the depths of pessimism. 'Hopeless!'

And then suddenly he was asleep.

He woke up in broad daylight. Drusilla was shaking his shoulder.

The events of the night flashed into Palfrey's mind.

'More police are here,' Drusilla said. 'Cartwright's with them. Their cars woke me up.'

She broke off as a tap came at the door.


TWELVE

## GATHERING OF FRIENDS

OUTSIDE, the sun was shining and the morning was crisp and fresh; even the moor, seen from the bedroom window, looked bright and cheerful. But there was nothing bright about Cartwright. He was a man with a purpose, a hard purpose. He marshalled everyone into the great hall, from Morne himself down to the servants; *all* had to be there, including Gerry, who was still silent and whose mouth gaped a little, as if he had not really regained control of his muscles.

'Why all this?' wondered Palfrey.

Cartwright stood by Morne's side, threw back his shoulders and boomed:

'The reason for this meeting is very simple. Sir Rufus has agreed that it is also essential. A man escaped from Wenlock Jail last night—a man who goes by the name of Kyle.' He did not look at Palfrey; he appeared to be deliberately avoiding his eyes. 'The man is either an American or pretending to be an American. He was arrested on a serious charge, and there is strong reason to believe that he came here.'

Palfrey nudged Drusilla: 'Identification parade,' he said. 'Not bad.'

Cartwright said: 'Inspector Wriggleswade of New Scotland Yard will scrutinize every *one* of you. . . .'

Kyle was not among the men and women in the hall, but Palfrey, seeing them all together for the first time, realized again how easy it would be for someone to hide at Morne House; there were twenty-three servants for the house itself, and many more for the grounds. When the scrutiny was finished, a sergeant came in and reported to Cartwright. Ruegg had taken him all over the house, but there was no sign of Kyle.

Reluctantly, Cartwright dismissed the servants. Wriggleswade, a portly, rather pompous man, stayed behind, equally disappointed. Morne put himself at Cartwright's disposal. Was there anything at all he could do?

'Nothing,' said Cartwright. 'But I would like a word with *you*, Dr. Palfrey.'

'I wondered when we could come to that,' said Palfrey. 'I suppose you do know that Lady Markham died here last night, and that there was a visitor who tried to break into Sir Rufus's room?'

'Yes,' said Cartwright. 'We will go to your room.'

What was the matter with the man? He was behaving as if Palfrey were a criminal, certainly giving the impression that he was under suspicion.

As they entered, Sergeant Whittle straightened up from the dressing-table, and for the first time Palfrey felt angry.

'What's this, Cartwright?'

'Your room has been searched,' said Cartwright, harshly.

'Oh,' said Palfrey. There was nothing diffident about him then; he looked taller and a man to be reckoned with. 'Arbitrary, aren't you?'

Cartwright said between his teeth: 'Do you know what happened last night, Palfrey?'

'No.'

'Half Wenlock was destroyed,' said Cartwright.

The shock was too great for Drusilla, who blanched and reached for a chair. Palfrey's face paled and his eyes hardened. Half Wenlock *destroyed*. His own anger and indignation vanished before the horror conveyed by the words.

Cartwright asked abruptly: 'When did you last see Kyle?'

'On the way here.'

'And you haven't seen him since?'

'No. Unless he was the man who was frightened away last night.'

Cartwright said: 'Palfrey, I put this to you: you knew that man was Kyle, yet you let him get away.'

No sharp answer rose to Palfrey's lips. He understood now what was driving the man, and felt no anger. He spoke gently.

'No, Cartwright. That isn't true. I hope you're not making yourself unpleasant for the sake of it,' he added.

'I am doing what I regard as necessary,' said Cartwright, and his voice was suddenly very weary.

'What you need is a whisky and soda,' said Palfrey.

Cartwright did not refuse. He talked more coherently of the effect of the explosion, and then he said something which surprised Palfrey; the explosion had been somewhere out at sea.

'*Out at sea?*' asked Palfrey, startled.

'Yes. I thought it was an ammunition ship, but I'm told there has been nothing in the estuary for weeks.' Cartwright finished his drink, and then said: 'Palfrey, what *do* you know about this man Kyle?'

'Too little,' said Palfrey. 'Where did you find him last night?'

'One of my men saw his woman,' said Cartwright, 'and she led us to Kyle. He was in the market-place. He made no fuss at all after the woman had escaped.'

'Escaped from where?' asked Palfrey.

'The market-place. Two men pounced on Kyle, two on the woman—Lee, doesn't she call herself? Kyle created enough confusion to allow her to escape, and then behaved like a lamb.

122

How he got away from the jail I don't know—and I never shall know,' went on Cartwright. 'Two men on duty there were killed last night in the explosion. The police station itself is badly knocked about.' He brooded for a few minutes, and then went on: 'There's one good thing about last night. Miss Morne wasn't hurt and the sanatorium was practically untouched. It was sheltered by a hill. A few panes of glass were broken, that's all.'

'How is Loretta Morne?'

'There's been no change,' Cartwright said.

Palfrey was now itching to get into Wenlock, to try to find Kyle at the *Rose and Crown*. There was the possibility that the inn had been badly damaged in the explosion, as well as the possibility that Kyle would give Wenlock a wide berth in future.

Cartwright said grimly that he was leaving plenty of men at Morne House, whether Morne objected or no. He did not say that he thought there might be a connexion between the explosion and Morne House, but Palfrey knew that he suspected one.

McDonald asked for a lift into Wenlock, on the excuse that he wanted to make sure that Loretta was all right. Cartwright had no objection. He left Hardy, now almost completely recovered, with a party of police eight strong, and followed Palfrey in his own car, with Whittle and two other policemen.

On the journey, McDonald was unusually quiet, and Palfrey did not feel like talking.

Palfrey thought that the explosion had unduly affected Cartwright. Damage there was in plenty, but it was mostly superficial. Only very few houses were uninhabitable, although glass had been blown out of many windows. The townsfolk were going about their normal business, but many had a dazed look.

McDonald got off near the sanatorium; Palfrey saw one of Cartwright's men follow him up the hill. Well, that was right enough. Cartwright must take no chances. He himself must; he had certainly not justified the new trust Brett had put in him.

He wondered how soon he would be able to see Brett, and when the reinforcements which had been promised would arrive. After a call at the *Rose and Crown,* he decided, he would make for Corbin and find out whether anyone had yet taken possession of the furnished house.

He left Cartwright at a house which had been taken over temporarily as police headquarters, the police station itself

123

having been damaged—worse, it seemed to Palfrey, than any other building in Wenlock.

He looked about him as he drove on, wondering if Cartwright would, after all, have him followed, but could see no sign of that. He asked a postman the way to the *Rose and Crown*.

It was small and pleasant, standing back from the road. The only damage it appeared to have suffered was to the hanging sign, which swung by one hook only. Palfrey pulled the car into the side of the road two corners away from the inn, and sat for a moment looking at Drusilla. 'It might be an idea for you to stay in the car. If I have to get away in a hurry, it would be useful. Not that I think anything will happen here. Kyle's almost certainly gone.'

The *Rose and Crown* was open. A murmur of voices came from the private bar, and someone laughed. There was a fire in the little office near the narrow staircase. There, a young girl with red cheeks and a snub nose smiled at him prettily.

'Good morning,' said Palfrey. 'Is Mr. Pettigrew in?'

'I think so, sir. I haven't seen him go out.' She slipped off her stool and went to the telephone behind her. 'He'll be down in a moment. Will you please wait in the lounge?'

'Thanks,' said Palfrey.

He felt deflated. This did not square up with anything he had anticipated. Everything was far too normal. The inn was too attractive; the girl's smile was too frank; Kyle had not disappeared without trace.

Would Susan Lee be with him?

There was one odd thing—odder than anything else, he thought. Kyle, apparently, took no precautions against an unwelcome guest. The police might have some reason to suspect 'Pettigrew'.

'He probably saw me coming from the window,' thought Palfrey.

Suddenly he heard footsteps on the stairs.

'The gentleman is in the lounge, sir,' called the girl from the office.

There was no answer. The footsteps drew nearer. Palfrey waited, tensed, suddenly fully aware—as he had been subconsciously all the time—that the very normality of everything here was in itself abnormal.

Then the door opened and a man stepped in, a short, broad-shouldered man who most certainly was not Kyle, though there

124

was a look of Kyle about the set of his lips and his dark, tanned face.

'Good morning,' he said.

'Oh, hallo,' said Palfrey, looking blankly surprised. 'Are *you* Mr. Pettigrew?'

'Yes.'

'Then,' said Palfrey, as if with a flash of inspiration, 'the name must have led me astray. I'm so sorry. I won't keep you, and——'

'No one led you astray,' said Pettigrew. 'Kyle told you to come here and ask for me.' Then, with the twinkle in his eyes deepening, he went on: 'Surely you didn't expect Kyle to be here, with the police looking for him round every corner.'

'Kyle is so unpredictable,' murmured Palfrey. 'Why let the police catch him and then put their backs up by getting away?'

'We had been told that a gentleman of some importance in this affair was at the police station, and there was only one way of finding out. Kyle got himself arrested.'

'That was pretty drastic.'

'Don't you think that drastic methods are necessary after what happened last night?' asked Pettigrew. The smile faded from his eyes, the words were only just audible, but he impressed Palfrey more in that moment than before.

Palfrey said: 'Yes, I do. But I doubt whether Kyle and you are the people to carry them out. All this rushing to and fro, cocking a snook at the police, making difficulties where there are none, waylaying and shanghaiing——'

'There was no other way,' said Pettigrew. 'Have you an hour to spare. If you have, I'll tell you something about it. Or are the police lurking round the corner?'

'No tricks this time,' said Palfrey. 'If they are, it's of their own accord. I don't think you need worry about that. But my wife is waiting not far away, in case I need to make a sudden bolt for it. She'll get anxious.'

'Supposing I send her a message that you'll be a little longer?' suggested Pettigrew.

'All right,' said Palfrey. 'A note from me will be necessary, of course.' He scribbled a note and Pettigrew took it. 'Trusting fellow, aren't I?' asked Palfrey. 'The truth is that I ought to make you come to see me.'

'My dear fellow, *I* won't do you any harm,' said Pettigrew. 'We're after the same thing.' He rang the bell and a boy came, shiny-faced and beaming.

'You will find a lady in a car round the second corner on the right,' said Palfrey. 'Give her this note, will you?' When the boy had gone, he pulled up a chair and sat down.

'I'm glad you've done that, Palfrey. You've shown the one thing we have badly needed while we have been working—some measure of trust in us. You are a responsible person, and I was very glad when I heard you were down here.'

'Are you Kyle's employer?' asked Palfrey.

'Yes.' There was no hesitation about the answer. 'A better worker you won't find anywhere, Palfrey. I can say the same about Susan Lee. You've guessed that they were in American Intelligence service at one time, I suppose?'

'The thought had passed through my mind.' The air of unreality which Palfrey had felt earlier had returned. This short, powerful man with the friendly twinkle in his eyes was at variance with everything else he knew about the case—except, perhaps, with Kyle. It did not make sense, but perhaps it would do before Pettigrew had finished.

'Well, now,' said Pettigrew. 'It all started with Garth. A most dissatisfied Garth. Brilliant fellow, of course, but peeved because his own ideas were passed over and other men's were adopted. Rightly passed over, of course, but Garth isn't the type of man to realize that. He was ripe for exploitation. He had spent all his money on his experiments; there was no way of getting it back; the British Government was, as always in such cases, miserly in its treatment of him. Garth's contention, from the first, was that the conception of atomic warhead development was too vast. He believed that it could be done without the great expenditure and the building of enormous plant. He envisaged manufacture on a small scale and in small quantities. I am speaking very generally, you understand.'

'Yes,' said Palfrey.

'Well, there he was in America, helping without much heart,' said Pettigrew, 'when he was approached by the man Fyson. At that time Kyle and Susan Lee were attached to Washington Intelligence Bureau and they knew Fyson as an agent of powerful reactionary forces in both England and America. *Not* a Nazi; not a Fascist; not an anarchist. If you want it reduced to political terms, you might say that he favoured a benevolent autocracy and worked for those who also favoured it. Several otherwise admirable people did. The conception in their minds was that no nations subject to ordinary democratic rule should have control of things like the atom bomb, but that control should be centred in a small group of individuals high-minded enough to be above politics, above nationalism, above failings, and consequently above the *laws* of mankind. This may sound fine theoretically. There were five of them, as far as Kyle knew, and four he was prepared to admit were high-minded and incorruptible people. Of the fifth, a man named Gorringer, he had his doubts, although Gorringer's reputation stood high. When Garth returned to England and Fyson followed him, Kyle and Susan Lee were on the same ship. Kyle had been refused permission to go officially ; when he disobeyed orders and came to Europe, out he went. You follow that?'

'Yes,' said Palfrey.

'Good! Kyle, then, was in England, foot-loose, chasing a hare. Fyson, and this man whom he knew and distrusted, had an interest in Garth. He wanted to find out what the interest was. Garth continued experiments, getting far more money than he had ever had before. Kyle suspected that Fyson's employer was backing him, and began to press his inquiries. Garth fell ill. The substitution was arranged at the nursing-home and Kyle lost trace of Garth, but not of Fyson and the other people—you met Frenchie, Sol Krotmann and one or two others, didn't you?'

'Yes.'

'Satisfied that trouble was in the making, Kyle sent a full report to Washington,' said Pettigrew. 'I have a copy of his report. Washington ignored it. Urgent representations were made, and it was found that certain officials in Washington thought Kyle was making a case out for himself in order to get his job back. Inquiries were made about Garth,. of course. The impersonator was at the nursing-home, everyone was satisfied that Garth was suffering from overwork, and that was that.'

'Remarkable official attitude to a thing like the Bomb,' Palfrey murmured.

'A typical official attitude, I'm afraid,' said Pettigrew. 'The very vastness of the subject prejudiced officials against believing him. How could one man, Garth, do what an army of scientists, tens of thousands of workers and limitless financial resources were doing? Garth's project, you see, wasn't considered practical. Kyle was wasting his time. A report was sent to Whitehall about his activities, and he was officially repudiated by Washington. That made it more difficult, but Kyle isn't easily discouraged. His money was running short, but Susan helped

127

there. She did a column for one of the American syndicates—a report on affairs in England—and they managed to carry on, chasing their hare, unable to find Garth. Then Susan lost her job. Possibly some pressure was exerted, I don't know about that. They were flat broke, they hadn't found Garth, and, although they had talked with Sol Krotmann, Frenchie and others, they could not learn a great deal. What they had learned was that these people sometimes visited Cheddar Gorge, that the little syndicate was still powerful and wealthy, and that an unknown sixth member had joined them. Fyson told them about that, boasting that it added to their resources. Now, Palfrey'—Pettigrew leaned forward and took his pipe from his lips—'Kyle first of all assumed that only one of the original syndicate of high-minded humanists was of doubtful quality. This man Gorringer. You've heard of him, I suppose?'

'Vaguely,' said Palfrey.

'Most people are only vague about him,' said Pettigrew, 'but his reputation was sound, he did all the right things, and he certainly convinced the others of the syndicate that he was all that could be expected. There was one queer thing about him—contact with people who were certainly not incorruptible. Kyle found that out. He soon found that Gorringer's motives were open to suspicion.

'Kyle kept busy. He came to the conclusion that there was another member of the syndicate, one whose name he did not know, a mystery-man, if you like, but someone powerful. And all the time there was the great peril—"all power corrupts, absolute power corrupts absolutely". This is the nearest thing to absolute power we know.'

'Yes,' admitted Palfrey.

'So he was worried in case the possession of it had turned them from their high purpose. However, there soon came reason for doubting that. You know that Lord Anster died a few months ago, don't you?'

Palfrey said in a sharp voice: 'Anster wasn't in this!'

'Oh, yes he was,' declared Pettigrew. 'I know what you're thinking. Anster was a really great man—so was Cunningham and the Swiss Grayle, and Scottish Lord Malcolm. Four of the men most respected, most loved in the world, men whose power for good has been tremendous, pacifists each one, yet not dreamers.'

'But——'

'Let me finish,' said Pettigrew. 'Anster died. Only a fortnight

128

later, Grayle met with an accident near his house and also died. I don't think it's generally known that Cunningham and Malcolm have been missing from their homes for some weeks. Their families have not reported to the police. *I* think that they were two of the men found dead at the foot of Wenlock cliffs, although I can't prove it. I think Morne saw one of them there —he was questioned after one body was found, wasn't he?'

'Yes,' said Palfrey, somewhat dazed. He could hardly keep pace with the information and the thoughts which it engendered.

Pettigrew said: 'In Kyle's opinion, and in mine, those men have all been killed because Gorringer—which may be a false name—intended to exploit Garth's discovery. And Gorringer has a partner, the man about whom Fyson boasted. So far we don't know who that man is.'

'I see,' said Palfrey. 'Where do you come in?'

Pettigrew said: 'I was in America on Government business some years ago and met Kyle then. Our friend is a realist. He knows that I am wealthy; he believes that I am reliable; and he knows that I am not without influence in Whitehall. He took a chance and told me everything that I have told you. He emphasized, as if emphasis were necessary, that it was vital not to spread the information. The struggle had to be in secret, with or without official help. He asked me for help if I could not win it for him from Whitehall. I promised it, and I have given it. I should tell you that when I approached the people at Whitehall, I was immediately told that Kyle was a dissatisfied ex-agent, a braggart and a headstrong fool. The general opinion was that he was absolutely discredited and I was wasting my time on him. Whitehall, when it chooses, can be the most deadly obstructionist in the world, as I know to my cost. I wasn't satisfied, but all I could do was to finance Kyle and keep trying to help. Not until you actually found Garth in Cheddar Gorge was there any change in the official attitude. Then I was delighted to see that Brett came down here, and I had no doubt that you were going to work officially. When you first appeared on the scene, Kyle, Susan and I had a mild celebration. We thought that Whitehall had stirred after all. You disappointed us, but that's all worked out now. Now things have gone so fast that we can really hope for action, can't we?'

'Yes,' said Palfrey. 'This mystery-man in the syndicate—haven't you any idea who he is?'

'No. I might make a guess—Rufus Morne.'

'Do you know if Markham is concerned in this at all?'

'I've no reason to think he is,' said Pettigrew. 'I once thought that his son and young McDonald might be involved, although they're hardly the type.'

'I think I can explain their part,' said Palfrey. He briefly told McDonald's story, and Pettigrew seemed to find it satisfying. 'Well, now,' said Palfrey. 'A word first with Brett and, when I've heard from him, a gathering of the clans, I think.'

'What clans?'

'Yours and mine,' said Palfrey. 'After today I shall not be working alone. All right?'

Pettigrew said: 'I'm going to put the thing in your hands now, Palfrey.'

'Not mine, but Brett's. And Whitehall's, but a Whitehall which now really means business. Thanks. You've been very good and very helpful and I won't forget it. Er—do you know where the explosion started last night?'

'It was somewhere out at sea,' said Pettigrew, 'and I've an idea that the workings of some of the old tin mines go fairly far under the sea. It might have been an accidental blow-up, or it might have been an underwater experiment. From the blast, I've wondered if it happened from a boat.'

'From a boat,' Palfrey said, firmly. 'A safe experiment, after all. Put one of the infernal things on a small motor-boat, set its course, let it get a few miles out, and then—oh, well, we'll find out all the details sooner or later. Did I tell you that I think an attempt has been made to murder Morne?'

Pettigrew stiffened. 'Think?'

'Yes. I can't be sure. He's well-guarded now. An early talk with him is indicated. The number of things I want to do at once are legion,' Palfrey went on. 'Where shall I find Kyle?'

'At Bristol,' said Pettigrew promptly. 'These people are known to have a meeting-place there.'

'I've heard the Theatre Royal mentioned.'

'I don't think the theatre is actually concerned,' said Pettigrew. 'I don't see how it could be, but it's somewhere near there.'

'And Kyle's trying to find it, with Susan Lee?'

'Yes.'

'What about the Lancastrian who looks like Kyle?'

'He's with them, too,' said Pettigrew. 'He's an old employee of mine, and as deeply involved as any of us.'

'One other thing, to get it all squared up,' Palfrey said. 'Who

130

was the man believed to be under arrest, and so important that Kyle had to find out?'

'Gorringer,' said Pettigrew, promptly.

'Oh. Does he live down here?'

'He was down here last night, so Kyle told me,' said Pettigrew. 'I have had as little to do with Kyle as I could, of course ; I didn't want to land him in trouble, and the police have had their eye on me, as Whitehall knows I'm in on this. There's still one other point you will want to know,' went on Pettigrew. 'The place where we keep Fyson and Frenchie.'

'Ah, yes. Where?'

'My house, near Oxford,' said Pettigrew. 'You see, Palfrey, I have taken some risks over this business.'

'Yes. Congratulations.' Palfrey stood up. 'One urgent thing is to make absolutely sure that Morne's all right.'

'I'll leave that to you, now,' said Pettigrew. 'Oh, there are two small points. Gorringer once rented a flat in Mayfair, the telephone number being 01341. He leased it to his friends—that explains one puzzle, doesn't it? And they put a man on the staff at the sanatorium. He told Fyson you were going to visit Miss Morne, and he poisoned your tea. Now I'm off!'

'Where will you go?'

'Home,' Pettigrew declared, and took a card from his pocket. It read: 'C. K. Pettigrew, Lyme House, Nr. Oxford.' 'You'll find me there any time you like. What message do you want me to give to Kyle?'

'Come to *Sea View*, Middle Bay, Corbin,' said Palfrey, 'but not before eight o'clock tonight. If he does get picked up by the police, he can tell them they must refer it immediately to Cartwright. I'll fix things with Cartwright. Happier?'

'Much,' said Pettigrew.

Palfrey left the *Rose and Crown* without any interference and with Pettigrew's firm grip lingering on his fingers. Then he saw McDonald sitting on a seat in the courtyard of the inn.


THIRTEEN

## GATHERING OF CLANS

McDONALD stood up and waited for Palfrey. He was smiling ; his long face seemed to reflect genuine amusement, and the

131

broodiness which he had shown at the house that morning had gone.

'Hallo, bloodhound,' said Palfrey.

McDonald laughed. 'Don't remind me of those brutes!'

'Then don't be one,' said Palfrey. 'How's Loretta?'

'I think she's making progress,' McDonald said, seriously. 'I didn't stay for long. She recognized me for the first time.'

'How did you find me here?'

McDonald said: 'I once followed Kyle to this place. I saw him talk to Pettigrew. I came along to see Pettigrew today, and was told he had a visitor. I described you and learned I'd got it in one.'

They walked along the road towards the car. Drusilla was sitting at the wheel.

'Why did you come to see Pettigrew?' demanded Palfrey.

'I'm curious about Kyle.'

'I'm curious about you,' said Palfrey. They reached the car and he beamed upon Drusilla. 'Look what's blown up,' he said.

'It does appear in unexpected places, doesn't it?' murmured Drusilla.

'That's exactly the point,' said Palfrey. 'Will you drive while Mac and I sit in the back?' He opened the door, trying to decide what attitude to take. Someone at Morne House was involved. For the first time it occurred to him that he had never checked McDonald's story of having arrived in England only recently. Glancing sideways at the man, he found it hard to distrust him, but——

'Well, what about it?' asked McDonald.

Palfrey said: 'I am going to make one or two inquiries about you, Mac. It's time they were made. You haven't an alternative story for me, I suppose?'

'I'm afraid not.'

'All your past reticence has been to make sure that Loretta wasn't caught out in some discreditable business?'

'All.' McDonald was emphatic.

'And you once told me that you had little regard for family tradition!'

'None,' said McDonald, 'but I also told you that I have a great deal of regard for Loretta.' He laughed, and there was a bitter note in his voice. 'Would you like to know why I so dislike King Rufus?'

'Yes.'

132

'I want to marry Loretta,' said McDonald, 'and His Majesty won't hear of it.'

'Oh,' said Palfrey, and added, after a pause: 'Is Loretta a girl to allow her father to dictate to her?'

'In that one matter, yes.' McDonald stirred restlessly. 'At one time I thought she would defy him. Then something happened and she changed her mind.'

'Someone was blackmailing her, you know.'

McDonald snapped: 'Are you suggesting that *I* was?'

'No. Suggesting that she thought you were.'

'Oh,' said McDonald, and then shook his head. 'I doubt that very much, but you may be right. Where are we going now?'

'To temporary police headquarters,' said Palfrey.

'With me as prisoner?'

'Not yet,' said Palfrey.

Drusilla pulled up outside the police building. Cartwright was resting, but Wriggleswade was there. He was still pompous, but treated Palfrey with some deference. The reason soon materialized; special instructions had been received from Scotland Yard concerning the facilities to be offered to Palfrey.

'Oh, splendid,' said Palfrey. 'First, if you don't mind, tell the Bristol Police that I might look in on them, and would be grateful for help. Then, if Kyle is caught, I'd like him to go to *Sea View*, Corbin. Under escort, if you prefer it, but there and not here or to a police station. You're being very good, you know.'

'We've got to *find* these devils,' Wriggleswade said. 'There is one thing I meant to say to you, Dr. Palfrey. You oughtn't to go out anywhere without an escort.'

'What I will do is tell you when I'm travelling and ask you to arrange for me to be passed from village to village, as it were. A benevolent eye while on the road.'

'That's a good idea,' said Wriggleswade.

'And if at any time I have to leave my wife alone, you'll ease my mind by looking after her,' said Palfrey. 'And now, if I could have a room with a telephone for half an hour. . . .'

He was soon speaking to Brett. Brett made notes, asked occasional questions, but said nothing until Palfrey had finished.

'Well, now,' Brett said. 'I haven't been idle. Unhappily, Pettigrew's story is largely true. He has been in touch with some of our people on Kyle's behalf. Washington was firmly against Kyle, and that verdict was accepted here. Further inquiries should have been made, of course, but we can't worry about that, now; the job is to get the thing done. I think you can accept Kyle and Pettigrew at their face value.'

'Splendid!' said Palfrey.

'I'll inquire into the deaths of Anster and the others,' said Brett. 'There is one thing I seem to remember—Anster lost a lot of flesh a little while before he died.'

Palfrey's heart seemed to contract. 'Like Garth, you mean?'

'Yes. What does it convey to you?'

'Effect of radioactive elements on the human body,' said Palfrey harshly. '*Now* I'm beginning to understand.'

He was pale with the shock of the realization. Garth's emaciated condition could be explained by radioactivity, proof that Garth had been working on atomic power *recently*.

'This gets worse,' he said, aloud.

'Could it be worse?' asked Brett, and, when Palfrey did not immediately answer, he went on: 'Let me settle your mind about McDonald as far as I can. He has recently returned from Far Eastern submarine service. He had been in attendance at the Admiralty recently. As far as I know, there's nothing wrong about what he has told you about his movements in London and his opportunities for being concerned in this affair. There are rumours, too, that he was at one time engaged to his cousin, but that Morne put his foot down.'

'I should be glad to think he was telling me the truth,' said Palfrey.

'I suppose so. Now, this is of great importance,' said Brett, 'and greater since the explosion. At all costs we must not allow any rumours to be spread about the case. The need for secrecy is greater now than ever. It has been suggested in London that a widespread search be made of the whole of the moor down there. I'm against it, because it will give rise to speculation. What do you think?'

'I'm with you. We want the thin end of the wedge first.' Palfrey told Brett about the possibility that one of the mines on Morne's estate was being used as an experimental station, and went on: 'If we can find the right mine and get one or two of our fellows into it, we can get busy with a wholesale raid. Until then——'

'It's much too dangerous,' Brett said. 'We now know what these people can do. For the time being, you will concentrate some of your forces on finding the mines and the others on finding the leaders. Gorringer may be your man.'

'Yes,' said Palfrey. 'Well, what help are you sending me?'

134

'Daniel is at *Sea View* with several others,' said Brett, 'and will work under your orders. You can have more if you need them. I shouldn't concentrate too many in one place yet, if I were you. The police are looking after you now, aren't they?'

'Yes, very well.'

'Good! Then I'll let you get on with it,' said Brett.

Palfrey next called at *Sea View*. A man with a rather high-pitched voice answered him, that of a Z.5 man named 'Dan'.

'How many of you are there?' Palfrey asked.

'Seven. Bandigo, Trollop, Carmich——'

'Leave those three at the house and take the others to Morne House,' said Palfrey. 'Go as police ; I think Morne won't object then. Watch him and, if necessary, hold him. You'd better take two cars and keep close together. When you get near the village of Henson, be careful. A police car crashed there yesterday, and the cause isn't known.'

'Right-ho,' said Dan. 'When will you be along?'

'Some time this afternoon. If Kyle turns up—you've heard about Kyle, I suppose—make him welcome until I come. Is that all clear?'

'Admirably clear, Doctor!' Dan laughed and rang off.

Palfrey got up and joined Drusilla and McDonald, who were in the next room.

'I know you're going to say that you want me to return to Morne House,' McDonald said, with a grimace.

'I do. I've reason to think that King Rufus is in greater danger even than we thought before,' said Palfrey. 'Watch him carefully, won't you?'

It was nearly half-past two before McDonald left for Morne House in a hired car. The Palfreys saw him off, then started for Corbin. They reached *Sea View* a little after four o'clock. The house stood in small grounds not far from the sea, and it was rightly named, for they could see the Cor Estuary from the front windows. Two cars were standing in the carriageway.

'Did Dan get off at once?' asked Palfrey, when they were sitting in a pleasant front room.

'Five minutes after you'd called,' said Bandigo. 'Two cars as instructed.'

'Now,' said Palfrey, 'when we've seen Kyle and discussed his story, here's the plan of action. Check on all the mines on Morne's estate. Get plans of them. Find out which one is like

135

the plan which I've already obtained. Having found it, put it out of action.'

'Ah,' murmured Bandigo. '*Very* simple. Especially the last part.'

Palfrey said: 'They are experimenting somewhere on that estate with new forms of atomic energy, and they've got to stop experimenting. A large-scale raid will probably mean that they'll blow the place up. The risk is too great. We've got to find a way of getting inside that mine, and you fellows must do it, because I'm already too well known. Sorry, but there it is.'

Carmichael laughed. 'Why apologize, Sap?'

'The job is elementary,' declared Trollop. He had dark hair and a pale face, and his little finger was missing. 'What about Dan and the others?'

'Who will take over at Morne House?'

'I will,' said Palfrey. 'I can work there without too much trouble, I think.'

'When do we start?' asked Carmichael.

'Tonight,' said Palfrey. 'After Kyle's been here; and I'm expecting him soon after seven o'clock.'

'What are you going to do while you're waiting?' asked Trollop.

'First have tea and then a nap,' said Palfrey. 'I can hardly keep my eyes open. Then the gathering of friends, and after that the dispersal of forces. Which reminds me,' he added, thoughtfully, 'someone will have to go to Bristol, but we'll know more about that when Kyle reports.'

'Do we look on him as one of ourselves?' asked Trollop.

'Yes.'

Palfrey went upstairs to rest. He felt he must have a couple of hours' sleep if he were to be fresh enough for the coming session.

It was dark when he woke up, and only a faint light came into the room from the passage. 'Hallo,' he said, and sat up. Drusilla, who had been asleep on the bed next to him, stirred.

'Telephone, Sap,' said Bandigo, from the door.

It was Susan; she did not beat about the bush, but, once sure that she was speaking to Palfrey, said abruptly: 'Nick's disappeared, Palfrey. He was all set to come to see you tonight. We had one last look round Bristol. He went to the Theatre Royal—and didn't come out again. Pettigrew was watching and was injured—not badly, but enough to put him out of action. He gave me your number.'

'Oh,' said Palfrey. 'Anything else?'

'Yes,' said Susan. 'Gerald Markham was also near the theatre. I thought you were going to keep him at Morne House.'

## FOURTEEN

## THEATRE ROYAL

'WELL, what was it?' asked Bandigo. He was still standing by the door, and his head was bent a little because he could not pass through when standing upright. Behind him were Trollop and Carmichael.

Palfrey explained and added thoughtfully: 'One night shouldn't make much difference in the hunt for the mines, but if you fellows try Bristol and we don't pull anything off, you'll be recognized afterwards. You'd better carry on, I think. 'Silla and I will go to Bristol. I'll ask Brett to send some more men down there.'

Carmichael asked: 'What about Morne House?'

'Dan will have to look after it,' said Palfrey. 'It's odd that Gerald Markham got away and Dan didn't ring through to report it.'

Brett immediately promised to send men to Bristol, and Palfrey had finished speaking to him before Carmichael managed to get through to Morne House; Corbin Exchange was working under pressure because so much damage had been done in Wenlock. At last, Daniel Fayre came on the line to say that all of them had reached the house after an uneventful journey.

'No,' said Dan. 'I haven't seen Gerald Markham. This man Hardy told me that, as far as he knew, everyone except McDonald was still here. McDonald came in about three hours ago. But anyone can get out of this place without being seen.'

Palfrey and Drusilla started out a little after half past seven. Palfrey was low-spirited, almost hopeless. He felt that he had to go to Bristol, and yet it seemed such a waste of time. If Kyle had been outmanœuvred, it meant they were up against clever people. It was even possible that Susan Lee had been impersonated over the telephone.

When at last they saw the city in the distance, lights twinkling on the Severn hills and deep in the great valleys, it was barely eleven o'clock, so they had made good speed, but the Theatre Royal would be closed. They drove straight to the Grand Hotel, and hurried through the swing doors and into the large, bare reception hall. Susan Lee jumped up from a chair near the grill-room.

'Hallo,' said Palfrey. It was a relief to see her safe and unhurt. 'Situation unchanged?'

'Yes.'

Palfrey glanced at the tiny cubicle where the night porter was standing at his desk.

'Let's get upstairs,' he said, and they walked up the stairs to the lounge, which was dimly lit and nearly empty.

'Everything that has happened has been near the Theatre Royal, and Nick went in. I'm sure he went in.'

'During a performance?'

'Yes, and he didn't come out when it was over. I was watching. Even had he wanted to avoid me, he would have made sure that I saw him. Palfrey, in all the time that I've worked with Nick, this has never happened. I almost went to the police.'

'Yes,' said Palfrey. 'We can now. They'll do what we want without asking us questions. First job, police, to get the place surrounded. That shouldn't be difficult, except that it might be noticed. We'd better impress on them that we don't want to attract attention. Then I'll go in.'

He was not surprised that the police were prepared for his call ; and when he got back to the hotel from the police station three men were sitting with Drusilla and Susan in the lounge. They were men of the same character as Carmichael, Bandigo and Trollop. Susan had already explained the situation, and they got up as Palfrey entered.

Palfrey said: 'It's all set. 'Silla, you and Susan will stay here.'

'But——' protested Susan.

'Sorry,' said Palfrey. 'Stay, please.'

He drove with the others towards the Theatre Royal, but stopped at the end of the street. Few people were about, but there was the sound of traffic on the main road. A man came out of the shadows of a doorway.

'Is that Dr. Palfrey?' The man was in uniform, Palfrey had already seen him at the police station. 'Everything set?'

'Yes, sir.'

'Thanks,' said Palfrey. 'Bill, come along with me, will you?'

He and Bill walked quietly along the street. A few yards

138

from the theatre, he turned and looked round. No one was in sight; the street was dark and empty. It was not likely that anyone watching had observed the police.

They reached the door.

Palfrey's companion shone a torch on it, made a quick examination, and said: 'This shouldn't take long.' Palfrey had chosen him for the first sortie, for Bill Wyatt was reputed to be able to force any lock and open any door. He used a small tool, working swiftly, with little sound. Soon they stepped into the foyer and closed the door behind them.

The foyer was pitch dark. They stood listening to their own breathing, then Palfrey shone his torch. The beam travelled down the long passage towards the auditorium. Near them were the electric light switches. Palfrey pressed one down, and by good chance a light at the far end of the hall came on, one that would not be noticeable from the street.

They walked along the passage. A staircase led up on the right, and there was a closed door marked 'Gallery'. Together they went up the stairs. The wood creaked under their footsteps, and Wyatt whispered: 'How old is this place?'

'Early eighteenth century, isn't it?' asked Palfrey.

'They do say it's the oldest in England.'

They looked into several offices, all tidy and clean, then found themselves outside a door marked 'Circle'. They put out the light in the office, crept into the circle and stood listening. There was no sound, nothing at all to suggest that anyone else was there. The dark void of the auditorium was immediately in front of them; they might have been standing on the edge of a black chasm. Palfrey shone the torch backwards, saw a light switch and pressed it. Several lights came on at the back of the circle, showing the array of green plush seats. The stage looked tiny; the scenery, a drawing-room, looked like a large doll's house.

Above them was the gallery, and they could just see the ceiling there, but not the ceiling of the auditorium, which was lost in the darkness.

'I think we ought to have more light,' said Palfrey.

They walked back up the steps, pressing down all the light switches they could see as they went along. The upstairs passage and the stairway were well lighted now and they went downstairs, putting on more lights.

They looked into the auditorium again; the perspective was different from the stalls. The stage seemed very high; no stage lights were on, but they could see the set much more clearly.

'Let's go back-stage,' said Palfrey.

'What are those doors neither on the stage nor off it?' asked Wyatt. Although he whispered, his voice seemed to echo.

'The proscenium doors,' Palfrey said. 'Interesting survival, I'm told.' He smiled. 'Nothing very sinister, is there? But I have heard it said that there are passages leading to other buildings. We'll see.'

There was a narrow doorway and a flight of narrow wooden steps. Palfrey found a light switch, and they walked down, pausing for a moment to look at the complicated wooden machinery under the stage. There was no one there.

'Well,' said Palfrey, 'that leaves only the gallery.'

They were on the stairs. His arm was outstretched to push the door wider open. He had heard a movement, perhaps a footfall; and then the door pushed against his hand. Someone was trying to close it from the wings. He stiffened his arm, moved the other to support. Someone gasped on the other side of the door. The pressure grew greater, and Wyatt squeezed up to help him. They pushed until at last the door gave way. It banged back and they lost their balance. Footsteps sounded on the stage, echoing noisily. One of the proscenium doors slammed.

'After him!' snapped Wyatt.

'This way!' called Palfrey. He ran across the stage, pushing the furniture out of the way, and saw the figure of a little man running up the side passage of the auditorium.

Then the lights dimmed.

Palfrey thought he saw the man reach the central doors and rush out. A door slammed and there was silence. Palfrey measured the distance between the stage and the floor of the auditorium; it was a long one, over the orchestra pit. He drew back, ran and leapt, making it with only an inch to spare. Actually his heel scraped against the curtain of the pit.

He raced up the side, hearing Wyatt scrambling into the stage box of the circle. He could hear footsteps now on the stone floor outside. He went into the cold passage but could see no one. He thought he heard movements above him, as if someone was going up the stairs.

Wyatt came hurrying after him. 'Oughtn't we to fetch the others?' he whispered.

'Not yet. Let the beggar think we're on our own,' said Palfrey. 'The gallery, I think.'

The gallery steps were narrow, and made a hollow noise as they walked up, approaching each corner cautiously. They reached a little bar which smelt of beer. Together they went out into the gallery and looked down into the dim auditorium. Wooden seats, which looked centuries old, were on either side of them.

'Supposing we do find these beggars, what can we do on our own?'

Palfrey said: 'If they think we're on our own, they're more likely to get reckless. We want them reckless.' He withdrew to the narrow wooden staircase of drab light brown. There was still no sound save their own breathing. There were several doors and one more flight of steps, much narrower than the others. He went up them, and found himself in a tiny loft.

Wyatt cried: 'Palfrey! Pal——'

And then his voice broke, and there was a gurgling sound. Palfrey swung round, dropping his hand to his gun. As he touched it, a shot rang out, echoing and re-echoing through the theatre. He backed down the stairs, fearful of being shot in the back, but nothing happened. He saw Wyatt leaning against the wall, gun in hand and blood streaming from a cut in his cheek. Wyatt was pointing down the stairs.

A man said: 'You won't find it so easy to get down, Palfrey.'

Wyatt straightened up, without speaking. He walked to another door, just behind Palfrey. It was little more than a hatch, standing about as high as his waist and fastened by an ordinary catch—a cupboard, probably. As Wyatt bent down, blood dropped from his cheek, and he padded his handkerchief and held it against the wound while he explored. Palfrey went to Wyatt's side.

'Anything in there?' he whispered.

'An empty cupboard,' muttered Wyatt.

'There's another on the other side,' said Palfrey. 'I think we might find them useful.' He was whispering, and the man on the stairs certainly could not hear them. 'Can you squeeze in there and sit down for ten minutes. Then he'll probably come up to find out why we're quiet.'

Wyatt squatted down and Palfrey helped him to squeeze into the cupboard. It was dusty, but fairly clean. The door closed on him.

Palfrey crept towards the cupboard opposite Wyatt's. It was about the same size. The door faced the head of the stairs, and,

141

if he crouched inside, he would be able to watch the stairs and cover them with his automatic.

He did not think he had a great deal of chance to outwit his opponent. They were above the gallery; that was the worst of it. At gallery level they would have had a chance to climb over, drop to the balcony, and then into the stalls.

'*Palfrey!*'

'Hallo,' said Palfrey. 'Are you still there? I'm just patching up my friend.'

'You'll want patching up before long.'

'Oh! Threats!' said Palfrey, disparagingly.

He was puzzled by the hidden man. What kind of man would talk like that? What manner of man would use those brave threats, threats uttered almost as if he were intent only on keeping up his own spirits? Not a particularly clever or resourceful one, thought Palfrey.

'Yes, *threats.*' It was getting absurd.

'Well, good-bye,' said Palfrey. 'Come on, Bill, let's get out. Mind your head!'

Palfrey squatted inside the cupboard. It was more difficult for him than for Wyatt, who was so much shorter, but he managed it and looked out over the top of the door. He had his automatic in one hand and Wyatt's in the other. He could see the head of the stairs; and after a few tense seconds he saw a hat, a trilby hat, moving upwards. Then he saw the man's eyes, narrowed, and darting to and fro. Was the man entirely alone? It seemed like it.

He came further up the stairs until Palfrey could see his head and shoulders. He was peering across the tiny room and looking straight at Palfrey, who did not move. The man took another step upwards.

Palfrey shot him through the shoulder.

The noise of the shot was deafening inside the cupboard. The smell was pungent. Palfrey choked as he flung open the door. The man on the stairs had toppled backwards, but was trying to hold on to the hand-rail. He fell as Palfrey reached the head of the stairs. The crash reverberated about the landing, but as it died away there was no other sound except a call from Wyatt.

'All right, Sap?'

'Yes. Come out,' called Palfrey.

The man on the floor was staring at him in bewilderment. His face was blank and nondescript—the face of a man with

142

little intelligence. Why had he been left here alone? What had he been doing? He was so thunderstruck that he did not speak nor utter a protest as Palfrey ran through his pockets and took out a knife and an automatic ; the knife was stained with Wyatt's blood.

There was no time to look at the wound on his shoulder.

Palfrey lifted him and carried him up the stairs, took off his tie and knotted it about his wrists, with his hands behind him. Then he bundled him into the cupboard from which Wyatt had come. The man endured all this without protest.

Wyatt was trying to smile. 'Not bad,' he said.

'Not good yet,' said Palfrey. 'Can you manage to get down the stairs on your own?'

'Yes, I think so.'

'We'll have the others in,' said Palfrey. Palfrey watched Wyatt going unsteadily down the stairs. He himself went on to the gallery, looking about him. He thought he heard a sound of movement, but could not be sure.

Suddenly he saw the proscenium door open!

It opened slowly, and Palfrey stood tense, well in the shadows, to avoid being seen. A man appeared—someone whom he had never seen before. The man peered about him, then turned and beckoned.

A second stranger appeared.

They stole across the stage towards the door leading to the under-stage machine room, then disappeared. Palfrey peered over the gallery rail, wondering what were his chances of climbing down. He might easily fall, but he desperately wanted to follow these men, and if he went down by the staircase he would have little chance of catching them.

He swung himself over.

He hung at full length, his feet a little way above the balcony of the circle. He was close to one of the reeded pillars ; with one arm about it, he slid down. For a moment he thought he would topple over, but he regained his balance and stood on the balcony, with his back to the auditorium, breathing deeply.

There was a sharp crack ; *someone was firing at him!*

He did not look round, but moved forward, reaching the circle floor, and dropped out of sight. Two more shots were fired, but neither touched him. He crawled along a few yards and then peered over the balcony. The man who had fired at him was standing by the side of the curtains, looking towards him, a gun in his hand. He was a short, dark, sturdy man ; from a distance he looked rather like Markham.

Palfrey crawled further along, towards the next pillar. Then he stood up, for the pillar hid him from the stage. He might have a chance of winging the fellow down there. As he began to take aim, there were footsteps, and the sound of voices downstairs. The man on the stage started and moved back. Palfrey fired and missed. The man disappeared, while the door leading to the auditorium burst open.

*The police had come in strength.*

So, too, had a tall man, well dressed and very angry.

'I don't care whether all the police in Bristol are here, you shouldn't have come in without my permission!' He glared at Palfrey. 'Who the devil are *you*?'

'Mine the responsibility for breaking in,' said Palfrey. 'Sorry. Urgent job of work. Are you the manager?'

'Yes.'

'Yes, it's Mr. Wells, sir,' said one of the policemen.

'Then you can help us,' said Palfrey. 'Two or three gunmen have gone to earth beneath the stage, I think.'

'*Gun*men!'

'I did say it was urgent, didn't I?' said Palfrey. 'Do you mind telling me whether there is any secret passage leading from the machine-room down there?'

'There used to be a tunnel, but it's blocked up. The theatre is full of hidden passages, you know. Well, full's an exaggeration, but it's so old that——'

'In short, a good hiding-place for rogues and vagabonds,' declared Palfrey. He offered cigarettes, and Wells took one. 'The rest of the force is near the stage,' Palfrey went on, 'trying to get below, I expect. Is there another way to the machinery down there?'

Wells said: 'There is. Yes.'

'You couldn't have timed your arrival better!' marvelled Palfrey.

Wells laughed. 'You've got a nerve,' he said.

Three men were trying to open the door which led below. Perry looked round with a one-sided grin, and said: 'They've fired at us three times, Sap.'

'Yes. Desperate men. But we've a friend in need in Mr. Wells here, the manager. He knows another way in.'

Wells led them out by the opposite wing, through the proscenium door and across the theatre. He turned into a small room

144

where three doors led off, and went immediately to the middle door.

'I'll go first,' said Palfrey.

'You won't,' declared Wells.

He opened the door and walked into a small passage, where another door was ajar. 'It's all right,' he said, and led the way again.

At the top of a flight of stairs he motioned them to stop. The stairs were in darkness, but the room below was lighted, and Palfrey saw two armed men leaning against a wooden bench. The thump, thump, thump of the police who were hammering at the other door filled the air.

The men below obviously had no idea they were being watched.

Wells whispered: 'When are you going to do something?'

'Wait just a moment,' said Palfrey.

He had hardly finished speaking before another man appeared; and for the first time Palfrey thought that he was looking at the leader of the gang. This man was well dressed, good-looking in a swarthy fashion, and very sure of himself. He appeared as if from nowhere, and Wells whispered: 'The old tunnel entrance was near there.'

The swarthy man said clearly: 'How much longer can you hold out?'

'We're all right,' said one of the others.

'Can you stay for half an hour?'

'We can try.'

'You'd better make it,' said the swarthy man. 'It'll be good for your health.'

'And what will be good for yours?' asked Palfrey.

All three men below spun round. One raised his gun, but Palfrey fired and sent the gun spinning out of his hand. 'I shouldn't move, if I were you,' said Palfrey, and he stepped forward, into the light. By then, the other door was open, and the police were crowding down the stairs.

The swarthy man moved like a flash. Palfrey fired after him and missed. The swarthy man disappeared. One of the others also started to move, but two policemen jumped at him and they went down in a struggling heap. Palfrey, Wells and Perry followed the swarthy man, and saw a door slam.

'That's it!' cried Wells. 'The old tunnel!'

He was the first at the door, trying to find a handle by which

145

to pull it open, but the handle was on the other side and the door looked a part of the wall.

'Do you know this exit?' asked Palfrey, sharply.

'It leads down to the docks,' said Wells.

The Bristol police inspector had joined them and caught the last words. 'The docks, does it?' he said. 'Do you know just where?'

'Yes,' said Wells.

'We'd better hurry,' said the inspector.

It was all so quick, so confused, Palfrey had to concentrate to get his thoughts in order. A tunnel leading from this room towards the docks, perhaps to the river mouth. Probably these men were making for a ship. That explosion had taken place out at sea. If they could catch these men and find the ship they might find the key to the mystery. But wasn't it better to leave that search to the police and Wells, and concentrate on this door?

'Coming, Dr. Palfrey?' asked the inspector.

'You carry on,' said Palfrey. 'Leave a couple of men, will you?'

'Half a dozen will stay,' said the inspector. He hurried off with the eager Wells, leaving Palfrey, Perry and one uniformed policeman in that under-stage room ; the other policemen were presumably somewhere upstairs.

They set to work on the door.

Once the door started to open, it swung back easily on well-oiled hinges. Palfrey did not open it wide, but waited, half-expecting a shot. None came. He opened it wider ; only darkness lay ahead. He took out his torch, but the policeman stepped forward and offered his. 'Mine's more powerful, sir,' he said.

'Thanks,' said Palfrey, gratefully.

The long white beam carved its way through the darkness.

It fell upon a man's head with fair hair. The man was on the floor against the wall. A faint, mildewy smell came from the tunnel, and when Palfrey stepped forward, his foot slipped on the slimy floor. He trod more carefully, and the policeman kept the beam steady.

'Well, well,' said Palfrey, blankly.

The light shone on Gerry Markham's face. There was an ugly gunshot wound on his throat. He lay much as Rose Lindsay had done in the caves at Cheddar Gorge.

## FIFTEEN

# THE BRIDGE

GERRY MARKHAM had not been dead for long.

There was an expression of horror on his face, as if he had seen death coming. His hands were clenched, and in them were hairs, hairs probably pulled from a man's head in his struggle with the murderer.

'Nothing we can do for him, I suppose, sir?' said the policeman.

'Nothing at all,' said Palfrey.

At first the tunnel was high enough for them to walk upright, but after a while they had to bend their heads and then their knees. At one point they had to crawl for a few yards, and their hands and knees were covered with evil-smelling slime. Apart from the torch, there was no light.

When they reached a spot where they could stand upright again, Palfrey murmured: 'Let's stand still for a moment.'

They did so, their breathing hushed. Vague, muffled sounds travelled along the tunnel; it was even possible to make out a man's voice. The sounds drew no nearer, and Palfrey said: 'All right. We'll go on.'

It was some time before they saw light.

It was at the end of the tunnel, a faint, dull light which grew slightly brighter as they walked carefully along. When they were close to the opening they saw that it was water, with light reflecting from it. After another few minutes, they reached the end of the tunnel, and found themselves standing on a narrow ledge in the side of a dock. Further on, in another dock, was the flood-lighting which Palfrey had noticed earlier in the evening. Here, at the exit of the tunnel, it shone only faintly, but it was bright enough to show a motor launch which was moving fast towards the Severn. The dock gates were open, the level of the water was the same as the level of the river. The moon had risen, making vision clearer.

The harsh roar of the engines filled the night air.

Policemen were running along the side of the dock, and there were people standing and staring from the dock-side—people from the little houses which lined it. Then there was another roar, and a second motor-boat, a police launch, started off in the wake of the first.

'Quick work,' Palfrey said. 'Well, we can't do anything.'

'We *can*, sir!' The policeman's voice was pitched high in excitement.

'What can we do?' asked Palfrey.

'If we cut across to "A" Dock, sir, we can cut the first boat off,' said the policeman. 'We shall have to commandeer a car.'

'Good work!' exclaimed Palfrey. In the light of the rising moon, he could just see the first boat, making good speed, a heavy wake behind it. The police launch did not seem to be travelling so fast. He followed the policeman, using a flight of narrow, slippery steps, to the road, and ran after the man towards the main road, past gaping crowds, many in their nightclothes. He stopped a small car that came along and explained the situation in a few words to the driver who raised no protest. They drove at speed to 'A' Dock. As the car drew up, the policeman shouted loudly to the night-watchman.

'We want a launch, and——'

'You don't want no launch,' said the watchman. 'They've gone back, up along the Avon.'

'*What!*'

'S'fact,' said the night-watchman. 'Just come down from the roof. I saw them. Your fellows are a long way behind.'

'Never mind,' said Palfrey, as cheerfully as he could. 'They'll probably catch up.'

'Not in *that* old barge they won't,' said the night-watchman.

'Along the Avon,' said the policeman. 'I know what we *can* do.' He turned to the driver of the commandeered car, a young fellow who seemed eager to help. 'Have you got plenty of petrol?'

'The tank's half full,' said the driver.

'Know the road to the bridge?'

'You mean Clifton——'

'No, under the bridge.'

'Oh, yes, the Avonmouth Road.'

'That's it. As fast as you know how,' ordered the policeman. He was evidently a man of resource and initiative, a man after Palfrey's own heart.

The car started off immediately. The driver reversed, drove back towards the town, then up past the big hotel, forked left off the Clifton Road and found speed along a flat, wide road where there was little or no traffic and no people except an occasional policeman. They passed ships and warehouses on their left, but soon were in a built-up area. The driver seemed

148

to know the road well. He took one wide swing to the left, then put on an extra burst of speed and the headlights shone on great wooded cliffs across the river.

Other lights came on, near them.

The driver pulled up by the side of the road, while Palfrey looked about him, amazed. The police had lost no time at all. Cars were stationed about the road, their headlights were already turned towards the river, while the motor-launch, some way off, was swinging its searchlight from side to side.

Lights came on above them.

Palfrey looked up. In the moonlight and against the beams of headlights he could see the giant span of the suspension bridge; it looked an infinite distance away. The cars seemed to be half-way down the cliff on their side of the river; only on the other side were there no lights.

The noisy *chug-chug-chug* of the motor-launches could be heard clearly—two separate engines. Palfrey watched the searchlight of the second as it swayed from side to side, and saw it catch the leading boat, not more than two hundred yards in front.

*The leading boat was heading for the opposite bank.*

The policeman said, gloomily for the first time: 'I think they'll get away now, sir. I was hoping they'd come this way, or else try to get out by Avonmouth. Not much chance *there*, believe me.' He sniffed with disappointment.

Palfrey said: 'We've tried. Can't we get on the other side?'

'Only over the bridge, sir, and we'll have men up there by now. You can tell that from the lights.'

'Yes. They've been very quick,' said Palfrey. 'Still, we might try the other side—if,' he added, turning to the driver with a beaming smile, 'you can still run to it.'

'I'm game,' said the man.

Police cars were now on the lower road, shining their headlights towards the river, and the launch searchlight was pointing steadily towards the bank. Another launch came up, and its light was added to the other. Palfrey could see the wooded banks on the far side, and many people moving about. The police launches looked like toy boats on the broad surface of the river. Close to the opposite bank was another launch— the one in which the gang had escaped. They could see no one on board her.

The policeman said: 'They might be in the tunnel.'

'Another tunnel?' exclaimed Perry.

'The railway tunnel,' said the policeman. 'There's a single-track railway over there, and a tunnel almost opposite where the boat's tied up.' He shook his head. 'I don't think we'll catch them now.'

They stood watching for a few minutes. In the tense silence Palfrey began to feel unnerved by the height at which they were standing. He was about to turn away when he saw a flash far down in the depths of the valley, not far from where the policeman said there was a tunnel. A sound came echoing upwards.

'That's a shot,' exclaimed Perry.

'And another,' said Palfrey.

Their attention was riveted on the point where the shooting was coming from—near the mouth of the railway tunnel, the policeman told them. At first Palfrey thought it was aimed at the policemen who were now clambering ashore from the launches. But they were some distance away from the tunnel, and it seemed unlikely that the gunmen could see them clearly enough to aim.

'Someone's running!' cried Perry.

Now they could see a man running down from the lower slopes of the cliff towards the river ; and they could see the men following him, and shooting at intervals. Seen from that distance, the tiny running figures seemed unreal, like toys in motion ; but there was no doubt in the minds of the watching men of the stark reality of that hunt.

The searchlights of both launches were now turned towards the spot. Palfrey could see the man darting from bush to bush, and at least three others following him, all of them with guns. Police were climbing up the hillside, working their way round to get behind the gunmen, who must have been desperately anxious to stop the man from getting away, for they were rapidly losing every chance they had of escape.

*Crack-ack-ack-ack!*

The fugitive was near the river now, and running across a clear patch of ground. He put on an extra spurt of speed ; probably he knew that if he could get away here, he would be safe from his pursuers. He ran fast, but from that great height he seemed to be crawling. Flash after flash followed him, and the echoes of the shots rumbled about the gorge. The man reached the edge of the river and plunged in. They could see the tiny splashes. There were more flashes as the gunmen

150

loosed their last rounds; then they turned and disappeared among the trees.

The chug-chug of a motor-launch started again. It moved towards the swimmer. Palfrey saw him tread water and wave. Then he dropped down again. He seemed to move very little. Palfrey wondered how badly he had been hurt. The launch was alongside now. Palfrey could see men leaning over, to help the swimmer in. They seemed to stay there for a long time, bending over the side; then there was a concerted movement upwards, and Palfrey saw the man brought on board.

'I wonder who it is,' said Perry.

'I'm hoping it's Kyle,' said Palfrey, 'and I'm also hoping that he's not badly hurt. We'd better go down.'

They moved towards the car.

Sharp across the quiet came the sound of another shot.

It was much closer to them and followed by a sharp clang. The driver said: 'What's that?' There was another clang, and then Palfrey realized that the bullets were hitting the car.

At the same moment, Perry snapped: 'Look out, Sap!'

He pushed Palfrey, who dropped behind the car. They all stared upwards. On the right of the bridge, on high ground, they could see the dark shape of a man crouching, and they saw the flash from his gun. He had probably been up there for some time, watching, waiting this chance to shoot at Palfrey.

The policeman shouted: 'Get him! There he is. Get him!'

He began to run. Other police followed him. Palfrey felt a sudden stab of fear. He jumped to his feet and called out a warning. There was another shot. In the garish light of the headlamps, he saw their policeman escort suddenly pitch forward and lie still. The policemen swerved aside, but went on. Then other policemen arrived from *behind* the gunman, who stood up for a moment and looked desperately about him.

It was the swarthy man.

He darted to one side and for a moment was lost in the shadows. A policeman called 'Spread out!' The men obeyed. With men above and men below, there seemed little chance for the swarthy man to escape; he might do more damage with his gun, but he was too heavily outnumbered to get away.

He tried!

Palfrey saw him clearly in the beam of a headlamp, moving downwards to a spot where the cliff seemed to drop sharply down towards the road. He ignored the path up which the police were streaming, and jumped. He disappeared. Two or

151

three policemen turned and ran back, past the bridge.

Palfrey ran onwards, towards the stricken policeman. The shouts and confusion about him did not concern him just then. He went down beside him. He stayed for a moment, with his hand on the man's chest; when he took it away, it was wet. That one shot, that one chance shot, had gone right through the heart; his hand was wet with the man's blood.

Savage anger filled him.

He stood up and looked along the bridge. The headlamps of several cars had been trained along it now, and he saw the swarthy man leap over the turnstile. He sped towards the far side, but police were approaching him, and there was now no possible escape.

Palfrey joined in the chase. The fugitive was half-way between the two squads of policemen, about fifty yards from each. He hesitated only for a moment, then turned and climbed on to the railings of the bridge.

There was a gasp from a dozen throats.

One moment the man was astride the railings, the next, he swung himself over and disappeared. Palfrey leaned over the side. The ironwork immediately beneath the road itself was probably heavy enough to enable the swarthy man to move with reasonable safety, but he could have no chance of getting away, unless he esayed the almost impossible feat of climbing down the ironwork to the cliff.

Torches were trained on the man now, and some of the cars were being moved so that lights would converge on him. Only by leaning over dangerously could Palfrey see the man. With Perry, he left the bridge and went down the grassy slope on the left side. Now he could see the man, moving sure-footed along the ironwork, oblivious of the people watching him. He was too self-confident, thought Palfrey; no man could move at such speed on that ironwork and retain his balance for long.

He *was* trying to climb to the bank, in the hope of evading the police among the wooded slopes. And he still moved swiftly, although he had fifty or sixty yards to go, and the great stretch of water yawned before him, hundreds of feet below.

A policeman swung over the railings and began to follow him. The tension was almost unbearable. The policeman moved more slowly, and hung on more carefully; obviously he had gone to make sure that the swarthy man could not double back on his tracks.

Forty yards, now. . . .

The swarthy man slipped!

Every moment Palfrey had been waiting for it, but now that it had happened, it was with a sense of shock. One moment the man was there; the next, he was falling without a sound into the stillness of the gorge, into the waiting waters below.

No one moved or spoke. Every eye followed the falling body of the swarthy man. He disappeared. There was no sound to indicate when he had hit the water or the road below.

There was complete silence.

A short, sharp blast on a car-horn broke it absurdly. The man who had sounded the horn looked sheepish; but the tension had snapped. Men moved about. Some went to the aid of the policeman under the bridge. Palfrey, feeling cold and damp with perspiration, lit a cigarette and went back to the commandeered car. An inspector in uniform came up.

'You'd better get back and have a rest, sir.'

'Rest!' echoed Palfrey. He laughed mirthlessly. Of course, you're right. But I shan't rest until I know whom they found in that launch.'

'Better get below then, sir; they'll be able to tell you there. Or, better still, go to the police station; the latest reports will be in.'

'Thanks. I will,' said Palfrey. He got into the car next to the eager driver, who was silent and glum after the tension. Perry climbed in the back.

They reached the police station, and the driver gave his name and address and then drove off. Palfrey walked wearily into the station, and was received by a man in plain clothes who introduced himself as Superintendent Cox. He was a breezy man, eager to do everything he could to help. No, they had not yet got the name of the man who had been picked out of the river, but they knew he had been slightly wounded in the leg but would be well enough to be brought to the police station after treatment at the hospital. He would not be long. No results had yet come in about the chase on the other side of the bridge. Some of the men might have got away.

'Some?' asked Palfrey.

'There were five in all.'

Palfrey telephoned the Grand Hotel, and was not surprised when Drusilla answered almost as soon as he had given her room number.

'Much action, but all safe,' Palfrey said.

He thought Drusilla caught her breath. All she asked was: 'Are you coming back soon?'

'In about an hour, I expect,' said Palfrey. 'Excitement is over for the night, and you can both relax.'

'I see,' said Drusilla, and then Palfrey heard Susan Lee's voice asking whether there was any news of Kyle. 'I'll telephone you as soon as I've got any news at all,' said Palfrey. As he spoke, the door opened and the inspector who had been on duty at the theatre came in. 'Just a moment,' said Palfrey, and looked eagerly at the inspector, who obviously had news of some kind.

'Well, that wounded man is *Kyle*,' said the inspector, in some excitement.

'Nick's all right,' Palfrey said into the telephone, and then replaced the receiver. 'That's fine,' he said to the inspector.

'You want him, don't you?' asked Cox.

'Yes,' said Palfrey. 'He should have quite a story for us.'

Some time later an extraordinary figure limped into the room. It was Kyle. His clothes must have dried on him. His trousers were shrunk and tight, the bottom of one was cut away and bandages showed beneath it. One lapel of his coat was torn and he wore an old muffler instead of a collar and tie. He looked on the point of exhaustion as he dropped into a chair, but when he glanced at Palfrey there was all the humour and devilment imaginable in his eyes.

'Why, hallo, Palfrey!' he greeted. 'You don't know how good it feels to be rescued by the police instead of hunted by them. You haven't fixed the rest of this business yet, I suppose?'

'Not yet.'

Kyle shrugged. 'I thought that would be asking too much. But I've got quite a story, Palfrey. . . .'

Kyle's story added little to their knowledge of the affair; it was logical. It explained all that had happened that night, but it was not a vital contribution. Palfrey wondered, as the Amercian talked, whether he were keeping anything back. The police seemed to entertain no such suspicion.

Kyle had been convinced for some time that, usually after it was closed, and sometimes during performances, the theatre had been used by Fyson and his men. He had gone there again that night, at the beginning of the performance, and scanned the audience from a seat in the front of the circle. During the interval he had seen a man he knew as Darkie.

'Good-looking and swarthy?' asked Palfrey,

'You've placed him,' said Kyle, and went on.

He had followed Darkie up the stairs to the gallery, and then lost him. Like a fool, he said, he had ventured further and gone up the top flight of stairs. There he had been ambushed and knocked out. When he came round, he was tied hand and foot and crammed into one of the cupboards about which Palfrey knew only too well.

After the performance—a long time after, he imagined—he had been taken out and his legs freed. He had been hustled downstairs to the room beneath the stage. There he had been questioned; the bruises on his face and chin showed the way the questioners had set to work. Kyle showed no resentment about this. The questions, he said, had all been to one purpose: did he know anything about the mine? At that, Kyle cocked an eye at Palfrey, and Palfrey nodded.

'I thought you would know something about that by now,' went on Kyle.

Palfrey, it appeared, had figured largely in the questioning. Did Kyle know whether Palfrey was working officially for the British Government, or was he simply interfering? Did Palfrey suspect Morne of any part in this affair? Did he suspect any of the others at Morne House? If so, whom? Kyle had answered none of these questions. He said simply that he had not opened his mouth. Not even when they had brought Gerry Markham in . . .

A frightened Gerry, as much a prisoner as Kyle. Nothing was said about what he was doing there. They started to work on him. If Palfrey had examined his fingers, he would have seen that the little and third fingers of his right hand had been broken. Kyle said that he knew that nothing must make him talk, not even the same treatment, if meted out to him.

Then someone had come in and said that entry had been forced into the theatre.

Kyle grinned across at Palfrey.

'When I heard your name, Palfrey, I certainly thought of you as an angel from heaven! There was panic for a while. Then Darkie sent one of his men to find out where you were looking. Gerry Markham and I were pushed into the tunnel with the crowd. We were there when you came down. You couldn't see the stairs from the doorway, otherwise I don't think you would have got out again,' Kyle added.

The man whom Darkie had sent to watch Palfrey and Wyatt

155

had been away for some time. Darkie had planned to go after him, but had timed his moment badly. When he had gone, there had been shooting—the shooting when Palfrey had been hanging over the gallery.

'Then the panic really broke,' said Kyle. His face was bleak, and he was looking at Palfrey. 'Young Markham went crazy— just plain crazy. He was terrified of that tunnel. Darkie shot him through the throat—you've seen that, haven't you?'

'Yes,' said Palfrey.

'I guess I needn't tell you much more,' said Kyle. 'You know that we were rushed through the tunnel and there was a motor-boat waiting for us. I had a chance to jump overboard then, but thought I might find out where they were heading, so I kept quiet. Then the police launches got busy and we had to double back. Everything went too fast for me. Darkie had left us near the dock—I don't know what's become of him. The other decided when they went ashore that I would be better dead than alive, but they said so at a silly moment, and I ran for it.'

Palfrey smiled faintly. 'Well, Darkie won't trouble us any more. That's one thing on the credit side.'

Kyle was trying to be bright, but was clearly tired out, and he could walk only with difficulty. Palfrey made sure there was a room for him at the Grand Hotel, and went there with him, together with a police escort. He still had no idea whether the other men had been caught, but he did not think that greatly mattered. Darkie had seemed to be the only man of any importance.

He was so tired that he could hardly keep his eyes open. Drusilla had to help him undress. He grinned at her weakly, got into bed, and closed his eyes. . . .

It was past mid-day when he woke up.

'I've arranged for some tea and then for a cold meal,' said Drusilla. 'Will you bath before or after?'

'After. I would like to stay here all day. How are the others?'

'Nick was still asleep when I looked in half an hour ago.'

'Nick?' Palfrey raised his eyebrows.

'I've seen rather a lot of Susan,' said Drusilla. 'What else can I call him?'

'No news of any kind, I suppose?'

'They caught three of the men last night,' said Drusilla, 'but Superintendent Cox or Fox or something says that he doesn't think we shall learn much from them.'

'Nothing from Brett?'

156

'Nothing from anyone.'

'Have you telephoned *Sea View*?'

'Yes, and Morne House. There is no news of any kind ; everything is normal. Bandigo and the others spent this morning looking up surveyors' plans of the mines on the Morne estate, but at twelve o'clock they hadn't any results. I mean,' went on Drusilla, 'they hadn't found one with a plan like the map.'

'What about the news of Markham's son?'

'Cox or Fox told me that he isn't going to issue any news at all until he's seen you,' said Drusilla, 'and I told him you would be available at three o'clock this afternoon, *if* you were awake.'

'Protective, eh?' smiled Palfrey.

'Wells called about half past eleven,' Drusilla went on. 'The police told him a little about what you're doing, and he came to apologize for leading off last night.'

'Great Scott! *He* was all right,' declared Palfrey.

'Apparently the night-watchman and the cleaners who work there in the morning thought that someone was using the place,' said Drusilla, 'but Wells thought it was one or two of the cleaners having a quiet smoke against orders, and took no action about it. But he has watched the place at night now and again, and felt curious last night. That's how he happened to be passing and why he came in.'

'Lucky he did!' said Palfrey. 'If he hadn't shown us that other way to the under-stage room, we would have been in serious trouble. Meanwhile, how far have we got?'

Drusilla said: 'Susan and I have been talking, Sap, and it seems to us that we've weakened the other side but not got much further.'

'That's about right. Still got a good opinion of Susan?'

'Very good.'

'Splendid!' said Palfrey. 'Any news of Wyatt?'

Wyatt was patched up, Drusilla told him, and would be off duty for a few days. The police had failed, so far, to get any intelligent statement from the prisoner in the cupboard at the theatre, or the other prisoners.

Palfrey felt that he ought to get up quickly, but he was still very tired. Bandigo and the others would lose no time in telling him when there was anything of interest to report ; there was no point in killing himself. A telephone call from Brett, when he was in the middle of his breakfast-cum-lunch, reassured him further.

'I suppose there's nothing else about Gorringer?' he asked.

'Except that he's been missing from his home for several days, nothing,' Brett told him.

Palfrey finished his lunch, and then went in to see Kyle, who was sitting up in bed, eating. Susan, fresh and delightful, was sitting by his side, and Palfrey was in no doubt as to her feelings for Nick Kyle.

Kyle was depressed because of his injured leg.

'Nothing is likely to blow up quickly,' Palfrey comforted him. 'You'll be about again in a few days, and——'

'I'm going to be about today,' declared Kyle.

There was little that Cox could tell them beyond what Drusilla already knew. He beamed when Palfrey told him what he thought of the organization, and reminded him that orders had come from Whitehall, with instructions for the police to be ready for any emergency. When Palfrey had called to suggest that trouble might develop quickly, Cox had made arrangements for all the main roads out of town to be watched, and for radio calls to be sent out directly trouble developed at any one point. What was troubling him now was what to do about the Press. They were demanding a fuller story about what happened, and someone had told them of a murder. Should he give the name of Gerald Markham?

Palfrey said: 'Better call him an unknown man for the time being, I think. I'd rather tell his father myself.'

Cox's cheerfulness spurred Palfrey to quicker thought and action. He must see Morne that night. He must, if necessary, force an issue. Bandigo and the others must trace that mine and get busy. There must be no delay; any minute might bring another disaster like the explosion in Wenlock Bay.

Kyle was well enough to travel, but not well enough to take any active part for the next day or two. He and Susan must stay at *Sea View* with Drusilla.

'Urgent thoughts?' asked Drusilla.

'More urgent thoughts. "Begone dull sloth!" Hop next door and tell the others we're starting for Corbin at once, will you?'

'Ought Kyle to travel?'

'Yes.'

'Very well, sir,' said Drusilla, mockingly deferential.

They left Bristol at half past three, and before six o'clock the Talbot was standing outside *Sea View*, and Palfrey was helping Kyle out. Drusilla and Susan were on the porch, waiting for the door to be opened.

Kyle leaned on Palfrey's arm and said heavily: 'You've

158

hedged every time I've mentioned coming with you to Morne House. I want to see Morne. I want to look inside that house. I've earned it. A little bit of flesh out of my leg needn't stop me. *You* won't stop me, friend.'

'Oh,' said Palfrey. We'll see. I——'

He broke off, for the door opened and tall Bandigo stood on the threshold. His eyes were bright and there was a broad smile on his face as he said:

'We've got it, Sap. We know where that place is.' He laughed. 'The nearest mine to Morne House. That ought to interest you.'

## SIXTEEN

## THE MINES OF MORNE

THE discovery had been made an hour and a half earlier. The map of the old mine had shown almost the same markings as that of the plan which Palfrey had obtained from the minstrel gallery. The direction of some of the workings was different, but the variations were slight. The dimensions on the map were the same as those of the mine; there was no doubt at all that the vital discovery had been made.

Bandigo's inquiries had been assiduous, and he had learnt all that was known locally about the mine. It was called the Wenn, because it was within the parish boundaries of Wenlock, and was one of the few which had not been opened during the war, because the experts declared that it had been worked out long since. It had been derelict for years; there was no maintenance staff, not even a watchman. Much of the machinery had been dismantled during the war, to be used in other mines, but the wheel, shaft and cage were still there and, as far as it was known, could be operated.

There was another thing of importance. It was close to the sea, and there were under-sea passages. The shaft was sunk to a depth of about seven hundred feet below sea-level, and the opening was in the Wenlock foothills. That was why Palfrey had never seen it; it was some way off the main Morne House-Wenlock road.

'Are you going there first instead of to Morne House, Palfrey?' asked Kyle.

159

Palfrey said: 'I don't know yet. Carmichael and Trollop are there, you say?'

'They should be there by now,' said Bandigo.

'Is there any other known opening to the mine?' asked Palfrey.

'No'

'Good place to have one,' murmured Palfrey. 'In the foothills, a secondary shaft, difficult to find—yes, it wouldn't surprise me if it's being worked that way. *If* it's being worked,' he added. 'We must find that out without delay. Four men aren't enough.'

Kyle said quickly: 'You won't bring the police into this yet, will you?'

Palfrey blinked. 'Why not?'

'They'll be recognized,' Kyle said. 'Your men won't be—not at first, at all events.'

'No,' admitted Palfrey. 'I'm inclined to agree that it would be unwise to have the police there in strength just yet, but the police must be warned to stand by. So must the military. The nearest garrison town is thirty miles to the south, isn't it?' That was a rhetorical question, for he had already checked on these details. 'Have you told Brett?'

'I telephoned him, but he was out, and I didn't leave a message.'

'I'll have another shot at him,' said Palfrey. He got up and went to the telephone. His mind was hazy with the rush of plans and preparations, but one thing was clear: they had found the mine where Garth had experimented, there was no doubt of that; how could they make absolutely sure of getting in without warning the men still working there?

Brett came on the line, and Palfrey spoke quickly, giving only the bare essentials. There were a few moments of earnest consultation, and then Brett said: 'All right, Palfrey. I will arrange the military aspect of it. You talk to Cartwright and make arrangements with the police. You'd better tell them what they already suspect—that there are experiments with a new explosive going on down there. I doubt whether any of them will realize what kind of explosive, but they will work better if they're not kept entirely in the dark.'

'Yes,' admitted Palfrey. 'Any news of Gorringer?'

'None at all,' said Brett.

Palfrey rang off, satisfied with the situation except for one thing: Gorringer. It was a name to him, and nothing more, though a name which stood for all that was evil and dangerous. He did not even know what the man looked like. If it were Morne, now——

'I think we'll go to Morne House, Nick.'

Kyle's eyes brightened. 'We?'

'Oh, I can't keep you out of it,' said Palfrey. 'We'll work from there. It's near enough to the mine for our purpose.' He was on edge to be off, but wanted to speak to Cartwright before he left. 'You get ready, I'll be back inside an hour.'

'What about us?' asked Susan, glancing at Drusilla.

'Men must work and women must weep,' murmured Palfrey.

'You can't get away with that,' Susan declared.

Palfrey said: 'Don't make it more difficult than it is.'

Susan shrugged her shoulders. Palfrey went out and drove to police headquarters, where, Bandigo had told him, Cartwright had returned late that afternoon. Cartwright still looked tired, but he was cheerful in much the same way as Cox of Bristol. He listened attentively, and when Palfrey had finished, he said with a grim smile: 'Yes, I'd realized that it was an explosive, Palfrey. The Wenlock disaster proved that. I can arrange for a cordon to be flung around Wenn Mine and Morne House. Both are necessary, don't you think?'

'Yes,' said Palfrey. 'How soon can it be done?'

Cartwright looked at his watch. 'It's nearly eight o'clock,' he said. 'Shall we say by midnight?'

'Yes. Good work,' said Palfrey.

'And you say the Marquis of Brett will look after the military side of it?' said Cartwright.

'Yes. And naval—naval might be necessary.' Palfrey smoothed back his hair and smiled. 'We've travelled some distance, haven't we?'

'We have,' said Cartwright, heavily. 'You're going out to Morne House now, are you?'

'At once,' said Palfrey.

'You'll want a car escort,' Cartwright said. 'I'll look after it if you'll give me a quarter of an hour.'

Palfrey smiled. 'You're good,' he said. 'A quarter of an hour will do nicely.'

Morne House was in darkness. No flares burned. They did not know they had arrived until their headlights shone upon the closed gates.

Palfrey slowed down.

'That's the first time I've seen these gates closed,' he said. 'I wonder why.'

'Hardy's orders, I guess,' said Kyle.

Palfrey thought that he was probably right, and expected to see a policeman rise out of the darkness to question them. But no one moved. Both cars pulled up, and all the occupants except Kyle got out. Now that they had switched off the engines, the silence was absolute. Palfrey tried the gates.

'Padlocked,' he said.

'I can open them,' declared Bandigo. 'Show a light, will you?'

'It won't be so easy,' said Palfrey. He and another man held the light steady while Bandigo worked on the padlock. Palfrey remembered Wyatt opening the door of the Theatre Royal. How long ago that seemed.

Bandigo said: 'Here it comes.'

'I'll walk,' said Palfrey. 'You drive, Ban.'

Bandigo grunted agreement and went back with the policemen. Palfrey walked slowly into the courtyard. Soon the silence was broken by the purr of the engines. The headlights shone on Palfrey, but not far beyond him. He had not remembered that the house was so far from the gates.

The fountain appeared in the headlights as the cars drew nearer; the great bear with water spouting from his snout and folded paws.

*For the first time, there was no water spouting!*

Palfrey's heart contracted; it made the night seem more eerie and the mystery of those locked gates deeper.

His own car slowed down by his side, with the headlights shining on the great door of Morne House. Kyle called out, but Palfrey did not hear him. This quiet, this darkness, were alike inexplicable.

The cars pulled up. Bandigo knocked on the door heavily. Palfrey told him to find the bell. Bandigo pulled it; the deep clangour sounded, but there was no answer. *No answer.* By the time Palfrey reached the foot of the steps the bell had rung three times, but there was still no response.

Kyle limped by Palfrey's side.

'Can you make this out?'

'No,' said Palfrey. He looked at the illuminated dial of his watch. 'It's eleven o'clock,' he said. 'Cartwright's cordon should be here soon.'

Bandigo pulled the bell again, but it was a waste of time. One of the policemen asked whether they were going to break in.

'It's the only thing to do,' said Palfrey. 'Let's try the windows first.'

They split into two parties and made a complete circuit of the house, shining their torches on the windows and on the shutters beyond. All the windows were heavily shuttered, none would be easy to break down. Bandigo muttered an expletive, climbed up the pillars to the top of the porch to look at the first-floor window above it.

'Just the same,' he called down.

'What's happened to Daniel?' muttered Palfrey.

'And Inspector Hardy,' said a policeman.

Palfrey wondered if it would be worth trying one of the side doors, and looked along the front of the house.

As he did so, something moved near one of the cars.

He did not speak or indicate what he had seen, but looked away and then towards the car again. There was a man standing there, in the shadows; only his hands were visible. Palfrey looked away, hoping the man would come further forward. Instead, when he looked again, the hands had disappeared.

Palfrey said in a whisper: 'Stay where you are, all of you.' He turned to go down the steps, but as he did so the hands appeared again, and in one of them was an automatic. Palfrey dropped his own hand to his pocket; then the man in the shadows spoke sharply.

The voice was McDonald's.

'Don't move, any of you,' he called.

He stood forward so that the light of one car shone upon him, and then shone a torch towards them. It travelled slowly, on Bandigo's face, on that of the policeman, then on Kyle. It stopped for a moment, then went on and reached Palfrey. *'Palfrey!'* McDonald exclaimed, with a wealth of relief in his voice. He lowered his gun and came hurrying forward. 'Am I glad to see you!'

Palfrey gulped. 'That's good to hear,' he said. 'Where did you come from?'

'Inside,' said McDonald. 'Over the roof and down the wall. For the first time in my life I've been glad of those bears!' His relief was still evident in his voice as he went on: 'The only way to get in is the way I got out. That door is probably double-barred inside.'

'Oh,' said Palfrey. The anti-climax made him feel foolish. 'What were you doing there?'

'Locked in,' said McDonald.

'What about the others?'

'I don't know anything about the others,' said McDonald. 'I thought I was on to something and went up to the top floor. I was in a room punting around, and the door was locked on me. I'd no tools, nothing with which to try to get out. But they'd forgotten the window, or perhaps they thought I wouldn't be fool enough to try to get out by the window,' he added. 'I ought to have broken my neck.'

Palfrey said: 'Do you mean that no one else is inside?'

'I haven't the faintest idea,' said McDonald. 'I can only tell you that I've been locked in that room for two hours and couldn't make a soul hear.'

'All this is very interesting,' declared Kyle, 'but what about getting in?'

'Three of us will go with McDonald,' Palfrey said. 'The others had better stay here. We'll have to find a way out of the room upstairs and get down to open the door.' He looked at McDonald. 'Do you know where to get the ladder to light the flares?'

'Yes,' said McDonald.

'Show one of them,' said Palfrey, pointing to the police. 'The quicker we get some light, the better.'

McDonald lost no time and, five minutes afterwards, Palfrey, Bandigo and one policeman went with him towards the south side of the house. In a small stone building near it was an extension ladder; it would reach half-way up the house, McDonald said; after that, they would have to climb up the wall. By the time the ladder was in position and McDonald was leading the way, the flares were burning, and they could see everything clearly in the bright, lurid light.

McDonald was sure-footed, and did not seem nervous, although the climb from the top of the ladder was sheer. He reached a window which they could just see, and then disappeared. Palfrey said: 'I'll go next.' He started the climb, using the ornamental bears, finding the going easier than he had expected. McDonald hauled him through the window. Bandigo and the policeman followed. They found themselves in a small, low-ceilinged room. Bandigo paid attention to the locked door. He examined it carefully, and laughed.

'This won't be difficult.'

Five minutes afterwards, McDonald led the way to a narrow landing. Beneath them was a flight of stone steps, and they went down cautiously.

164

They met no one and heard nothing. McDonald switched on all the lights as they went, but all the time there was only darkness ahead of them. Soon they reached the great staircase leading to the main hall, only dimly illuminated by the landing light.

At a touch of a switch, one of the chandeliers lit up.

'Now we're moving,' said McDonald. 'We'd better let the others in.'

Kyle and the two remaining policemen entered eagerly, but were equally affected by the silence of the empty house. McDonald led the whole party in a complete search. Palfrey had never made this tour before, and it seemed unending. Nowhere did they find any sign of life. Eight or nine policemen, four of his own people, the staff and the family had been here at the time when McDonald had gone upstairs.

Kyle said: 'Is there a cellar?'

'I don't know of one,' said McDonald. 'We've seen everything but the outbuildings.'

'We might try the telephone,' Palfrey said.

He picked up the instrument in the small room between the hall and the music gallery, and waited, listening intently. There was no answer. He replaced the receiver abruptly, and said: 'Could they have left by the road?'

Kyle said: 'Be sensible, Palfrey. The doors were locked on the inside. All of them.'

'Yes,' said Palfrey.

The facts which faced them were chilling, uncanny. The great house had been emptied of people within the last few hours, and there was nothing to see how it could have been done.

Palfrey said: 'We'll have to make a more thorough search. We might find a door like that at the theatre. The devil is to know where to start.'

'Ground floor, anyhow,' said Kyle. He was perspiring freely, and had his leg up on a chair. 'I'll have to rest for a while, Palfrey. You fellows get cracking.'

'We may as well start in the gallery,' McDonald said.

They switched on all the lights in the gallery. Two men took a wall apiece. They tapped and explored, but found nothing at all helpful; they had nearly finished when the silence of the house was broken by a sharp cry: 'Palfrey!'

'That's Kyle!' snapped Palfrey. He rushed forward with the others. There was a scuffling noise from the inner room, and another cry. As they reached the door leading to it, a figure

165

appeared for a moment, someone Palfrey did not recognize, and the door slammed!

'Rush it!' cried Bandigo.

They flung themselves on the door, but it was locked. They could hear sounds of a fierce struggle within; then silence, followed by a sharp, cracking noise; and silence again.

Bandigo was working furiously on the lock of the door. He got it open in a few minutes, and Palfrey went forward cautiously, his gun in his hand. But the room was empty; there was no sign of Kyle.

The others crowded in. McDonald hurried over to Kyle's chair. The arm was smeared with blood. There were patches of blood on the carpet by the side of the chair. A little pool had gathered near the fireplace; someone had trodden in it and left a trail.

All of them looked at the floor, their eyes moving with one accord towards the last dark patch of blood near the bookcase built into the wall by the fireplace.

McDonald said: 'That's it.'

'We can't do much on our own,' said Palfrey. 'We must have more help.' He looked at the clock over the fireplace; it wanted a few minutes to midnight. 'The police will be on the moor by now,' he said. 'Somebody had better go and tell them all to come here; then we shall feel that we can take more action.'

'I want to stay here,' said Bandigo.

Palfrey said: 'Will you fellows go?' He was looking at the policemen.

They agreed without hesitation, and left immediately. Contact with the police cordon should be made about a mile from Morne House, and within half an hour, unless they met with trouble on the road, the police should be here in strength. Palfrey was uneasy at having to wait, but he knew that there was no choice left open.

'Are you going to try to open that wall?' asked Bandigo.

'Not yet,' said Palfrey. 'I think——'

He was looking at the bookcase as he spoke; and he saw it move. McDonald caught sight of it and jumped away. Bandigo dropped his right hand to his pocket.

One end of the bookcase moved outwards. It moved soundlessly, slowly, and a dark void became visible behind it. Palfrey took out his gun, stepped towards the fireplace and covered the gap.

A man said: 'Stand away from the opening, all of you.'

166

'Stand away,' the man repeated. 'Don't be foolish enough to think you can defend yourselves. Sir Rufus wishes to speak to you.'

One of the servants came through. He straightened up and looked at Palfrey's gun with a sneer. Another man followed him. Palfrey thought: 'They seem very confident.' He heard a movement behind him and looked round. There were two other men in the room, near the minstrel gallery door, and both were armed. The hopelessness of the situation came over Palfrey like a dark shadow. In this house it was impossible to defend oneself, impossible to know when one was safe. He put his gun into his pocket. Bandigo did the same.

*Morne* wanted to speak to him.

There was a movement from behind the bookcase. The servant stood on one side, his head bowed. It was fantastic. Palfrey, McDonald and Bandigo stood in a half-circle about the bookcase, with the armed men behind them.

Morne stepped through.

He was faultlessly dressed, and looked more composed than Palfrey had yet seen him. He limped slightly. His red hair was brushed back in waves from his forehead, his brow was unfurrowed, he looked impressive and remarkably handsome; there was something almost regal about him.

Palfrey smiled: 'So you're responsible, Morne.'

Morne smiled faintly. 'Sit down, Palfrey. All of you sit down, please.' He stood in front of the fireplace, looking at them, one hand in his coat pocket, the other held in front of him. 'I do not quite know what you mean by saying that I am responsible, Palfrey. If you mean that I am responsible for my daughter's accident, you are quite wrong.'

'I was thinking of Garth and Gorringer,' said Palfrey.

'Of Gorringer, you need have no further fears,' said Morne. 'I do not know how much you have learned. I suppose you know as much as Kyle knows. He has just been persuaded to tell me that. That is why I thought it best to talk to you, Palfrey.'

Palfrey did not speak.

'Of the early days of this adventure,' Morne said, 'you know much of the truth. Anster, Cunningham, Malcolm and Grayle were my friends. They knew what Garth had discovered. They believed that this discovery could not safely be left in the hands of governments swayed by power politics, fired by greed, intoxicated by their own power. I fully agreed with them,

Palfrey. I agree now. You are a reasonable man, free of prejudice. Don't *you* agree?'

Palfrey did not speak.

'I think, at heart, that you do,' said Morne. 'It was decided then to make sure that Garth's discovery should be made known only to a small circle of men on whom complete trust could be placed. Unhappily, Gorringer was included in that circle. He was not incorruptible.

'I was aghast when I heard of the death of my friends. At that time I believed that outside persons were responsible. I even suspected Nicholas Kyle. I am convinced now that he was driven by excellent motives, although undoubtedly he was misguided.'

He paused. Palfrey listened intently for the next word, fascinated by this man's calm confidence.

No one else spoke.

'When I discovered that Gorringer was, in fact, disloyal and had killed my friends,' continued Morne, 'I took the appropriate action. In such a matter as this, ordinary standards and ordinary laws are of small significance. I know now that Gorringer was responsible for the earlier accidents to my daughter; that she believed that he was blackmailing me; that she stole the papers, which you afterwards found, in the hope of helping me; that she had confided a little in Halsted, who got in touch with you. These things, doubtless, puzzled you.'

'Yes.' The word seemed wrung from Palfrey.

'Now one of the things which Gorringer did was to try to put pressure on Garth,' went on Morne. 'When I discovered that, I gave Garth sanctuary here. I was not aware, at the time, that I was harbouring traitors. I let it be known that Garth was engaged to Loretta, because it was a sufficient answer to all the questions which might be asked. I knew that I could rely on my daughter's discretion, you see.'

Palfrey did not speak in the pause which ensued.

'However, there *was* treachery,' said Morne. 'My nephew Gerald and his mother conspired together to work against me. *They* sent Garth away. Gerald, angered because I had refused to allow him to marry Loretta, became quite beside himself. *He* was responsible for the accident in the minstrel gallery. He was the man who nearly killed you in the gallery. All of these things he confessed only last night, a little while before he died. He pretended that he was trying to help Loretta; he used that as an excuse for his many journeys, for his interference, for his

168

appeal to Bruce McDonald to help. Last night, loyal supporters of mine discovered the truth about him just before his death. They would have brought him back here alive had he not made difficulties. You also made difficulties, and the proper course was taken. You see, Palfrey, I am being very frank.'

'Yes.' Palfrey's voice was hoarse.

'Let me explain a little about the theatre at Bristol,' said Morne. 'It was used by those who worked for Gorringer. What Gorringer did not know was that for some time some of his workers were, in fact, in my employ. Those workers escaped from the river last night, after hearing Gerald's confession, and since have reported to me everything that happened. The theatre itself was not used except as an entrance to the tunnels which led to the docks and which enabled some men to move secretly by night. Gorringer first discovered it, and preferred to use it at considerable trouble, because he wanted—wisely—to distract attention from this house and from the mines.'

Palfrey's lips tightened.

Morne smiled serenely. 'So the mines surprise you, Palfrey? They should not. Garth had been working in them for a long time.'

Palfrey did not answer. The dominant thought in his mind was that Morne did not realize that they were on the track of the mines. That mattered more than anything else. Carmichael and the others were working near there now, might even have found the secret entrance to Wenn Mine.

'Do you or don't you realize the significance of that?' For the first time, Morne's voice was sharp.

Palfrey said slowly: 'No, not altogether. You talk as if you were the only person who held this knowledge. You are not. It is well known to the Government here and in America.'

Morne said: 'I thought you would see more clearly than that, Palfrey. The United Nations—united!' he added, scornfully, and suddenly there was fire in his voice and in his eyes. 'Split asunder by dissension, by trivialities, standing by while half the world is ravaged by disease and starvation—what weaklings they are, what puny creatures guide them!'

Palfrey said, with a faint laugh in his voice: 'Most people would rather trust the Great Powers than you, Morne.'

'Do you understand, Palfrey, that you are completely in my power? I have been patient with you. I have encouraged you to stay here. I wanted, you see, a reliable messenger to take my information to the proper quarters, and I wished you to be that messenger. But I am not everlastingly patient——'

Palfrey said: 'My patience isn't inexhaustible, either.'

Morne said harshly: 'You do not appreciate the seriousness of the situation. I will acquaint you with it. The trial explosion at sea two nights ago failed only in one thing ; the power of one small unit was under-estimated ; it was not intended to cause such damage. There are many other units in my possession. The work is complete. That is why I have prepared to leave this house. I shall go, with my staff, to a place where I shall not be easily found. A ship is waiting off Wenlock Cliff to take me tonight. Its cargo is already loaded. The mine where the experiments were carried out will be destroyed when I have left. *This house will be destroyed.* I shall cut myself off completely from my earlier associations. I must take no risks, Palfrey, and I *shall* take no risks.'

Palfrey said: 'How many are you taking with you?'

'As many men as I need,' said Morne. He looked impatient. 'If you are worried about the police who were here, and those friends, of course, you are worrying yourself unnecessarily. They have been taken to a place of safety, and they will return when I have left the country. You see, Palfrey, most of this part of the moor is mined. There are entrances in many unexpected places. Halsted found one.' He laughed, and then went on more quickly. 'I do not want to prolong this interview, Palfrey. I have no personal animosity against you or the police or anyone who has helped you. I wish them well. I want you to act as courier to Whitehall—keeping, you see, to my original plan. I have prepared a letter. You can take it tomorrow. Tonight you will spend beneath the house, and you will be freed in time to escape before it is destroyed.'

Palfrey said: 'You know, I can't understand you. Only a few days ago, I thought you were about to commit suicide.'

Morne said harshly: 'That was after I had discovered that Gorringer had betrayed me. I thought he had won, but I was able to defeat him. If you are still interested in trifles, Palfrey, you may like to know that Gerald Markham poisoned me ; he used nicotine ; doubtless, the symptoms of my attack are now obvious to you.'

'How long ago did you first start on this, Morne?'

'Years ago,' said Morne. His voice was low-pitched. 'I shall succeed, Palfrey. Nothing *must* prevent it. You know the situation as I do. You know, in your heart, that the leaders of the

170

nations today are not fit to lead. You know they cannot be trusted——'

'I know nothing of the kind!' snapped Palfrey.

Morne raised his hand.

Palfrey was thinking: 'The mine and the ship; they must both be taken.' How could anything be done *quickly* unless he or Bandigo or McDonald got away and told the story?

Morne said: 'Do as I tell you, Palfrey. Go to the bookcase and through the wall.'


SEVENTEEN

THE MINE

THE armed men were standing behind Palfrey. The two guards were by the bookcase. Morne was pointing towards it. Bandigo and McDonald moved towards it as if they could not help themselves. But Palfrey continued to sit on the arm of the chair, trying to look unconcerned. Now he could think of nothing else but Cartwright's police, who must surely be near at hand.

If they arrived in time, they might stop Morne from getting away. King Rufus! The sole arbiter of success or failure. The man who ruled over his staff as if indeed they were his subjects.

Get *him* away, and the rest would be easy; nothing would be done without him.

'*Palfrey!*'

Palfrey sat still. 'I'm not going,' he said.

'I do not want to use force, but——'

'You hypocritical madman!' said Palfrey, harshly. 'You dare to say you don't want to use force! You used it on Wenlock. You killed and maimed. You will kill and maim again! You started off with lofty ideals, and they turned your mind. You are no longer sane; you are the Devil incarnate, and I shall do *nothing* to help you. I shall not stir a finger. I shall stay here, dead or alive.'

Morne said heavily: 'Do as you are told, Palfrey; I shall have no more of this.'

'I shall not move from this chair,' said Palfrey.

The futility of it sickened him. Morne's men would be watching; even if the message had got through to the police, their approach would be seen. It would take but a few seconds for Morne and his men to go behind that wall, leaving only the dead behind them, and the police would be as befogged as Palfrey had been when he had found the deserted house.

Morne said: 'Carry him.'

He turned away. Two of the men from the gallery door approached Palfrey. He sat watching them. There were six men in the room besides himself and Bandigo and McDonald. The odds were hopeless; nothing he could do could help him now.

The two men moved quickly; one struck him across the head and another lifted his legs. They carried him swiftly through the gap beyond the bookcase, down a flight of stairs into a small, lighted room, with walls of dark stone. The others followed. They walked through a long, narrow tunnel until they came to a door which opened on to another small, well-furnished room.

Markham and Rachel McDonald were sitting there.

'You will wait here,' said Morne.

He went out through another door. Guards stood outside the doors. Palfrey dropped into a chair, McDonald stood staring at his mother, and Bandigo stood quite still with his arms by his sides.

McDonald said in a cracked voice: 'Mother, you——'

Markham growled: 'You may as well keep your mouth shut. She's as mad as he is.'

She asked quietly. 'Will you come with me, Bruce?'

'*No!*'

'You should,' she said. 'There is no other wise course. Loretta will be with us.'

McDonald cried: 'He can't take her!'

'He took her from the sanatorium today,' said Rachel. 'She was well enough to be moved with care. He might leave the house and all his possessions here, but not Loretta—you should know that. Why don't you come, Bruce?'

McDonald did not answer.

Morne came back. Markham got up, scowling; he had only spoken once. Rachel McDonald rose from her chair and looked smilingly at her son. He returned her gaze, but did not speak. The servants went out.

Morne looked at Palfrey, and said: 'There is a steel door on the other side of the door you can see leading to the house. It will open at six o'clock tomorrow morning. You may then leave, to take the message which you will find by your side. You will be wise to hurry, and to make sure that all human beings are away from Morne House and a radius of three miles—and a radius of three miles from Wenn Mine also. I shall be beyond pursuit, but radio messages will reach me.'

Palfrey did not speak.

Morne led the others out, and the door closed on the three men who remained. Bandigo got up at once and tried one door, then the other, in a futile gesture. He even spent some time examining the locks. McDonald stood in silence. Palfrey, glancing at his watch, realized that they would have to stay here for five hours before they were released; five hours in which the situation would get beyond repair; five hours while the ship made its course——

The *ship* could be stopped!

He felt a moment of wild elation, but that quickly faded. Morne would have left nothing unprepared. The obvious solution to the getaway was a submarine. It seemed ages since Hardy had told him that U-boats had been suspected of using Wenlock Bay.

He looked round the room. It seemed bare now, and lifeless. For some reason, he thought of Kyle. Why had they taken Kyle with them?

*A door opened!* It was the door through which Morne and the others had gone, the door leading towards Wenn Mine. Into the room stepped a sturdy old man whom Palfrey recognized; Ruegg, the man who had guided him across the moor. Ruegg closed the door behind him, softly.

'Make no noise, gentlemen, please,' he said. He smiled at McDonald and held something towards him. 'Your mother asked me to give you this, Mr. Bruce.'

It was a key.

McDonald said, in a hoarse voice: 'I don't understand——'

'She asked me to tell you that *she* has sanity,' said Ruegg, with a gentle smile. 'The key will open the door into the house, and I am able to tell you how to move the steel door. There is not long at our disposal, gentlemen; the ship is due to leave in two hours' time.'

It was a feverish moment. McDonald's hand trembled as he inserted the key; Bandigo stood watching him impatiently, Ruegg was smiling. Palfrey was trying to make sense of this development. Rachel McDonald had realized that active opposition would be futile; she had chosen this way of making sure

173

that the mad venture was stopped. They had to make sure that no time was lost now.

The door opened.

Palfrey said: 'Ruegg, how long is the tunnel?'

'About three miles, sir.'

'Will they walk?'

'Oh, no, sir, there are electric cars.'

'Is there one this end?'

'Not now, sir,' said Ruegg. 'The shafts are very difficult to negotiate, sir, especially for someone who does not know them. I think it would be wiser to work from the house.'

'Not all of us,' said Palfrey. 'I'm going——'

'I'm coming with you!' snapped McDonald.

Bandigo said reluctantly: 'I suppose you're right, Sap.'

'I think so. Get word to Carmichael and Trollop as soon as you can, explain the whole situation to Cartwright and ask him to telephone Brett. Ruegg, I would like you to come with us, but you may have to find your way across the moors; it's possible that there will be a guard on the roads. You do understand that, don't you?'

'Yes, sir,' said Ruegg.

'How do we open the other door?' asked Palfrey.

'By the same key, sir.' It opened easily, and Ruegg stepped forward and pressed a switch which opened the steel doors beyond. Palfrey was thinking: 'Rachel McDonald. Thanks to Rachel McDonald.' It was like a refrain in his mind.

'Come on,' exclaimed McDonald.

'We'll want torches,' Palfrey said, 'and some idea of the tricks of the tunnel.'

'I will get the torches, sir,' said Ruegg, 'and, if you will come with me, I will explain as much as I can.'

Two tracks in the floor of the mine were hard from the frequent passing of the electric trucks. On either side of these tracks the earth was damp and loose. Rats scuttled out of the darkness, their eyes glowing pink in the beam of the torch.

Palfrey and McDonald walked steadily on.

Palfrey found it impossible to concentrate; his mind refused to obey him. Perhaps the darkness affected him. Perhaps those dark, scurrying shapes chilled his blood. Perhaps the drops of icy water that fell from the roof and fell on his face and hands numbed him. There was certainly something the matter.

For some minutes he had been aware of a soft, padding

174

sound, like a footfall. It kept pace with him. He told himself that it was imagination. Or the echo of his own footsteps. But it was no good; the padding sound continued in his ears.

He whispered: 'Go another few yards, Mac, and stop.'

'Did you hear something?' he asked.

'I thought I did.'

'So did I.'

'Let's go on,' Palfrey said.

Immediately he started walking, the sound came again.

McDonald stopped suddenly, and Palfrey bumped into him. His heart raced.

The sound stopped.

McDonald said: 'I'm devilishly cold.'

'We might run a bit,' said Palfrey.

They broke into a trot. It was difficult to make themselves move quickly at first. Palfrey was conscious of shambling along. Gradually he warmed up. It was better to be warm, but it did not take that dull noise out of his ears. He saw the beam of torch light disappearing into the distance, and knew that the tunnel ran straight for at least two hundred yards. 'Quicker,' he said. McDonald lengthened his stride, and Palfrey found himself running well. But he could not quell his fear. The impulse to look round was now overwhelming.

He glanced back swiftly, but he saw nothing. Still the sounds were there, between their footsteps. They were running side by side and keeping pace. Sometimes water splashed up to their knees, once or twice they ran into a pool so deep that they were slowed down and the water splashed up into their faces. Palfrey was reminded of the moor, when he had ridden out with Ruegg; the creepy moor, with mist rising from the stagnant pools and the treacherous bog all about them. There could be no bog here, and there was no sense in believing that they were being followed, and yet that awful fear was deep within him.

*Why?*

McDonald said: 'I suppose they can time the damned thing?'

He gasped the words out.

'What thing?' asked Palfrey.

'The bomb.'

So that was it! That was the thought that held those awful fears, as different from anything he had ever experienced. They were running towards that 'unit'. They were running towards and not away from the thing which had caused such damage in Wenlock, the thing which was allied to the terror that had struck Hiroshima. They were running towards it, and he wanted to run away.

He had to go on.

He managed to glance at his watch. They had been on the move for twenty minutes; it seemed much longer. They had covered a little over a mile, he thought; not very much more, because they had lost some time standing and listening. But at this rate they would reach the mine in less than an hour.

McDonald said: 'Stop a moment.'

Palfrey obeyed. He saw why McDonald had wanted to stop; they were out of the narrow tunnel and running into another, wider one. The floor level of the wider tunnel was higher than that of the one along which they had been running. They stepped into it. The floor was much drier, and Palfrey laughed in sheer relief.

'Do we go right or left?'

'We follow the tracks.'

The tracks turned left. They walked along for a few yards, and then broke into a trot again. They were further apart now, and the floor was much harder—almost as if it had been cemented.

Then along the tunnel there came a whine, a high-pitched whine like a sighing wind. McDonald gasped: 'What's that?'

'Let's keep going,' said Palfrey.

At the first sound his heart had started to beat very fast; now, to his satisfaction, it was steadier. Being confronted with an emergency had steadied him. He put his hand to his pocket and touched his gun.

The sound came again, high-pitched, whining; like a dog.

Palfrey thought of the bloodhounds on the moor.

There were other sounds now; someone was running. McDonald put a hand on Palfrey's arm. 'Put that light out!' he gasped. Palfrey obeyed. They stood in pitch darkness, listening to the noises travelling along the tunnel. Running footsteps merged with that whining sound; there seemed to be a note of excitement in the whining. The bloodhounds *were* ahead. Suddenly the noise grew louder, there was a baying note; yes, the bloodhounds were coming towards them.

Palfrey said: 'You've got your gun, haven't you?'

'Yes, of course.'

'We'll stand on either side,' said Palfrey.

McDonald pressed against one wall, Palfrey against the other, and they stood waiting in the darkness. The baying was getting nearer and nearer. Then a faint light appeared, not far away. It grew brighter. They could see another bend in the tunnel. Suddenly a figure appeared, a man, running fast but swaying a little from side to side. They did not see his face, but they could see the terror which was reflected in his movements, in his desperate speed.

Two hounds leapt into sight, not more than thirty yards behind him, and a moment later a small truck appeared. Its single headlight, low down, spread a bright glow along the tunnel, on the hounds and their quarry.

*On Kyle!*

Palfrey fired at the dog nearer to him, and the beast dropped in its tracks. It had been a lucky shot, there was not even a squeal. A gasp of alarm came from the man in the truck. Then McDonald fired, twice, and the second hound fell over and kicked his feet in the air and squealed, a horrifying sound. McDonald fired again and the squealing stopped.

The driver of the truck was standing up, with a gun in his hand. 'No thanks,' said Palfrey, absurdly, and shot him; there was nothing else to do.

The man slumped back.

Kyle was now leaning against the wall and gasping for breath. McDonald hurried to his side, while Palfrey looked at the driver of the truck. The man had died instantaneously.

Kyle was trying to smile, but his lips were set with pain. Palfrey ran his hands over him; the trouble was in that wounded leg, which had been tried far too much.

They carried Kyle to the truck. There was ample room in the back for him to lie full length. He was grinning more cheerfully now.

'How far away is the mine?'

'Most of two miles,' said Kyle. 'And they're all set to leave.' There was a wondering note in his voice. 'One of the servants slipped me a knife. I was able to cut myself free.'

'He slipped us a key,' said Palfrey.

'I'm looking forward to meeting him again,' said Kyle. 'You know what they're doing, I suppose?'

'Morne told me.'

'There are twenty-five or thirty of them along there, including the women,' said Kyle. 'They fetched that girl, Loretta. We three won't be able to do much against them.'

'There will be help,' Palfrey said. 'Our people will move on the mine pretty quickly, and the bay is being watched closely.'

'That makes it easier,' said Kyle.

'Makes what easier?' asked McDonald.

Kyle said: 'Getting that damned bomb formula.' He grinned. 'It is a formula. Morne's got it in his pocket. There aren't any copies. He told me about that. He talks too much, does King Rufus—you dubbed him well, McDonald.'

'I know him,' growled McDonald.

'Do you think you can drive this thing, Mac?' asked Palfrey.

'I can try,' said McDonald. 'I wonder how far we can go before we're heard.'

Palfrey said: 'That doesn't matter; they'll expect the truck back; the sound won't worry them.'

'The man who always keeps his head,' said Kyle, with an eyebrow raised. 'Stay in the back with me, Palfrey, I can talk as we're going along.'

The whine of the engine was deafening. At first Palfrey could not hear what Kyle had to say. He crouched down, with his ear close to the man's lips, and concentrated on listening.

Kyle said: 'The man we must get first is Morne, Palfrey. I don't think he'll want to be taken alive. He's convinced that he's the new saviour of the world—that makes him a sight more dangerous.' Palfrey nodded. 'After that, we must stop the mine from being blown up,' Kyle said, quite calmly. 'You should see the laboratory, Palfrey! It's worth millions. If Morne is telling the truth, and I think he is, an eggful of this damned stuff will blow it to perdition—and us with it.' Palfrey nodded again. 'But the real trouble will be with that ship,' said Kyle. 'It's a submarine. No one dare fire on it; if they do——'

The coast for many miles could be ravaged.

'So we've got to get at it from this end,' Kyle finished.

Palfrey felt the perspiration dripping from his forehead.

How could they do these things?

'You two will have to go on,' said Kyle, 'but come back for me when you can.'

'All right,' said Palfrey.

Once more the feeling came over him that this thing was too much for him, but there was nothing to do but go on.

McDonald drove as far as the next tunnel, much wider even than the one through which they had come. He stopped, and they got down and stood looking along the tunnel.

There was light some distance ahead, then lines of light forming a rectangle, presumably a door, leading to a well-lit room. Kyle called: 'I don't think that door's locked. See if they've

178

gone.' Palfrey said: 'Right-ho,' and they walked on.

They reached the door and stood outside, listening, but they could hear nothing. Two or three trucks were standing in the wide space near the door. Palfrey touched the handle and opened it an inch. He could see no one inside. . . .

He opened the door more widely and stepped through into the underground laboratory.

It was a vast chamber, well lighted, and fitted up with benches. In the middle stood a huge bulk of machinery. The place was scrupulously tidy, and much warmer than the tunnel.

'I'll go back for Kyle,' said McDonald.

'Good man,' said Palfrey.

He walked round the laboratory, marvelling at the intricate apparatus, and wishing that he could spend time examining everything fully. It was some minutes before the earlier, sickening fear returned: how could they make sure that the place was not blown up? How could they save this plant?

The truck drew up outside the door.

Palfrey went out to help to carry Kyle in. There was another problem: how much could they handle Kyle?

Kyle, much more himself, grinned broadly as they sat him in a small easy-chair. Palfrey pushed a stool under his leg, and Kyle said:

'So this is it? I always thought I'd find it, Palfrey. What are we going to do next?'

'Do you know where they've put the bomb?' asked Palfrey.

Kyle said: 'No. But I know what it looks like.'

After a pause, McDonald said: 'We ought to start looking.'

'Do you know when it's timed to go off?' asked Palfrey.

'No,' said Kyle.

'Morne said that the house would go up at six o'clock,' Palfrey said. He stared at his watch, as if that would give him inspiration. 'We've time to follow Morne and get back and look for this.'

McDonald said: 'There might be a hundred men outside, searching for the entrance, Palfrey. We can't take chances with them!'

'We've got to get Morne,' said Palfrey, flatly.

Sharp and clear from somewhere outside there came the crack of a shot. It echoed about the laboratory, and set glass tinkling. They looked at each other in startled inquiry.

'If anyone starts shooting,' said Kyle, 'the thing might go off!'

There was another shot.

Palfrey walked slowly towards the door at the opposite end of the laboratory. He was hardly conscious of anything but his terrible fear.

## EIGHTEEN

## THE SUBMARINE

PALFREY opened the door. His heart was unsteady and his fingers trembled as he touched the handle. He looked into the semi-darkness of a room beyond, and called out in a high-pitched voice: 'Anyone there?'

It sounded ludicrous even in his own ears, and the echo came back to him. He called again, and immediately afterwards there was a flurry of movement. If some of Morne's men had remained behind, anything might happen now.

'Sap!' cried a voice.

'Carmichael!' exclaimed Palfrey. His fears dropped away, and he hurried forward. 'Where are you?' He had recognized the voice, but could not see Carmichael. 'Where——'

Carmichael stepped forward into the light. Trollop followed him, and immediately afterwards the outer room seemed filled with men. Some were in police uniform, there were a few in khaki battle-dress, and several men in lounge suits. All of them stared at Palfrey incredulously.

Palfrey said: 'Who fired that gun?'

'I did,' said a man in Service uniform. He sounded a little sheepish. 'I saw something move.'

'Well, I shouldn't fire, whatever you see,' said Palfrey. 'There's an explosive somewhere here that might go off if we play tricks, and that wouldn't be healthy.'

Carmichael said: 'They know what it is, Palfrey.'

'Oh,' said Palfrey. He pulled himself together as a youthful major came forward. 'We've quite a job,' he said. 'Hidden somewhere in the next room is the container which is set to go off at six o'clock or earlier.' He saw men flinch at the word 'earlier'. 'Even when we find it, I don't know that we can do much about it,' he added, 'except take it out on to the moor and get away as quickly as we can.'

The major said: 'We'll have a try, anyhow.'

'Kyle knows what the thing looks like,' Palfrey said, and Kyle waved from his chair. 'Do you know about what is happening outside, major?'

'I'm afraid not,' said the major. 'What about Morne? Have you got him?'

'No. But I know where he's gone.'

'We'll have to get after him, too,' said the major.

Palfrey said: 'Yes. Two parties.'

It was surprising how much better he felt now that the others were here. It was good to hear the major give orders precisely and to see his men obey without question. A party of twelve, including four policemen, Palfrey and McDonald, was to set out in the electric truck after Morne. The others would stay in the laboratory; some were already searching, under the supervision of a little, sharp-featured man from the Wenlock police station.

As Palfrey waited for the trucks to start, anxious thoughts filled his mind.

Would they find the bomb; and could they get it far enough away in time?

Was there any reason to think that it would be greatly different from other bombs? Could bomb-disposal men hope to work successfully on it? Could anyone be found who would know how to dismantle it?

Carmichael did a great deal of talking, the gist of which was that he and Trollop had wandered about the foothills near the old entrance to the mine and eventually seen lights moving in the distance. Closer inspection had revealed what Palfrey had long suspected—a second shaft sunk to the mine. The machinery had been slightly damaged, but the major's men had repaired it quickly, and the party had arrived almost at the same time as Palfrey and the others.

The trucks moved off, hurtling through the darkness, without any attempt to drive slowly and quietly. McDonald sat at the wheel, with Palfrey next to him. Two other men were sitting at the back.

They came upon a wide bay, where several trucks were standing empty. McDonald slowed down. All three trucks pulled up, and the men gathered together in the bay. In front of them was a semi-circular wall with two doors; they could not see any light at all.

Palfrey led the way to one door, a lieutenant to the other.

181

Only Palfrey's door was unlocked. He opened it gently and peered through.

No one appeared to be in the room beyond.

It was another great chamber, cut almost in two by a stretch of water nearly twenty yards across. The water was moving gently, and reflected the bright roof-lights and the figures of the men who approached. There were benches on either side ; the room was a workshop, where, undoubtedly, repairs were carried out to submarines which had put in here. Palfrey wondered whether Morne had known about this place during the war. It was a perfect hide-out for U-boats. He had heard rumours of secret repair-shops off the Corshire coast even before Hardy had mentioned these suspicions. Certainly this workshop had been established for some time.

The water-cut led through a tunnel where there was a foot-path on either side. The soft lapping of the water was the only sound.

Palfrey led the way on one side of the water and peered ahead at another lighter chamber.

If Morne and his party were already at sea, what could happen?

They reached the second chamber. *The ship was there.*

They could see it some distance ahead, moored to the quay-side. Roof-lights were shining on its glistening sides. Gangways were in position. There were several men on deck, and two or three people were standing on the quay. Someone on the ground was hidden from Palfrey, who kept as far back in the shadows as he could.

A man moved and Palfrey saw Loretta Morne on a stretcher. Her face was turned towards him, and he had never seen such a look of hopelessness.

Morne came out of the turret, walked slowly down the plank and looked at her. She returned his gaze and said something which Palfrey could not hear. Morne bent down and put a hand on her forehead. She spoke again, without removing her gaze. Morne slowly shook his head.

McDonald, just behind Palfrey, stirred a little. Palfrey touched his hand. Morne raised his voice, and two men picked up the stretcher.

'They mustn't take her down there!' McDonald was almost frantic, and his voice was too loud. Palfrey expected Morne to look round, but there was no indication that they had been heard. The stretcher was raised. Morne stood watching.

Palfrey whispered: 'They'll never get away now, Mac. Don't worry.'

Palfrey moved forward slowly. He stopped and whispered again.

'I'm going forward before Morne goes aboard. I'll get him into the water if I can. Four of you go to the other side. Remember, no shooting.'

Four men silently filed back.

Other things were being taken aboard. Suddenly, Markham appeared from behind a stretch of wall which hid part of the quay from Palfrey. He glared at Morne, but went aboard without any outward protest. He stood on deck while Rachel walked past Morne.

Palfrey moved forward.

If they looked towards him now, they must see him. He went steadily, his hands held a little in front of him. He saw Rachel glance his way. She stiffened, then looked away again. The servants, only two of them clad in sea-going clothes, had gone behind the wall. Morne was standing with his back to Palfrey, quite unaware of any danger.

Then Markham looked his way.

Palfrey was ten feet from Morne by then, with hope high in his breast; but Markham cried: *'Palfrey!'*

Morne swung round.

Palfrey leapt at him. The man had no time to defend himself, no time to fend the attack off. They met—but Palfrey had underestimated Morne's strength; he did not give way, only swayed back and flung his arms about his assailant. For a moment they stood struggling, while the men came rushing from behind the wall and Markham shouted orders.

That was the thing which impressed Palfrey most, even as he struggled: *Markham gave orders.*

Morne's grip was powerful. Palfrey felt the breath being squeezed from his body. He was seeking Morne's wrist. If he could get a proper grip, the man would be helpless. Markham and those on the quay had not seen anyone on the other side, but the four men were there, waiting at the water's edge.

Palfrey got his grip; Morne gasped and his pressure slackened. Palfrey was just aware of men passing him, going into the attack. He did not see Rachel McDonald leap from the deck to the quay. He did not see Morne's men close with his own supporters. He was aware only of the fact that Morne was powerless in his grip, and that in Morne's pocket were the vital papers.

He swung the helpless man round and caught a glimpse of his face. It was distorted with rage; there was malignance in his eyes, all the hatred that he could summon was focused on Palfrey. Remorselessly, Palfrey forced him towards the water's edge. The sound of the struggle between the others was loud in the cavern.

Someone reached Palfrey's side. 'Take his coat, take his coat!' It was Rachel McDonald. Palfrey said: 'Pull that sleeve!' Morne was still helpless in his grip; he tried to fend the woman off, but failed. She pulled off one sleeve, and the coat hung from one shoulder. Palfrey released Morne, pushed him suddenly away from him and grabbed the coat. Morne staggered and Rachel tripped him. He fell headlong into the water, and a wave came up over Palfrey's legs and nearly made him lose his balance.

The coat was in his hand.

Men were spilling out of the submarine now, and Markham was rushing towards Palfrey. McDonald and his supporters were already outnumbered and struggling desperately—a fantastic struggle of armed men who dared not use their guns. Palfrey saw Markham coming, saw Rachel turn and block his path, crying: 'Take the coat! Take the coat!'

But men were behind Palfrey now; McDonald was out, unconscious; two others were down, and there were men to spare to attack Palfrey. He rolled the coat and flung it as far as he could across the water. He saw his men standing with arms outstretched. Morne was still in the water, but swimming powerfully towards him. He did not see what happened to the coat.

Then Markham sent Rachel staggering to one side and leapt at Palfrey. They closed. The rush was so fierce that Palfrey went back helplessly. He was near the edge of the water, and felt himself toppling. Markham kept a hold on him and dragged him back.

Someone was crying, 'The coat! The coat!'

Markham struck Palfrey across the face. Palfrey felt pain shoot through him and lost his balance. He went into the water as Morne began to climb on to the quay. He did not see Morne stop, turn and look at him; and he did not see the man plunge in after him again.

He did not see the men on the other side fish the coat out of the water and turn away. He was conscious only of the chilling coldness of the water, and a sudden twinge of cramp in his right leg. He reached the surface, drew in a gulp of air and went under again. Something brushed past him. When he came up for the second time he was more collected, and started to strike out for the side. He wanted now to help Rachel McDonald.

Something pressed against his back. A man was gripping the back of his neck and forcing him under.

He went down, not knowing whether he would be able to come up again, but the pressure relaxed under water, and with a wild heave he flung himself towards the bank. He broke water again, flung the hair out of his eyes, saw blurred figures on the quayside, some still struggling, some watching. Then he heard a splash behind him.

Morne was there, reaching out for him again.

Palfrey went over on his side, turned on his back, kicked and caught him on the head, but not heavily enough to do any damage. Morne gripped his right arm.

Palfrey tugged desperately and Morne released his arm and grabbed at his neck. His fingers slid off the wet skin. Palfrey heaved, turned over and struck out for the bank on the other side. His ears were filled with loud, drumming noises; the cavern seemed to echo as if with thunder.

As with thunder. . . .

The engines of the submarine were turning!

Then something touched his shoulder; he thought of Morne, and in a panic wrenched himself free. He was submerged for a moment, but came up again.

Someone cried: 'Don't struggle! Don't struggle!'

There was something reassuring in that voice, and he kept still. He felt someone take his shoulders and raise him. He could not help himself, but he knew that he was being dragged across the water to the far side. Another man was standing there, and bent down to help him. He collapsed on the quay, hardly conscious, hardly aware of thought. There were voices and that awful droning.

And a sharp explosion.

A shot!

He opened his eyes, but could see nothing beyond the water dripping from his forehead. Someone said: 'Keep down!' There was another shot; did the fool not realize what might happen?

He dashed his hair from his eyes, crouched low, and stared

across the water. Markham was standing there, firing at him. There were two or three people in the water, and he wondered whether Morne was one of them.

He felt a bullet strike his thigh.

He gasped, and stopped moving, but still stared towards the far side. He saw Rachel McDonald get up from the ground and throw herself at Markham.

Markham. . . .

Someone shouted. Markham turned his head. The submarine was moving slowly; a man on the deck was beckoning Markham. Markham levelled his gun, the shot roared out, and Palfrey heard the bullet strike the floor near him. Then Markham turned and ran towards the submarine.

Morne was not aboard; Morne was somewhere in the water. But the ship was moving, and Markham was in control. The facts came to Palfrey in a vivid flash. Markham had all the time worked for this; was Kyle's mystery man. Markham had known the truth and had waited, prepared to take over from Morne at the first opportunity. And this was his opportunity.

Markham reached the deck. The submarine was gathering speed. Somewhere within its cabins or holds were those 'units', those bombs which could be used to bring about such fearful destruction.

Palfrey tried to move; he succeeded only in flopping forward a few inches. The submarine was getting further away. He saw several men leap aboard, but none of Palfrey's men; all Morne's—or Markham's.

*Then Morne appeared!*

He was swimming powerfully by the side of the ship. He reached her and hauled himself aboard. Markham was still staring at Palfrey, and noticed nothing. Two or three members of the crew helped Morne aboard, and still Markham seemed to notice nothing. Morne stood for a moment, his huge figure dripping water, his red hair glistening in the roof lights. He did not speak, but moved forward.

At last Markham realized that he was there.

Everyone on the quays was staring at the two men. Markham backed away. Morne stretched out his hand. His fist was clenched. Markham raised his gun, Morne knocked it aside with a contemptuous gesture, then his hand shot out and gripped Markham's throat. Palfrey could see the strength of his grip, saw Markham's mouth open and his tongue protrude, saw his eyes bulging. The whole scene was moving away from

Palfrey; and all the time the droning of the engines reverberated through the cavern.

Markham collapsed.

Morne maintained his pressure for a moment, and then flung the man into the water. As Markham fell and water splashed up over the deck, Morne seemed to shake himself, as if he had rid himself of something unclean. Then he stood quite still, looking at the quayside, looking towards Palfrey.

He was magnificent.

And he was getting away.

The submarine moved slowly towards another tunnel; it was half-way through and still Morne stood immovable, watching; when the deck reached the tunnel, his head was almost level with the roof, but he did not move.

He disappeared.

The droning of the engines was duller now.

Palfrey forced himself to look away. A man was bending over him, asking if he were all right, but he did not answer. How could anyone stop the submarine now?

There was a coat lying near him, sodden, shapeless; in the pockets was the formula of Garth's secret, but the bombs themselves were on board the submarine, and there was the one in the laboratory.

'Look!' cried someone on the other side of the water. 'Look!'

As he spoke, men burst into sight from the tunnel from which Palfrey had come. The major led the way, Carmichael followed him, then the others who had been left in the laboratory streamed through. Rachel McDonald, on her feet now and approaching her son, started to talk and point. Palfrey saw the men streaming off in the wake of the ship; and for the first time, too, he saw a small motor-launch moored to the quayside. There were others on the far side that had at first been hidden by the submarine.

Palfrey croaked: 'That launch—that launch!'

There was hope again, a faint flicker of hope which he dared not fan into flames.

Two men carried him to the boat, which rocked precariously, paining his wounded thigh. The others climbed in, and they started off just as another party in a larger boat on the opposite side began to move. They chugged through the darkness of the tunnel, unable to see anything at all, in imminent danger of collision, but soon there was light ahead of them and they saw that the larger boat had travelled fast.

The light looked unnatural.

They came out of the mouth of the tunnel, and saw that searchlights from ships standing out in the bay were all converging on the submarine. Small boats were moving towards it, and aeroplanes were flying across the bay, their lights shining down upon the water. The submarine itself, with Morne still on deck, was moving slowly, uncertainly. The great side of the cliff was above them, and behind them the small tunnel opening, like the mouth of a cave, which led to the workshops.

The small boats were nearing the submarine; one, much larger, was closing in on her. It was a destroyer, and Palfrey could see the men lining its deck, preparing to board. He watched the whole scene breathlessly; he saw the destroyer and the submarine touch; the submarine heeled over, then righted itself; and as it did so, men streamed aboard.

Morne moved; one moment he stood there in the blaze of light; the next he disappeared over the side. From the deck, Mrs. Bardle watched him.

Morne had gone and the submarine was stopped; the bay was seething with small craft, and aeroplanes still droned overhead. Palfrey felt the relief almost too much for him, but there was still anxiety in his heart. Had the bomb in the laboratory been found, and so released the men who had arrived just too late to prevent the submarine from leaving its berth? If so, where was that bomb now?

He was too tired to think.

The men with him said: 'Had we better go back?'

'No, we'd better head for Wenlock.'

'Yes. I think so.' The rest of the men in the boat were obviously relieved. Palfrey sat back as comfortably as he could and looked about him. Another, larger motor-boat drew near, and someone hailed him. It drew alongside, and he saw Kyle sitting in the bows, grinning.

'Ahoy, Palfrey!'

Palfrey grinned back. 'Did you find it?'

'*And* dismantled it!'

'*What?*'

'It's a fact.'

Palfrey found himself laughing. . . .

It was half an hour before he reached the crowded quayside in Wenlock Bay. It was brightly lighted and thronged with people. He was glad to be lifted on to a stretcher, to have his injury attended to quickly, and to find that it was no more than a flesh wound. He felt utterly exhausted. He closed his eyes as he was carried through the crowd towards an ambulance, but opened them suddenly when he heard *Drusilla* cry: 'Sap!'

'Why, hallo!' said Palfrey, and gripped her hands. She was gasping for breath; she had seen him and run and forced her way through the crowd. Susan was behind her, eager questions in her eyes. 'It's all right. Nick's there,' said Palfrey. 'All over. Did you see them board that submarine?'

'Yes,' said Drusilla. 'Yes. Is it *all* over?'

'Everything,' said Palfrey. 'I—at least, I think so! That coat —where's that coat?'

One of the men who had been in the boat with him was standing nearby, and raised the coat.

'Thank the Lord for that,' said Palfrey. 'Yes, *all* over,' he said. 'Morne's gone. Did you see him?'

'Yes,' said Drusilla.

'And Mac and Loretta will probably live happily ever after,' said Palfrey. 'I know what you didn't see: Rachel!' He began to talk quickly. He told her everything that had happened since they had reached Morne House. His mind was very clear. He understood everything, the explanation that Morne had given him, the story of Pettigrew, the part that Markham had played. Markham, of course, always working—first through his wife, then his son—a dark and sinister man who pretended to help Morne but planned eventually to hold that dreadful power in his own hands . . .

There was a remarkable gathering in the small ward. Cartwright, and the Bristol Cox, Hardy—who had been released from a disused mine several miles away from Morne House— Kyle and Susan and Drusilla, Bruce McDonald and Rachel.

Rachel was as much the dominating figure there as Morne had been on the submarine's decks.

Much of what she told them was already known, from Morne's talk in Morne House, but she added touches which Palfrey did not know. That for some months they had all been afraid of being murdered; that the family had united against the threat; that the man Gorringer had tried to blackmail Morne, and eventually Morne had defeated him; that Markham—she uttered that name with withering contempt—had worked with Gorringer, although she and Morne had not known that until that day. Morne had intended to take Markham away and deal with him at sea.

She told them that Gorringer had visited Morne House through the mine workings, and had been killed only two days before.

She told them that she had not known the truth about Garth, nor suspected it. She told them, too, that on the night of Palfrey's arrival someone had tried to break into Morne House, and the servants, most of whom obeyed Morne with unquestioning loyalty—had gone after him with the hounds.

'And what of Loretta?' asked Palfrey.

'I think that Loretta discovered a little, perhaps not all, and confided in Halsted, who sent for you,' said Rachel. 'I think Loretta was frightened of the thing which her father was doing, but would not openly betray him.'

Later, Kyle was wheeled along. He was bright and cheerful, fully satisfied, he assured Palfrey. When Whitehall had moved, there had been no mistake about it.

'We're getting ready to return to the States when the inquiry is over. Maybe I shall get my job back. I shall need a job. I'm getting married.'

'Splendid! Congratulations.'

'Well, I'm taking on plenty with Susan,' said Kyle, but there was a merry gleam in his eyes; he was certainly very pleased with himself. 'Are there any things you feel aren't cleared up yet?'

Palfrey said: 'Only the incidentals. Why did Gorringer use Cheddar and Bristol when there were plenty of hiding places nearer the mine?'

'That's an easy one,' Kyle assured him. 'You ought not to have missed it. Don't forget that Gorringer was fighting Morne, although trying to hide it. He needed a separate force. Morne looked after the workmen and employed the physicists, paying them well without telling them why he was working with Garth. Gorringer set up a different army, and he made all the mistakes. Except for Fyson, all of his people were modelled on Al Capone. It's a good thing they were.'

'Yes,' said Palfrey, and added, quietly: 'Morne himself might have got away with it.'

'What was there to stop him?' asked Kyle.

There had been nothing; with the loyalty of his staff assured, and the Wenn Mine so close to Morne House, it was doubtful whether there would have been any leakage; the world might never have known until the submarine reached its port and Morne's ultimatum had been issued.

Palfrey said: 'I wonder why he told me that Garth was the man who had stayed at his house.'

Kyle said: 'Don't ask me.'

It was a puzzling question, and, much as Palfrey pondered over it in the next few days, he could find no answer, save one; it had been Morne's first mistake.

Palfrey's wound quickly healed. Brett came down to see him. The newspapers, day after day, carried long stories about Morne and his plans. Repair squads and relief organizations came to Wenlock, but the road across the moor was closed, for Morne House still stood, and somewhere within it was the last of Morne's bombs. Villages and cottages nearby were emptied; no one went near the place; to risk life would have been purposeless.

After ten days, Palfrey was well enough to travel.

On the same day, Loretta Morne was able to move a little for the first time. The adventures of the submarine had not affected her recovery, and there was now little doubt that she would walk again.

Palfrey badly wanted two things: to hear Loretta laugh and to see Morne House again.

'You are not going near Morne House,' declared Drusilla.

'No, dear,' said Palfrey, meekly.

They went to the sanatorium, however, and were led by the eager Ross to Loretta's room. She was sitting up a little, her hair was dressed and her eyes were bright; and McDonald was sitting by her side. Something he said made her laugh. Brightness and sunlight seemed to fill the room.

She looked at Palfrey with radiant eyes, and held out her hand.

'I want so much to thank you,' she said.

'You started it,' Palfrey said. 'Let me ask just one question. How much did Halsted know?'

'No more than I,' said Loretta, 'and I knew little; but I was afraid. I found that drawing and those figures on my father's desk and took them; and from that moment I lived in fear.' For a moment the radiance of her eyes was clouded. 'I was afraid he wanted to kill me, but I should have known better. Halsted talked a great deal about you. He promised to ask you to help. I was against it, but——'

She broke off, and Palfrey smiled.

'All over,' he said. 'No need for regrets.'

Then across the silence came a roar, distant and yet deafening, terrifying. They stared at one another. The rumbling continued, and the blast came, but it whistled only softly in Wenlock and that room.

Loretta said, in a low voice: 'I'm glad the house has gone. I can really forget now.'

McDonald was holding her hands.

The Palfreys went quietly out of the room.